"*The Santa Run* is a warm delight full of laughter and heartfelt romance that will gift wrap readers in the holiday spirit. Pugh's fresh, spunky voice is a star on top of the Christmas tree that shines beautifully in the rom-com genre."

—Jessica R. Patch, best-selling author of the Seasons of Hope and Honeyhaven series.

"Heartwarming, wholesome, and perfect for Hallmark fans, *The Santa Run* is a poignant, engaging love story. Relatable characters Eliza and Bennett have chemistry to spare. Eliza's journey through loss and uncertainty to rediscovered hope is bolstered by seriously swoonworthy Bennett, an outsider striving to repair his own past. A joyful gift to romance readers everywhere."

—Tracy Gardner, Mary Higgins Clark Award– and Edgar Award–nominated author

"Warm and cozy from beginning to end, *The Santa Run* is a feel-good charmer! A Christmas visit to Beth Pugh's Pine Valley is like stepping inside a snow globe, and readers will be made to feel right at home. If you love Hallmark Christmas movies, you'll thoroughly enjoy watching this delightful romance come to life on the page."

—Bethany Turner, award-winning author of *Plot Twist* and *The Do-Over*

"It's always a pleasure to find a new author who can create a story you can't put down. Beth's love for Kentucky and talent for writing sweet romance shines in this wonderful Christmas story. You will endure all the feels. I highly recommend *The Santa Run* to my readers."

—Mindy Steele, best-selling author of *An Amish Flower Farm* and *Christmas Grace*

"*The Santa Run* features all of my reader catnip: a smart, zesty voice, favourite TV Christmas movie tropes, and a fish-out-of-water story liberally peppered with warmth and community. A poignant tale of loss and love found, I loved the tradition of the train and its railway run providing a unique new offering in a veritable Candy Cane land of Christmas romances.

"As delicious as whipped cocoa, Pugh's voice and irrepressible romanticism wrap you up like the warmest sweater. I would happily spend time with Eliza and Bennett in picturesque Pine Valley for many seasons to come.

"Fans of Debbie Macomber, Denise Hunter, and Robyn Carr won't be able to get enough. I, for one, am so happy to have found a fresh voice to add to my insatiable love for all things Christmas romance!"

—Rachel McMillan, author of The Three Quarter Time series and *A Very Merry Holiday Movie Guide*

Other Books by Beth Pugh
The Valentine Proposal

The Santa Run

BETH PUGH

Birmingham, Alabama

The Santa Run

Iron Stream Fiction
An imprint of Iron Stream Media
100 Missionary Ridge
Birmingham, AL 35242
IronStreamMedia.com

Copyright © 2022 by Bertha Pugh

The author is represented by Julie Gwinn, president of The Seymour Agency.

Library of Congress Control Number: 2022940964

Scripture quotations are from the Authorized (King James) Version. Rights in the Authorized Version in the United Kingdom are vested in the Crown. Reproduced by permission of the Crown's patentee, Cambridge University Press.

Cover design by For the Muse Designs

ISBN: 978-1-64526-387-6
ISBN: 978-1-64526-355-5 (e-book)

1 2 3 4 5—26 25 24 23 22

To my parents
Your love continues to inspire me. I miss you more than should be possible and long for the day when I will see you again. Keep waiting at heaven's gate.

Acknowledgments

At times, writing can feel like an endless stretch of lonely road paved with self-doubt. When I began my publishing journey, that sums up my emotions quite nicely. It was a few months after burying my daddy, and the grief nearly suffocated me. But God showed up and walked alongside me. He turned my sorrow into joy, bringing Romans 8:28 alive for me and I will forever be grateful. I pray you see Him in this story and in life because there is nothing more beautiful.

The road might have started off lonesome, but God didn't leave it that way. He placed people in my life to help me along the way, like an outstanding agent. Julie Gwinn, you are at the top that list. Thank you for taking a chance on this story and on me. You are a blessing.

As is my writer tribe. Meghann Whistler, thank you for walking this road with me. You are an amazing critique partner and a wonderful friend. Danielle Grandinetti, our chats uplift me so much. After talking to you, I feel renewed and ready to face the keyboard again. Thank you for meeting me in my mess time after time. To Stephanie Jay Taylor, you are one of the best encouragers I have ever met. I am blessed by your heart for others and beyond honored to call you friend. Susan Tuttle, I was working on this very manuscript the first time I messaged you out of the blue. I was humbled when you offered prayers for me then and even more so as you continued to check in with me throughout the years. I will always be thankful for your friendship.

Special thanks to my editors, Jessica Nelson and Nancy J. Farrier, who weeded through a plethora of exclamation marks to find the heart of this story. You taught me not only the proper etiquette of punctuation but the power of show rather than tell, and I won't forget either. Thank you for the care you poured into these words, and into me, while never letting me settle for less than the best I had to offer. Your hard work and knowledge made this book shine.

To Buddy, Bree, Jill, Sarah, Breanna, Julie, Bea, and all my beta readers: You took the time to read this story before anyone else and I can't thank you enough. Your encouragement and support pushed me to keep going. To my friends, coworkers, and family who cheered me through each rejection and every revision, thank you. I love you so much. I don't know how you keep from muzzling me when I go down the rabbit hole of book talk, but your patience is much appreciated. Kat, Madison, and Nicole: you ladies made me believe in this story and in myself. I thank God for you. I love you all from the bottom of my heart.

Last, but never least, to my husband and son—I am undeserving of the love you show me, but I will forever love you back with all that I have. Izaiah, being your mommy is my favorite thing and that will never change. Watching you grow is a gift I treasure. I am so proud of you. Ryan, you are the love story I want to read for the rest of my life. I would be lost without you. Your unconditional support leaves me in awe, and I can't thank you enough for being everything I need exactly when I need it, whether that be a kick in the pants to get me moving or a bear hug to hold me together. I will always love you like coffee loves donuts.

Chapter One

Lights from the Christmas tree in the far corner of the office flashed rhythmically, their reflection barely visible on the computer screen as Eliza Lee Elliot checked her newly cleaned-out inbox for the umpteenth time. The room emanated an eerie somberness instead of the usual coziness she'd come to associate with the Appalachian Express, her home away from home for the last two years.

Most days, she'd rather stay late at the office than make the trek to her house on the edge of town. Moving out of Grandpa Walt's had been the right decision. The time to stand on her own two feet had come, but living alone took some getting used to and she simply hadn't acclimated yet. She'd get there. *Eventually*.

But not today, not with her new city-slicker manager on his way.

Needing reassurance, she swiveled her chair to face her brother, Jett. When he looked up, his furrowed brows and telling silence ushered in the reality of the situation. Concern instead of the comfort she'd hoped for shone in his eyes. Eliza squeezed her fingers around the armrest and rocked her chair back and forth. Without a word, Jett stood up, walked around behind her, and placed a hand on the back of her seat to still the motion. She wished harnessing her nerves were that simple.

"Sorry." Eliza offered her apology without looking up, feeling a slight warmth on her cheeks. "I still can't believe Sean and Ava sold the railroad. Retirement is one thing, but selling?

The Appalachian Express has belonged to the Peterson family longer than I've been alive."

"You're preaching to the converted, sis." Jett shook the back of her chair gently. "I don't like it any more than you do, but I don't blame them. It'd be hard to turn over the reins to a stranger. Heck, even a friend. But no kids mean no successors. Selling makes sense."

"I hear what you're saying, but I don't want to." Eliza sent a cutting gaze toward the computer screen. "And why sell to this bigshot company from New York? Pine Valley is nothing more than a dot on the map to them. They won't understand us. Did you see how that last email was signed? *Mr. Bennett M. Olsen, McCoy Railway Supervisor.* Too proper and important to leave it on a first-name basis. That middle initial is egotism at its finest." She crossed her arms, daring Jett to argue.

Undeterred, he met the challenge. "That's the way it's done in the city."

Eliza glared at him while her toes went to tapping, a nervous habit she'd picked up in college.

"Be still, jitterbug." Jett patted her shoulder. "You'll tap right outta your shoes if you don't calm down."

Eliza let herself lean into his touch, savoring the connection. For the past few months, she'd worked so hard to prove her independence. Doing so meant distancing herself from her family more than she liked, even at work. Today, though, it was nice to know she wasn't alone. "You're right. I'll try to chill. I just wish I knew when to expect our *guest*. That's all."

Spinning the chair around, Eliza caught Jett off guard, nearly rolling over his foot.

Jett yelped and jumped back. "Watch it!"

She stood, side-stepped, and braced herself mentally for the impending reprimand. Jett's lips bent into a frown as he scowled at her. The look made her feel too much like the bratty sister of yesteryear instead of the responsible woman she'd grown into. It was almost sobering enough to take the humor out of the moment. *Almost.*

"Oops. You OK?" Eliza touched his elbow as she clamped her lips tight, locking up the laughter threatening to escape.

Jett nodded. "Yeah, you missed, but not by much. I knew you were a dangerous driver, but apparently, anything with wheels becomes deadly when you're around."

Eliza smacked his arm and let loose a giggle. "Oh hush. You're fine. How about a fresh cup of coffee to make it up to you?"

"It's a start, I guess."

After pushing her chair under the desk, Eliza scurried to the break room. The rich notes of coffee wrapped around her halfway down the hall. Welcoming the familiar scent, she inhaled deeply as she poured her brother's coffee. The fresh brew looked too good to pass up. She poured herself a new cup as well and returned to the front. There, she set her cup beside her keyboard before taking Jett his. He mouthed a "thank you" and pointed to his headset.

Eliza nodded and returned to her seat, passing Hanna as she did. Hanna, sister-in-law extraordinaire and the much-needed voice of reason between Eliza and her brother, had found her comfy spot by the main phone. Her feet sat on a box of copy paper beneath the desk and her back rested against a throw pillow. If the setup wasn't doctor's orders for Hanna and her growing bundle of joy, it would have been comical. Eliza waved at her, scrunching her lips between a grin and a pout at the adorable sight.

The sounds of the office settled softly around her as she resumed her work. The click of Jett's keyboard, the rustling of papers being sorted, the tick-tock of the second hand circling the clock. Eliza focused on the medley of familiarity until her nerves got the best of her and she reopened the email from her unseen supervisor. If only she knew what to expect.

Maybe I can find out.

A company as vast as McCoy Railway surely had an expansive website that might include bios. After a quick internet search, she found the page and clicked on the Staff subheading. There, directly beneath the CEO, a man with coffee-colored eyes and a jawline just a strong smiled at her.

"Hello, Mr. Bennett M. Olsen." Clicking the photo, Eliza zoomed in for a better look. Immediately, she wished she hadn't. At first glance, the man was handsome. Up close, handsome morphed to gorgeous. Dark brown eyes deep enough to get lost in, hair nearly the same shade with a few golden strands kissed by the sun, and a nose to make the Greek Olympians jealous.

Eliza closed the screen without so much as skimming the paragraph about him, too afraid whatever the website revealed would make her believe in love at first sight. *Nope, not interested.* Sure, if she were searching for love she'd try to find a man as unlike Austin Stone as she could, which made Bennett the perfect candidate. His dark gaze could never be mistaken for Austin's baby blues, and those hickory locks Bennett sported hit different than the blond waves of her former fiancé.

No matter. Landing a date ranked so low on the totem pole of Eliza's life she'd have to limbo to find it. Since extinguishing the torch she'd held for Austin, she had no desire for a new relationship, especially not with a big-shot businessman who called New York City home.

Eliza startled in her seat as a ringing phone pulled her away from her musings and back to reality. Hanna pointed to her, letting her know she was transferring the call, and the line lit up.

"Appalachian Express, Eliza Lee speaking."

"Hello, Eliza Lee. How are ya this morning?"

Eliza smiled and crossed her legs as she answered. "I'm blessed, Trish. And you?"

"If I was any better, I'd have to sit on my hands to keep from clapping."

"That's wonderful." Eliza tried to sound upbeat despite the frown that formed as she scanned her computer screen. Still no email. No word as to when the new supervisor would arrive. She reached across her desk for her coffee and blew across the top for a moment before taking a sip. "I wish I were half that good."

"Listen to this and maybe you will be. We've got more toys and candy than ever before, oodles of gloves and hats, top-notch coats, and a thousand turkey certificates, up from the five hundred last Christmas. Our sponsors have truly gone above and beyond, praise the Lord."

Eliza nearly leaped from her chair, but seeing Jett on his headset kept her in check. She bounced up and down as she clenched the phone tighter. "That's such great news! It's been a rough year for so many. Mines have shut down left and right. Those still open are hanging on by a thread. I'm afraid Christmas is going to be tight for lots of folks this year."

Trish sighed into the phone. "I know, darlin' dear, but keep your chin up. This is going to be our best Run yet."

A slap sounded on the line and Eliza Lee imagined Trish striking the desk in front of her. She shook her head with a smile.

"I think you're right. I can't wait." Eliza took another drink of her coffee. Warmth filled her once more, not from the brew alone this time but from the joy reignited inside her.

The Santa Run had always been her favorite holiday tradition, but she loved it even more now that she was in charge of coordinating the event. Organizing the run was her first leadership role with the railroad, and it couldn't have come at a more opportune time. What better way to prove herself to the company and her family than overseeing the tradition her grandfather loved best? She had to get it right.

Another thud echoed through the phone, followed by Trish's belly laugh. "Me, either. Oh, I have to let you go, sugar. A truck just pulled up with more donations. I'll call again soon."

The line went silent. Eliza grabbed her pen and started tapping, wired with anticipation of the impending holidays. The Santa Run was the biggest event of the year for the Appalachian Express. The company provided transportation for the jolly man himself to deliver toys, warm clothing, and goodies of all sorts to hundreds of families every year. Well, *a* jolly man, anyway, dedicated to filling the shiny black boots as best as humanly possible.

A snapshot of Grandpa Walt surfaced, flushed face and fake beard, a broad smile stretched across his face. His tired eyes shone brightly under the brim of a velvet hat as he sang out "ho ho ho!" to the crowd. Eliza had stood front and center waiting for his instructions. Minutes before the train left the yard, the big man himself motioned for her, pulled a red bag from a hidden pocket, and handed it to her. Nestled inside was a plush tan-and-white beagle she named Spot. It was the last gift Grandpa had given her. Now, making sure the event went off without a hitch was the only gift she could give to him.

"Was that Trish?" Hanna's voice burst the bubble of Eliza's reverie.

Eliza stopped the pen mid-tap, quickly pushing the memory far away. "Sure was." She took a breath, hoping to inhale the enthusiasm the moment deserved and exhale the grief threatening to disrupt it.

Hanna smiled. "How's the planning coming along?"

"Great." Eliza mustered as much cheer as she could. "More coats, more volunteers, more grocery vouchers. I think the construction delay gave more time for donations. The late December run is working out wonderfully. Is Jett's 'ho,ho,ho!' ready?"

"Sure is." Hanna tilted her head to the phone Eliza had just hung up. "I know you're worried about the sale, but why don't you focus on the run for a while?"

"I'll try." Eliza blew at her bangs. "But can I at least hold my breath until our new boss shows up?"

"If you must." The phone rang and Hanna slipped into secretary mode as she answered.

Exasperated with the uncertainty facing the railroad—and herself—Eliza Lee crossed her arms on her desk and laid her head on top of them the way she used to when her class played Heads Up Seven Up in school. *I can't stand this, Lord. I know the future is in your hands. I trust you, but it's so distracting. Help me focus.*

Eliza raised her head. A sound so quiet she almost missed it rang from her computer speakers. She rolled forward to get a better look and scanned the screen. Her inbox screamed for attention as a new message arrived.

This is it. Eliza moved the mouse slowly, like syrup falling over pancakes. She paused and let her finger hover over the button, too fearful to click. *Come on, now, Eliza Lee. Boss man is coming whether you like it or not. Might as well find out when.*

Forcefully, she slammed the button down. Her stomach churned as she read, making her wish she'd skipped breakfast. By the time she got to the end of the message, she was the one in need of ginger ale instead of her pregnant sister-in-law.

Tomorrow, Mr. Bennett M. Olsen would make his appearance.

A song from an old movie Grandpa had made her watch popped into Eliza's head. She hummed a few bars, hoping the curly-headed kid was right. That despite all the changes headed her way the sun would still come out—tomorrow.

Chapter Two

Bennett sat in the driver's seat, weighing the need to get out and stretch against the longing to curl up for a nap. The drive had been long, and the soreness in his legs proved it. Tense muscles were a small price to pay, though. The feeling of a road trip was irreplaceable, and he'd made this one worth his while. Now, it was time to get to work with Expand Kentucky, his father's latest project and the first acquisition of McCoy Railway.

Bennett glanced at the box of donuts in the passenger seat. Hot and fresh from Country Confections, the only bakery he'd come across in the small town of Pine Valley, Kentucky. Smitten from the first whiff of glazy goodness, he'd promised himself he'd come back again while waiting in line to order. The place was a breath of fresh air with its verse-of-the-day whiteboard, prayer box, and free coffee. It was the sweet escape from the city he'd been looking for.

The whole town was. From the moment Bennett passed the green-and-white "Pine Valley" sign, his stress had fallen away. Most of the trees were now bare. The fallen leaves blanketed the ground with faded autumn colors, still beautiful despite the dulling hues. The first signs of Christmas dotted the streets and The B&B Inn he was staying at already had their tree up in the lobby even though Thanksgiving was still over a week away.

Initially, Bennett thought the early decorations were just a southern thing, but after chatting with a couple of the guests during breakfast at the inn, he'd surmised the town usually had a big community event—one of the Christmas variety—the first weekend in December, which explained Pine Valley's holiday fast forward as preparation.

Even more interesting, the Appalachian Express assisted with the event, a fact Bennett did not look forward to relaying to Pops. The passing of Bennett's mother two weeks before Christmas had ruined the holiday for his father. While Bennett had been able to rekindle holiday cheer, his father refused to even try. The bitterness he continued to harbor would make the discussion difficult, but when his father's financial discipline was added to the mix, Bennett feared the conversation would be unbearable. Worse than if the event threw off the budget.

A ding sounded as his phone lit up. The text notification proved his father's financial devotion.

DO WHAT NEEDS TO BE DONE, BUT KEEP A TIGHT REIN ON THE SPENDING.

"Really, Pops? Not even a hello?" At least this time his father wasn't backing out of vacation. Bennett rolled his eyes as the memory of the last week streaked through his mind. What he'd thought had been a breakthrough with his father ended up as a backtrack of epic proportions. How had he been so blind?

Bennett had seen what he had wanted to see, that's how. A caring father ready to mend their broken relationship with a quick trip upstate to the Adirondack Mountains. The father Bennett prayed for every night never showed though. Instead, he transformed from Pops into Mr. McCoy, the savvy businessman who needed to get to the office and strike while the iron was hot. His father's plan had worked, and Expand Kentucky was full steam ahead as McCoy Railway secured its first acquisition by purchasing the Appalachian Express. The addition had sent Bennett from the city to the mountains.

After tapping out a reply to his father's text, Bennett glanced in the rearview mirror. The man looking back at him was one he hardly recognized. All his ties had been left in the city, folded neatly in the top drawer of his dresser. A khaki sport coat and navy sweater had replaced his collared button-down and after a week without shaving, his stubble had sprouted into an almost full beard. Bennett ran his hand across his jawbone and down his chin. The new hairs stiffened against his palm.

No-shave November?

An excited grin broke loose as that truth settled in. Looks didn't matter today. At the Appalachian Express, Bennett was free, separated from the reputation he sought to uphold and miles away from footsteps expecting him to follow.

Carefully, he transferred the pastries from the seat to his lap. As he did, his vision snagged on the passenger door compartment. A bright pink scrunchie lay forgotten. *How did I miss that?* Should he message Janet and tell her he found it? If Bennett were still in the city, he could simply take the elevator down to the bottom floor of the office complex and find her. Not that he would have. That nearness had been partially what prompted him to take the job in Kentucky when his father proposed it. Having his ex-girlfriend start work in his building a week after the breakup hit harder than Bennett had expected. He had no desire to restart the relationship, but seeing her every day made him question their time together or rather the lack thereof that had caused her to leave him.

Refocusing on the task at hand instead of his romantic failure, Bennett opened the door and slid out. He pressed the box against his chest while he shut the door. The November chill greeted him, making him quicken his steps.

Upon reaching the front stoop, Bennett stomped to clean off any stray leaves he may have picked up as a gust of wind blew around him. The blast forced his gaze from the straw mat below him to the entrance in front of him. A holiday wreath welcomed him. The grapevine circle surrounded a whimsical snowman while curled strands of satin ribbon in bright white flowed freely from the bottom.

Confusion bloomed like the mesh bow before him. Had he done the right thing by coming to Kentucky? Sure, he'd wanted some distance between himself and Janet, but his eagerness in leaving the city ran deeper than getting away from his ex-girlfriend. Bennett searched his heart. *Lord, why did I agree to this?* He shook his head as the answer came.

Project Pops.

His plan to reconcile with his father. Perhaps a temporary break from the city, and from each other, might be just what the doctor ordered. Despite working together, Bennett and his father remained like ships passing in the night, sharing the same ocean but nothing more. Miles apart might put them in the same bay. Distance had helped connect their hearts before. Why not again?

McCoy Railway had gifted him a last chance to make his father proud. Get in, get the job done, get out, get his dad back. Bennett stood straighter as he repositioned his hand under the bottom of the donuts, resigned to be the man his father needed him to be, but his way. There had to be a happy medium between busy and the burnout plaguing him, between career and the family he longed for. Bennett was counting on his time in Kentucky to serve as clarification of that fact.

Still holding the doorknob, Bennett wondered if a knock was necessary.

No, they're expecting me.

Before changing his mind, Bennett pushed the door open, shoving aside his uneasy questions with it. Hot air laced with the scent of dust filled his lungs. A sneeze worked its way to the end of his nose, making it wiggle. He tightened the grip on the pastries, and turned his face into his shoulder, before the sneeze finally escaped.

His eyes popped open to find the receptionist watching him. The sudden attention made his cheeks burn before he regained composure, reminding himself it was only a sneeze. Everyone sneezes.

"Let me help you." The lady with a kind smile and very pregnant belly dissolved the awkward silence as she rose from her chair. Gingerly, she took the box from his hands and disappeared down the hall. In mere seconds, she was back in front of him, handing him a tissue.

"Thank you, Miss..."

"Hanna, and you're most welcome. Mr. Olsen with McCoy Railway, I presume?" Her eyebrows rose as she posed the question and Bennett nodded, deciding right away he liked the tone of the office. No titles, first name only. He could get used to this.

"Bennett, please. No *mister* and no *sir*."

Such titles were reserved for people who needed to feel important, who thrived on empty accolades and impressive appearances, people like his CEO father. At the New York office, Bennett continually corrected the staff, especially when a new hire slipped and referred to him as Mr. McCoy. The mistake was easy to make. A biological father and son should share a last name, but Bennett and his father were the exception. Their familial relationship was a complicated matter—one lending different monikers despite the blood that bonded them.

Realizing Hanna remained standing to be polite, Bennett pointed to her seat. "Please, sit."

"Thanks. I sure appreciate that. It's getting harder for me by the day." She looked up as she placed her hand atop her stomach. "What can I do for you?"

"I'm looking for..." He glanced at the paper he'd nearly forgot he was holding. "Lee Elliott. May I speak with him?"

"Lee?" The young lady searched his face like she was working a puzzle without all the pieces to make it whole.

"Yes, my associate gave me a contact name of Lee Elliott." Bennett shed his coat and hung it on the rack in the corner.

He double-checked the yellow slip in his hand, making sure he'd asked for the right person. Though he'd sent out the mass email alerting the crew of his arrival, he didn't remember a single name from the list. The paper he held served as a lifeline and it clearly said Lee Elliott.

"Excuse me." A voice somewhere behind him spoke up.

Bennett turned toward the hall where a woman now stood. Her green eyes shimmered, even under the poor lighting of the office, and her dark hair cascaded over her shoulders. She tugged on a slouchy sweater that engulfed her petite frame before listlessly taking hold of a heart locked around her neck. The action gave Bennett a good look at her left hand. No bracelets—or rings—he noted. Realizing he shouldn't be noticing such things, Bennett threw a sheepish grin and stepped back.

She passed and stopped beside him. Her fresh face of ivory skin, smooth and fair, lit up as she smiled. "Did you call for Lee Elliott?"

"Yes, I did," Bennett answered, trying to catch his off-the-track thoughts, currently concentrating on the pink of her lips. He snapped his eyes up to meet her gaze. "Do you know where I can find him?"

"I sure do." She wiped her palms down the thighs of her jeans and offered her right hand. "Right here, but it's *Eliza* Lee Elliot. And you are?"

Chapter Three

E liza held back her laughter as she watched the stranger's face turn too many shades of red to count. Gone were her chances of making a good first impression, but she didn't want the greeting to go from memorable to deplorable. Not when Bennett had the power to make or break her.

"Oh. Sorry about that." The man straightened his stance and drew in a breath. "Mr. Johnson must've torn off the first name when he handed me the sheet and not realized it. He was a bit under the weather last time we talked and—never mind. I'm getting off track."

Eliza took a half step toward him, her hand still extended. As she did, she gave her new boss a better look. The website photo had not done Mr. Bennett M. Olsen justice. His hair was thicker in person and the jawline more attractive now that it was covered in stubble. Add in his eyelashes for days and looking away became a chore. Hoping the businessman was too dazed from the name mix-up to notice her ogling, she kept talking.

"That's all right. I won't hold it against you." She smiled and glanced at her still unshaken hand hoping to elicit the formality. The longer they stood there, the more uneasy she became.

"How kind of you." He chuckled and finally took her hand. At his touch, a gasp worked its way up her throat while warmth spread from the point of contact. Her nerves were really working overtime. It certainly wasn't his chocolate gaze or deep voice having an effect on her.

Clearing his throat, he released her hand. "I'm Bennett with McCoy Railway."

"Nice to meet you, Bennett." Eliza's voice sounded strong, much to her surprise. She motioned for Bennett to follow her. Together, they made a beeline for her desk.

In his presence the office transformed from familiar to foreign. The shift stripped away her newfound confidence, leaving her weak and exposed. Thankfully, the last year had taught her how to adapt. Before the vulnerability could set in, Eliza squared her shoulders and pointed to a chair near hers.

"Please, sit. I know we have a lot to talk about." Eliza seated herself and waited for Bennett to do the same. A heavy exhale sent a sprig of hair flying across her cheek. She idly tucked the strand behind her ear, propped her elbow on her desk, and cradled her chin in her hand while he made his way to the chair.

He stopped halfway. "If you don't mind, could you point me to the breakroom before we get started? I think Hanna took the donuts in there." A loud growl rumbled from Bennett's stomach. "As you can hear, I need one. And probably a cup of coffee before we tackle the day."

"Of course." Eliza stood back up as she answered, once again putting her laughter on lockdown. Bennett didn't know she was the office java junkie, but it was common knowledge to everyone else. Out of the corner of her eye, she saw Hanna, a knowing grin plastered on her face. Eliza pointed a finger toward her, a silent warning to keep her mouth closed. "Follow me. I'll get the monkey off your back and then give you the grand tour, introductions included."

"Sounds splendid. Thank you."

As Eliza sidestepped around her desk, Bennett backed up to widen the path for her. She started down the hall and he followed. Trying to keep the silence from deafening her, she gestured to the Christmas tree.

"Whatcha think about our tree? Gorgeous, isn't it?" Eliza called over her shoulder as she turned into the break room.

"Yes, it's lovely." Bennett fell in close behind her. "But isn't it a little early for decorations?"

"You sound just like Jett." She grabbed a cup from the top of the Styrofoam tower beside the coffee maker. Was she the only one ready for Christmas? She was beginning to think so. "With the year I've had, I needed the holiday cheer to come a little sooner than normal. Cream or sugar?"

Eliza Lee turned to face Bennett. To her surprise, he'd been standing at the door watching her.

"Black is fine."

She poured and carefully handed over the cup. Bennett lowered his head and inhaled the steam like he was the judge at a wine competition instead of the new boss on the block. He took his first small sip.

"Good, huh?" She placed her hands on her hips and waited for the verdict. Eliza knew the truth as assuredly as she knew herself to be an asset to the railroad. Still, she needed to make sure management realized it.

"Indeed, it is." Bennett took another sip and smiled before setting the cup on the table in front of him.

Eliza joined him as he stretched his right leg out from the side of the table. His khakis and chocolate loafers were put on full display. No one wore those types of shoes to the office. Too much muck tracked in and out to keep them clean. *You should've left those at home, City Boy.*

After plucking an apple fritter from the donut box, she pushed the pastries toward Bennett. "So, how long have you been with McCoy Railway?"

"Po—Powers that be hired me a little over ten years ago, as soon as I moved back to the city."

Bennett snatched a strawberry iced donut and took a big bite. Eliza waited for him to swallow, expecting some side story about when he first started with the company or an inside joke to follow, but she was met with silence. The urge to keep the conversation moving overwhelmed her as the quiet unleashed her voice.

"I bet the city's beautiful during the holiday season. I've always dreamed of going to Rockefeller Center but haven't made it yet. Have you been?" Eliza took another drink while she waited for him to answer, wondering what in the world had gotten into her. First, she'd implied how awful her year had been. Now, she'd blurted her dream of visiting the city. She should be building walls to hide from this man, not baring her soul. *Hush, Eliza Lee.*

"Let's see," Bennett said, oblivious to the mental reprimand inside her head. "The last time I went to Rockefeller was seven years ago, I believe. It's nice but so crowded, and after you've seen it once, it loses its magic. Last year I ate leftover Chinese food and fell asleep on the sofa before the lights came on."

Bennett smiled and traced the rim of his empty cup with a forefinger, staring toward the door. While he did, Eliza studied his face. His smile never reached his eyes. She searched and found no signs of sadness, but no evidence of joy either. There was something in that puppy-dog stare too. Stillness, yes, but more. *Longing, maybe?*

Without warning, Bennett turned his head, meeting Eliza's inspection as he did. *Definitely longing.*

Quickly, she stood and nodded to the empty cup. "Want a refill?" Eliza poured the last of her coffee down the drain. Turning on the water, she rinsed her mug to keep her from turning around until the heat on her cheeks faded.

"No, thanks." The familiar screech of a chair scooting back chased his answer. When Eliza twirled around, Bennett stood beside the table. He tossed the cup in the wastebasket and stuffed his hands inside his pockets.

"Ready for the tour?" Her tongue nearly tied itself as the words raced out. She'd never seen a man look more handsome, an alarming realization that made her pause. Bennett was her new boss, the man with middle-initial arrogance and the authority to end her career with the Appalachian Express. She couldn't be attracted to him.

"Lead the way." Bennett gestured for her to exit first. His face warmed as he did, but his smile still didn't light his eyes. It was a picture-day grin that only went skin-deep.

Eliza gave the grand tour as she led them down the hall again. She pointed out the restroom and supply closet as she steered the two of them back to the office space. Hanna sat at her desk sorting a stack of papers nearly as tall as she was.

"Bennett, this is Hanna, our receptionist. She takes care of the phone system and keeps all our filing in tip-top shape. She just so happens to be my sister-in-love too. We dropped the *law* years ago." Eliza's heart filled with joy as she introduced the two of them. Hanna was so much more than just a secretary or even her brother's wife. She'd become the sister Eliza had always wanted.

Hanna placed a hand on her belly, drawing attention to the baby bump.

"Currently, she's working overtime growing my new niece or nephew." Eliza chuckled, knowing the pregnancy was impossible to miss.

"I can see that." As he shook hands with Hanna, Bennett's voice softened in tone. He gestured to the stack of folders on her desk. "I think the new scanning software we'll be implementing will make your life much easier, Hanna."

"New software?" Hanna cut a glance to Eliza. She shrugged, letting Hanna know this was the first she'd heard of it. *Great. Introductions aren't even done and City Boy's making changes.* Eliza's foot went to tapping.

Bennett didn't catch the action, but Hanna must've, if her exaggerated nod was any indication. "I'll take your word for it, Bennett. Can't wait to give it a go. In the meantime, if I can be of service to you in any way, from making travel arrangements to finding the best steak in town, you just let me know."

"I might take you up on that last one before I leave for the day." Bennett covered his mouth as he stifled a yawn.

For the first time since the acquisition had been finalized, Eliza realized she wasn't the only one affected by the sale. Yes, things were going to be different around the office for her, but Bennett was in an entirely new town with not a friend to his name. Following that epiphany, she chided her selfish behavior.

Silently, she prayed for forgiveness while the two of them waited for Jett to work himself free. He held up his finger and continued with the call. Eliza pointed to her desk nearby before sliding into her normal chair while Bennett took the empty seat closest to her. His woodsy smell wafted her way and her breath hitched. *First, my nerves. Now, my asthma?* She was beginning to think Bennett was either bad luck or an insta-crush. Since she had no intentions of admitting the effect her new boss seemed to have on her, she was going with the luck thing. *Yeah, that's it.*

She swallowed twice before continuing. "You said you'd been with McCoy Railway for over a decade?"

"Yes, it's been a journey, to be sure." Bennett leaned forward as he spoke and rested his forearms on his thighs. Having his full attention unlocked an array of emotions in Eliza Lee, ranging from lovely to disarming. The competing feelings made it hard to think, let alone carry on a conversation.

Luckily, Jett stepped in and she didn't have to.

"Sorry that took so long." Jett's voice boomed as he joined them, making both Eliza and Bennett turn their heads. "I'm Jett Elliott. Nice to meet you. Bennett, is it?" Jett extended his hand.

"Yes. Nice to meet you too." Bennett grabbed Jett's hand and shook as soon as his feet hit the floor. Eliza followed suit and stood as well, ready to offer her hostess skills to the conversation if needed.

"Thanks. Do you have any questions yet? I take care of the scheduling—both training for the new hires and the shipments for transport—public relations, customer service issues, anything along those lines."

"No questions, but several ideas I'd like to bounce off of you." Bennett pointed to the headset. "Has the office tried an automated phone system before?"

"No, I don't believe s—"

"Jett, I hate to interrupt, but Dawg's on line two for you." Hanna appeared behind the group before Bennett could answer.

"I'm sorry." Jett took a step toward his desk. "Will you excuse me?"

"Of course. We'll chat later."

Bennett sat back down as Jett returned to his desk, his lips turned up in amusement. In a moment, she realized the reason for his smirk. She was the only one still standing. Jett pretended to smack his forehead and mouthed the words, "sit down." Feeling like the clueless little sister once again, Eliza plopped into her chair.

"Dog?" Bennett asked, leaving out the southern drawl with the proper pronunciation. He tilted his head toward her, giving Eliza a better view of those long lashes. His brown eyes sparkled beneath them. They were dark, but welcoming, the kind of eyes that sent her pulse to skittering. *Because they have the power to see you to the door, girl. Nothing more.*

Reminding herself of the boss-man box she had firmly placed around Bennett, she shrugged. "Dawg is a nickname. His real name is Shannon, but no one ever calls him that. If you're associated with the coal industry in any way, from mining to transport, you've got a nickname."

"I see, but why Dog?"

Amused by his proper pronunciation, Eliza leaned further into the seat. "Well, I don't know for sure. But I have a theory."

"Let's hear it then." Bennett's voice registered as strong as before but a new curiosity lined his tone.

"Are you familiar with Harry Potter?"

He nodded slowly. "I've seen the movies."

Do you remember the sorting hat that puts all the students into their Hogwarts houses?"

"I do," said Bennett.

"Good. You'll get where I'm coming from then." Eliza smiled as she began her explanation. "I imagine there's a trucker hat somewhere that's a makeshift sorting hat. Names are scribbled on folded slips of paper and thrown in. When you fill out your new-hire paperwork, you pull one out, and that becomes your handle."

Bennett blinked as if stunned before losing his composure. He slapped his knee as big belly laughs rolled out. Eliza added giggles but let them fade as she focused on the sound of Bennett's laugh, the first hint of joy she'd heard in his voice all day.

Knowing she'd partially caused the reaction filled her with pride. She held both hands out, palms up. "It's the only thing that makes sense. I've heard Tiny, Bozo, String Bean, even Flap. How do you get a name like that unless there's a hat?"

"Your reasoning sounds plausible to me." The two shared another quick laugh and Eliza resituated her chair.

"With that mystery solved, what were we talking about?" She shook her head and tried to steer the conversation back on track. From the corner of her eye, she snuck a peek at Jett. He remained focused on the computer screen. Bennett, on the other hand, set his sights firmly on her. Feeling his gaze glide over her, she resisted a shiver and answered the question herself.

"Oh, I remember now. Your career with McCoy Railway. Ten years is a long time. I've been the human resource director with the Appalachian Express for the last two years, and running the office is already second nature to me. With your experience, I'd say you could oversee an acquisition in your sleep, huh?"

Her heart raced as she asked the question. Attempting to hide her nerves, Eliza folded her arms on the desk while her worries took flight. Bennett's response had the ability to ground them or send them to ridiculous heights.

"Actually, no. McCoy Railway has avoided such things until now. There are no protocols to follow, no timeline to be met, or even statistics to compare with. It's a risk, but it's one worth taking."

Eliza blinked at the unexpected answer. Instead of clearing things up, he'd muddied the waters. *First time? No protocols? Lord, what on earth is happening here?*

Hoping to hide her surprise, Eliza crossed her legs and smiled. "Well, I guess we'll figure it out together."

She hoped they would anyway. She needed the railroad, for her sanity as much as for her livelihood. And if she had to fight to keep it?

So be it.

Chapter Four

Hunched in the shadows of the darkened street, Bennett squinted against the glowing streetlamps as one by one the lights switched on at the end of the alley. Rats skittered across the worn tops of his shoes, squeaking with each pass over the threads. He shuddered, wiggling his bare toes farther back and praying the rodents didn't find the hole above his pinky.

From the end of the street, a man called. The voice loud but undiscernible. Bennett strained to hear, but the distance between them coupled with the blood rushing through his ears scrambled the words. His legs shook as he gathered his last bit of courage and stepped closer to the voice. The shouts continued, louder this time, and Bennett angled his head.

For a moment, the voice became clear. Two words—*son* and *home*—rang out over the pounding of his heart. But then, the voice faded. Muffles sounded once more. Bennett braced a hand on the wall, ignoring the slime his fingertips scraped against and the rancid odor wafting from the brick. He crept along the building as the intense need to hear the man again fueled his steps. The longing drowned out the warning in Bennett's head to stay put, drawing him out of the shadows and into the alley.

Another word broke free over the city traffic and his labored breathing. A "goodbye" spoken with such intensity Bennett's knees buckled beneath the finality. Urgency unlike any he'd ever felt before pulsed through his veins. He had to get to the man at the end of the street before the chance slipped by.

Remembering his training from the track team, Bennett prepped himself to run. With slow measured breaths, he drew oxygen in through his nose and expelled the air through his mouth. When the man spoke again, Bennett shot through the alley, pumping his legs like it was the back half of the hundred-meter dash. Each time his foot hit the pavement, the impact sent sharp tingles along the bottom of the broken rubber heels. Bennett kept going. Balling his fists tighter, he convinced himself that each new stride would be the last.

But the alley never ended. Bennett's eyes widened as the pavement stretched ahead of him, pushing the man in the street farther and farther away until sirens started to sound.

No, not sirens, an alarm. An alarm beside the bed in his temporary room in Pine Valley, Kentucky.

With a smack, Bennett hit the snooze button. *A dream. It was only a dream.*

Repeating the realization out loud, Bennett grabbed his phone and scrolled through the pictures. He stopped at the image of a sandwich shop he'd never forgotten.

After his mother's death, Bennett's world flipped on its axis, sending him flying without an anchor to tie him to the life he once knew. His dad had tried to hold it together. Taking him on fishing trips over long weekends, camping during fall break, even sitting through horror flicks to spend time with him. But Bennett pushed him away. Being a family without her was too hard, and he was worn out from trying. After catching his father on a date instead of at the office where he said he'd be, Bennett ran away. If his father could start a new life, so could he.

Closing his eyes, he saw the shelters, the soup kitchens, the streets that welcomed the angry high school drop-out he'd become as a runaway. He'd hoped to find peace, but the rage inside him escalated until Bennett couldn't stand himself.

Even legally changing to his mother's maiden name did little to comfort him. It took a dumpster dive, a pastrami on rye, and Jack Sanford to break through the bitterness.

Bennett opened his eyes and let his gaze focus on the photo of the shop that saved his life. After he'd finished his sandwich that night, Jack took Bennett home with him. The deli owner gave him a couch to sleep on, clean clothes, and a Bible. By the weekend, Jack had not only arranged work for him on his brother's farm in Maryland but had also led Bennett to Jesus and the peace he'd been searching for.

While on the farm, Bennett earned his GED. It wasn't the same as walking across the stage in a cap and gown, but since he'd run away before the end of his senior year, the GED worked to fill in the gap. He followed it up with an associate's degree in business from a community college. The degree bolstered his confidence, and Bennett returned to his dad in the city.

He knocked on the door to his old home with a diploma in hand and an apology on his lips. When his dad answered, though, the words Bennett had spent so long rehearsing flew out the window as two arms wrapped around him. His father's tears fell on his neck as he squeezed him tighter. It was the first time Bennett had ever seen him cry.

The last time too.

Bennett laid his phone on the nightstand. Knowing he couldn't change the past didn't stop him from running from it. Bennett was still that kid trying to get back to his father. Establishing the office in Pine Valley provided him with a chance to do so.

With that incentive in mind, Bennett hurried through his workout. He showered, dressed, and picked up the daily donuts for the crew. When he got to the office, though, he discovered he'd been beaten to breakfast by a pretty little girl distributing various pastries to the rest of the room.

Bennett shut the door and placed his dozen from Country Confections on Hanna's desk. The noise caught the attention of the mystery guest. Smiling, she set her box down and skipped straight to him.

"Hi. I'm Lori. What's your name?"

Returning her smile with one of his own, he answered. "Bennett. It's nice to make your acquaintance."

"Right back at ya. Want a donut?"

Pointing to his breakfast purchase, he shook his head. "No, thank you. I brought my own."

"OK. More for me." Lori shrugged, walked over to Eliza, and picked up a paper from the desk. "Do you really like the flyer?"

Eliza draped an arm over the child's shoulders and squeezed. "I love it. You did a great job helping your mom pick out the colors."

Snatching the paper out of Eliza's hand, Lori ran up to Bennett again. "What do you think? Since you're the boss now, I need your approval too."

Bennett scanned the sheet quickly.

Packing Party . . . Santa Run . . . Sponsored by the Appalachian Express.

"I think this looks amazing. The letters are the perfect mix of red and green. You might have a future in marketing, young lady." Bennett pointed at the flyer, rereading it to himself. "What exactly is the Santa Run?"

"The Santa Run is Santa's personal train. Where are you from that you hain't heard of it?" Lori explained matter-of-factly, in a mix of proper English and hillbilly dialect, the twang thick on the *hain't*.

"I'm from New York," said Bennett. "I'm afraid the train doesn't run there."

Lori's eyes grew wide as half-dollars. "The city is missing out. I can't believe you've nev—"

Interrupting Lori's disbelief, Eliza touched her shoulder and nodded to the door. "I believe your mom's waiting on you in the car, little girl. Scoot so you're not late for school."

Lori stuck out her bottom lip. "Do I have to?"

"Afraid so." Eliza released her shoulders and gently pushed her forward. "Don't forget to thank your mama for the donuts and flyers for me."

With a mile-long frown soiling her face, Lori opened the door. She called out her goodbyes while running down the steps and through the parking lot, to a car with exhaust rolling out the tailpipe. Bennett waited until she was in the vehicle to close the office door. He turned around wondering what it would be like to have sweet moments like that every day. The New York office didn't do sweet.

Eliza offered him a timid smile. "Sorry about her."

"Don't be." He dismissed her apology with a wave of his hand. "She's adorable."

"Thank you. As my first and only niece, I agree wholeheartedly. But she can be a handful."

"I can't speak from experience, but I've heard all kids can be." Bennett held up the flyer Lori had given him. "Can you tell me more about this?"

Eliza pinched the flyer between her finger and thumb, carefully sliding it out of his hands and turning it toward her. "Of course."

She perused the paper with an unexpected reverence. Her eyes softened and her ivory skin seemed to glow brighter than before. The change touched Bennett to his core as he imagined himself looking the same way at his new social security card after his name change.

Laying the flyer on her desk, Eliza sat down and motioned for him to do the same. Bennett followed her instructions. Once he was settled, she started her explanation.

"The Santa Run is a community outreach the railroad sponsors, along with local and national businesses. Winter clothing, grocery vouchers, candy, and tons of toys are handed out at stops from the yard at Pine Valley to the depot near the outskirts of Hickory Hills. This year—" She shook her head and started again. "The past few years have been tough for lots of folks. The Santa Run eases the burden. It breathes joy into this town, even to people who've forgotten what that feels like. It's our oldest tradition."

Eliza paused, laying a hand over her heart. "And yours truly is in charge of organizing it this year."

"I see." Bennett's mind immediately went to the numbers his father cared about most. Supply cost, payroll, and profit loss due to downtime. Most likely, Pops didn't even know about the event. He would have pulled out the Scrooge impression if he had.

Bennett would have to fill him in, dropping a bomb on his father—and Project Pops—in the process. Discussing the holidays would do nothing to repair their relationship. Pops closed the door on carolers without a hint of remorse. How fast would he shut down communication when Bennett mentioned the Santa Run?

Then, there was Eliza. After seeing her reaction to the flyer and hearing her explain the run, Bennett needed to tread lightly. Her adorable factor rose ten degrees with the twinkle now reflecting in her eyes. The enthusiasm made her even more beautiful than she had been while talking to her niece.

But, as supervisor, Bennett couldn't let his heart—or a pretty girl—get in the way of his head. Holding on to that thought, Bennett forced a follow-up question between his lips. "Who pays for the run?"

Tilting her head, Eliza blinked at him. "The railroad includes the cost in the budget at the beginning of the year. A little money is set aside each month. Why?"

"Because this is the first I've heard of the Santa Run, which means it's also news to McCoy Railway. The expenses will need to be examined, maybe reworked, depending on the funds."

"Reworked? This late?" Her brows furrowed. "Bennett, I don't know if that can be done."

"It can. I've seen mountains moved in a matter of minutes when P—" Bennett stopped himself from finishing "Pops." If his father pushed back against the Run, Eliza would hate Mr. McCoy. If she knew Bennett was his son, that hatred might trickle down to him and disrupt the transition. He didn't need an office mutiny on his hands.

Bennett did a quick search for *p* words, finally settling on a fill-in-the-blank answer that made sense. "When potential problems arise."

"But there are no problems. Everything is right on schedule."

"Yes, *your* schedule."

"Not *my* schedule." Eliza circled the room with her gaze. "The company's schedule."

Refusing to be like his father and show no sympathy, Bennett laid a hand gently on her forearm. "The company that has switched hands since the budget was approved."

Extricating herself, she slipped her arm free and retrieved the flyer from the desk. She stretched the paper close to his face, stopping inches from his nose. "The company that has sponsored this event longer than our ages combined."

So much for sympathy.

"The company that you and I both answer to." Bennett gently nudged her hand down, meeting her glassy green gaze with his own determined eyes. "I'm sorry, Eliza, but I must report this to Mr. McCoy."

And I have no idea how he'll take it. His father didn't like to use the railroad for nonbusiness purposes and cared for Christmas even less.

Eliza nodded slowly. "Of course, Mr. Olsen."

"I told you, just Bennett."

Darting her eyes away from him, Eliza examined the desk like her life depended on it. She finally landed her sights on the empty coffee mug. Swapping the flyer for the cup, she stood. "Coffee, *Bennett*?"

Her tongue sliced his name like a sword, cutting first with the title she'd purposefully used and again with the dirty-word tone of the correction. Sensing she needed a moment alone— and knowing he did—Bennett nodded. Eliza tightened her grip on the cup and headed toward the break room. Her shoulders slumped when her feet hit the hall.

Bennett held back a sigh, even as his heart longed to reach for her. Earning Eliza's approval might be more difficult than he originally thought. With a passion as hot as hers, the feat could turn into an uphill battle. Maybe a war.

Like Project Pops, Bennett hoped the challenge would be worth it.

Chapter Five

"Don't take this the wrong way, but you look like death on a cracker." Jenny shook her head as she sized Eliza Lee up. Being honest to a fault was just one of the many reasons Eliza's brother Jonah had fallen in love with her, and why she made a fantastic sister-in-law. That and her fabulous fashion sense.

Eliza sat down beside her on the bleacher. "Gee. Thanks, sis. I love you too."

In seconds, the cold of the metal seeped through her jeans, making her squirm. Friday night in the valley meant high school football. Tonight's game was even more special than usual as the peewee cheerleaders were performing with the older girls. The collaboration served as part of a mentoring project the high school had adopted a few years back. Stands continued to fill until fans were packed as tight as sardines. Aunts, uncles, grandparents, cousins, you name it. Everyone decked out in their respective team color, poised and ready to point out which child on the field belonged to them.

Eliza scanned the field for Lori before elaborating on her disheveled appearance. "I'm exhausted. I don't think I've ever been so happy to see the weekend in my life."

As she scooted closer to Jenny, a key poked her and she resituated the set. The carabiner around the strap of her purse made a terrible commotion, but at least there was no way to lose her keys. It had been one of the simple changes in her life to help gain her independence. More than once, she'd had to call Jett or Jenny to rescue her after she'd locked her keys in her car. But not now. Thanks to the new setup, no more being stranded.

"Boss giving you fits?" Jenny's voice rose over the familiar *click* of a phone camera behind them.

"Not exactly." Eliza blew her bangs with a forceful huff. The warm breath turned to fog as it clashed with the chill of the night.

"Lori liked him so he can't be all bad." Jenny elbowed Eliza softly.

"He's interesting." Eliza's cheeks heated as Bennett's handsome face popped into her head. Trying to hide her blush, she fixed her hair over her shoulders. "But Bennett's got all these new ideas for the office. Digital filing, an automated phone system, and I'm pretty sure I overheard him discussing the possibility of commuter trains with Jett this morning. He wants to change everything, maybe even the Santa Run."

Maybe even me.

Eliza kept the thought to herself. Jenny already had the look of matchmaker in her eyes and explaining her mixed emotions about Bennett would only add fuel to the fire. She might be over Austin, but that didn't mean she needed a new man. So what if Bennett simultaneously aggravated and intrigued her? Who cared if his voice sent tingles down her spine, even when she hated his ideas? *Not me. Nope. No, siree!*

"Don't take it personally, Eliza Lee." Jenny tossed the comment casually as she scoured the sidelines. "He's doing his job."

Eliza rolled her eyes. Her sister-in-law had hit the nail on the head without even trying. If Bennett were anyone but her new boss, she might be willing to change her mind about dating. His quiet consideration spoke volumes, even louder than their bickering. The way he brought her the first cup of coffee from the pot, the donuts he continued to tote to the office, tasking Jett with jobs to include him in the new procedures, even his trips out to the yard to poll the crew on what they'd like to see happen with the railroad. Bennett's thoughtfulness continued to wear down her defenses.

But she was *not* telling Jenny that.

Before the conversation dove deeper into the topic of Bennett and his ridiculously long eyelashes, the cheerleaders trotted out to the sideline.

Jenny tapped her on the shoulder and turned toward the field. "Hey, here they come. Help me find Lori."

Together they searched the uniformed girls, eventually spying Lori front and center. Her hair was pulled back in a ponytail with ringlets falling just to her neck. A blue-and-silver bow sparkled as she placed her hands on her hips and waited for the signal to start.

"There." Eliza pointed to the field. "See her?"

"I do." Jenny beamed as she spoke. After a round of hearty applause, she pulled out her phone. "Let's snap some pictures to send to Jonah. He hates that he has to miss her cheering."

Eliza obliged, glad to fulfill her auntly duty of collecting snapshots. When the routine had ended, she inspected the gallery, making sure the photos turned out.

"I got some good ones. Look." Eliza handed the phone over as she clapped a few more times for good measure.

With each swipe of the screen, Jenny's smile grew wider. "You did, sister. Thanks."

"Most welcome." Eliza paused and let the applause of the crowd die down. "How is Jonah?"

The question sunk the mood like a cannonball. Jenny's eyes grew cloudy, and though her smile remained intact, it lost its intensity.

"Good." She nodded as if trying to convince herself as well as Eliza. "Just missing everybody here, especially Lori. He can't stand to be away from her. But we're coping. And Alabama isn't too far away. Not really."

"Thank God for that."

"And the garage." Jenny held up her car keys.

Eliza Lee laughed, but it sounded fake even to her own ears. Being away from Jonah hurt more than she thought it would. His passion for automotive eventually landed him a job turning wrenches on big rigs. Diesel mechanic had been a safe career move in coal country when he completed his program, but all that had changed with the new mining cutbacks. Since he'd been the last to be hired, he was the first to be cut loose. After the unemployment ran out and with no prospective positions presenting, they'd been forced to explore other options. Eventually, he'd enlisted in the army and landed himself at a depot in Alabama.

"Who knew they let grease monkeys in the army?" Eliza offered the joke with a smile, an attempt to hide how difficult her brother's absence had truly been.

"I'm glad they did," Jenny paused and waved at a bouncing Lori. "I'll tell him to call you this weekend. Even if he doesn't say it, you know he misses you, right?"

"Yeah, yeah, and I guess I miss him too." Eliza fiddled with her purse strap, remembering all the times he played keep away with her pocketbook while they were growing up.

"Enough about Jonah." Jenny scooted next to Eliza as she spoke. "I bet his ears are burning off right about now. How are you doing?"

Suddenly a huge football fan, Eliza watched the field intently while she answered. "I'm OK."

"Really OK? Or OK as in you're still sleeping the weekends away and staying at the office long after closing?"

"OK, as in, thank you for asking, but I really don't want to discuss this tonight."

"Eliza Lee, I know you don't want to talk, but we're family. I love you. It's been almost a year since Walt died and with the anniversary coming up, I worry. You can't blame me for that."

"I know, Jen. But I'm doing better. If focusing on my work keeps me going, what's the problem?" Eliza swallowed as she tried to shrink herself. Why did people always have to ask?

Yes, losing Grandpa hurt her, broke something deep inside that she wasn't sure she could fix, but she didn't want to talk about it. Not that she didn't appreciate their concern. She did, but she had to walk through her grief alone, except for the career she let hold her hand. The Appalachian Express didn't ask questions or shoot sympathetic looks or offer worried hugs. The office just let her be. And there was no chance of losing work to death like she had Grandpa, making it all the more appealing. Work was safe.

Before the sale at least. Now each new day brought a plethora of new concerns. If Mr. McCoy didn't like the budget, would he shorten the run? Cut it altogether?

Against the metal footboard of the bleachers, Eliza tapped her toes. If the run ended, where would that leave her? The project gave her purpose, a way to combat the sorrow and depression that Grandpa Walt's death had ushered in.

Rubbing her hands together, Jenny turned to her. "The problem is grief will catch up to you, and, when it does, you're gonna need someone. I can be that person."

"I know that, but I had that person once and losing him almost killed me." Eliza's voice broke as her eyes begin to sting. She took her sister-in-law's hand in hers. "Jen, let me handle this. My way. Alone."

"But—"

"No buts." Eliza released Jenny's hand and stood. She pointed at her bottom. "Except this butt that's freezing off. What do you say we cheer a bit, huh? Get some blood flowing?"

Jenny rose to her feet. "Fine. If that's what you want."

"It is." Eliza reassured her while the fight song played behind them. "I promise I'll come to you if I need you."

Chapter Six

week had gone by since Bennett had first walked through the doors of the Appalachian Express, and he was finally hitting his stride. Like she did every morning, Hanna greeted him with a smile as he crossed the threshold. He responded in the usual way by holding up a box of donuts. Food might not be the only way to a man's heart, but Bennett counted on the sweets to win over his new crew.

His new crew that liked him for who he was, not for his father's power or prestige or influence. In Kentucky, no one slipped and called him McCoy, because no one knew him to be the owner's son. Likewise, whatever name he made for himself in Pine Valley would be a reflection of his merit alone. Exactly the way Bennett wanted it.

For the most part, the plan to woo the office with baked goods and charm them with his management skills had worked. Except with Eliza. She embodied the southern combination of sassy and sweet with the sass making an appearance whenever he implemented a new procedure. The two of them had disagreed on more than a few things, from the auto attendant script for the phone to how the files should be separated before digitization. When she was sweet, though? Bennett couldn't get enough, which posed a real problem.

If he gave in to his attraction to her and it didn't pan out, work would be a nightmare. His ex, Janet, merely graced the same building as Bennett and her presence unnerved him so much he'd run to Pine Valley. It was best not to get involved.

Pushing his romantic contemplations aside, Bennett set the pastry box down on Hanna's desk. "You hungry?"

With a grin, she threw the top back and chose the lone apple fritter in the lot.

"I'll get some paper towels from the break room. Be right back." Hanna's voice trailed off as she hurried past him, pastry in hand and much too fast for a woman with child. Her steps made a *click-clack* tune in rhythm with her gait. Jett glanced his way but didn't speak. Instead, he tapped on the headset while Bennett hung up his coat.

His eyes darted from left to right, surveying the room. Judging from the new strands of mistletoe and a light-up snow globe on the accent table, he bet Eliza Lee had worked the weekend. The new decorations had her name written all over them, but where was she?

Trying to ignore the quickening in his pulse, he searched the desk for clues. The top drawer was pulled open, and a set of keys lay in front of the monitor. Looking closer, he watched little wisps of steam rise from the cup next to the keyboard. Someone had been working in her spot this morning.

"Here you go." Hanna nudged his shoulder and handed him a couple of paper towels.

"Thank you." Feeling like a kid who'd been caught with his hand in the cookie jar, Bennett accepted the towels. He plucked his usual glazed donut from the box.

Without warning, Eliza Lee appeared at his side. "Coffee, Bennett?"

Surprised by her sudden entrance, Bennett turned quickly, bumping the flimsy cup against her. The hot liquid splashed out, turning her ivory sweater the same shade as the coffee she'd offered him.

"Oh! I'm so sorry." Bennett cautiously retrieved the cup from her hand as he offered his apology. He set it on the desk closest to him and reached for the rest of the paper towels by the donuts. Reflexively, he dabbed one against the spreading stain.

"It's all right. No use crying over spilled milk, or coffee, in this case." Eliza fanned her shirt in an attempt to dry it. "I'll grab the stain stick out of my car. Be right back."

"Sure. Sorry again." Bennett found himself speaking to the closed door. Eliza was gone. She'd rushed out so fast she hadn't even grabbed her coat.

While Bennett waited for her to return, he took small sips from his cup. He walked around the office to get a better look at Hanna's equipment. The new scanner had been installed on Thursday, along with the software and programs she needed. Today she was starting the daunting task of digitizing the company's files.

Bennett retrieved his computer bag from beneath his desk. Unzipping the bag, he pulled out the laptop and fired the machine up. The home screen lit up just when he heard the door creak open.

When he looked toward the front, he was taken aback, just like the day they'd first met. Initially, he'd attributed the instantaneous reaction to her as the shock of "Lee" being a lady. However, the surprise factor no longer fit into the equation. This time he was fully prepared for Eliza and the same warmth enveloped him again.

The lightest shade of pink kissed her cheek from the cold and her button nose resembled Rudolph's. The jeans she wore were faded in spots and the long sweater paired with them hung to her hips just enough to showcase her petite figure. More than her looks alone drew him in, though. The whole energy shifted when she walked in, her passion and care exuding from deep within.

During the first day or two, he'd thought she was trying to prove herself to him. But after listening to her phone conversations with employees and customers, he'd realized she was the real deal. She genuinely loved working for the railroad.

Her excitement for the day brightened not only the room but everyone around her, including him.

Especially when she aimed her smile at him, like she did as she reentered the office and sat down.

She pointed to the spot where the coffee had spilled. "See? No harm, no foul."

Squinting, Bennett looked hard to find any remnants of the accident, but none remained. He let out a melodramatic sigh and dropped into his chair.

"That's a relief. I really am sorry, Eliza."

She smirked and the mischief popped out her dimples, a feature he'd failed to notice until now. *Beautiful.*

"It's good. Really." Eliza reassured him a final time, touching the cuff of his sweater. Through the thick material, his skin warmed where her fingertips rested.

"Good." Bennett smiled, his gaze meeting hers for a split second before she looked down at her hands and began fiddling with her nails. Her sudden reservation caught him off guard. Until now, she'd been all smiles and southern hospitality. Something had caused a change in her demeanor.

Bennett stiffened in his seat. Was she bored? Upset? Frustrated? With her head down, he remained clueless. Bennett had learned right away she was the poster child for wearing her heart on her sleeve. The inability to see her face, though, made it a sleeveless shirt.

She lifted her head up and offered a half smile. "Are you flying home for Thanksgiving?"

"No, if I go back to New York, I'll be driving. I prefer road trips to flights, so I drove down."

"That car out front is yours? As in, not a rental?"

He nodded, wishing he could tell her the history of "that car" as she so delicately put it.

"Nice." Eliza bobbed her head.

"Thanks. Since I have no idea how long I'll be here, I opted to use my personal vehicle and spare the company the expense of a rental."

"Makes sense." Eliza mumbled in a register much too low for her usual sunny disposition. Though the quiet tone didn't suit her one bit, she continued with it. "Listen, I hate to, but I've got to ask. People are calling me in a panic, and I don't know what to tell them."

Bennett watched as she drew in a ragged breath and wrung her hands tight. The sight made his insides twist with equal intensity. He scooted to the edge of his seat, intent on moving beside her. Before he could, she continued.

"Are there going to be layoffs?"

With the question out in the open, Eliza Lee's uneasiness made sense. As head of human resources, she undoubtedly had personal relationships with most, if not all, the railroad's current employees. The recent acquisition had made their future uncertain. Everyone looked to her for answers, and until today, she had neither hope nor hard times to offer them.

Bennett relaxed, thankful he had the answer she was looking for. "For now, the crew will remain intact and, if all the changes go according to plan, will stay that way."

"Thank the Lord." She closed her eyes and folded her hands, the display of gratitude humbling to see. When she opened her eyes, a sigh passed between her lips.

Bennett opened his mouth to tell her with the way the crew produced, McCoy Railway would be crazy to change personnel. Before he could, Hanna called to her, wagging a finger at the scanner.

Not liking where the scene seemed to be heading, Bennett followed Eliza to the front.

"Tell me again how to make the computer see the device?" Hanna gestured between the computer monitor and the new machine. "A pop-up keeps saying there's no scanner connected."

Eliza Lee smiled but despite the motion, her brows furrowed. "Before you click scan on the screen, tap the power button. The machine goes into sleep mode and if you try to start scanning before it's awake, the computer won't recognize it."

"I held the button down," Hanna said, pitching her voice about an octave higher than normal.

"That's why it didn't work." With a side-eye to the scanner, Eliza continued. "If you do that, the scanner will turn off. Just push it once and release to wake it up."

Hanna tapped the top file in her stack of folders. "Maybe I should go back to the old system today and work on learning the scanner after I clock out. It won't take too long."

"That's not necessary," said Bennett. "Let me try walking you through it again." The last thing he needed was retrograde action. Up until today, Hanna had been excited about the conversion. He didn't want to lose her support.

Eliza Lee laid a hand on Bennett's forearm. "Maybe she's got the right idea. Going back to the paper filing won't hurt anything."

"No. That's unacceptable." Bennett flinched. He hadn't been expecting his father's voice to replace his own.

The words settled among the three of them. Hoping a casual pose would take the edge from his tone, Bennett stuck a hand in his pocket. Red swept across Hanna's cheeks as she placed a hand on top of her baby bump and patted. Eliza Lee watched her sister-in-law carefully, hands on her hips as she walked around the desk and stood beside her.

"With all due respect, sir, I think paper filing would be best. At least that didn't give Hanna a headache and high blood pressure." Laying a hand on Hanna's back, Eliza Lee rubbed circles.

"It's fine." Hanna tucked an arm around Eliza's waist and tried to hug her, but Eliza stepped away and into Bennett's space.

"No, it's not." She took another step, bringing her toe to toe with Bennett.

Caught off guard, he started to retreat. Was this the same woman thanking God for no layoffs? The same woman that waved off his apology for spilling coffee? The same woman that managed to take his breath away just by walking into a room?

When she turned her gaze on him, Bennett had his answer. *Yes, indeed.* The same Eliza Lee, but with a fierceness he hadn't seen from her.

Instead of stepping back, Bennett leaned in, feeling his own blood pressure kick up a few notches. Emerald fire danced in Eliza's eyes and the flush of her cheeks magnified her passion. Bennett matched the look with one of his own as he squared his shoulders.

Never once in the city had an employee dared to defy him, and, if one had, he would have never reacted like he found himself doing with Eliza. He would have been appalled, not attracted to the defiance. But on her? Rebellion looked good.

His pulse jumped like that of an adolescent boy playing Seven Minutes in Heaven for the first time. *Did the supply closet have a lock?* He shook his head, hoping to dislodge the inappropriate thought.

Bennett took a deep breath in through his nose and held it, intent on putting Eliza Lee in her rightful place as an employee and nothing more, in the office and in his mind. Before he could get a word in edgewise, she rushed on.

"The new system is doing the exact opposite of what you promised." Eliza pointed in her sister-in-law's direction. "It's not making Hanna's life easier."

Bennett narrowed his eyes at Eliza, sending as many darts as he could slip past his attraction her way. "It will, once she gets used to it."

"Kind of like our customers will love the automated phone system once they get used to it. Right?"

"Yes." Again, Bennett flinched as his father's steely tone rang in his ears. "That's right."

Eliza's shoulders fell but the fire in her eyes remained as strong as ever. "Bennett, our patrons trust us because we know them. We know their voices, their mamas, their kids. We know when someone in the family is sick or graduating from college. We care, and that's what prompts their trust. This automated system is never gonna fly. Trust me."

"I understand why you think that." Squeezing his neck, Bennett considered her argument. She made valid points. The business-client relationships he'd witnessed testified to it, but the office in Kentucky belonged to him and he intended to run it his way.

Bennett released his neck and stood straighter. "But the customers will eventually talk to someone they trust. The push buttons just get them to who they need faster. Plus, the system frees Hanna up considerably. She's not answering calls for Jett or you or Joe at the yard. Too, if the call was made by mistake, the person realizes that and hangs up before we ever have to say hello. It's a win for everyone."

"Do you like listening to recordings when you call a business? It feels like you're talking to a supercenter." Eliza stuck her pinky and thumb out, making a charade phone and holding it next to her ear. "Dial 1 to hear store hours. Dial 2 to choose the department directory. Dial 3 to reach management. Di—"

Throwing a hand in the air, Bennett cut her off. "Dial 4 to speak with human resources. Good luck with the director. She's as bossy as she is beautiful."

Bennett snapped his mouth shut before saying something he'd regret. He'd already outed his utter frustration—and annoying attraction—to his subordinate. That was more than enough ground to give up for one day.

The door up front slammed shut, interrupting the argument. Bennett took a few deep breaths as he watched

Eliza Lee do the same. The fire was gone when her gaze settled on his. In its place, a plea for peace shone back at him. Though he knew better, Bennett nodded once, letting her know he was in agreement for a truce.

For now.

Immediately, her posture loosened. She tugged at the hem of her sweater and smoothed her hair, almost like they had been making out in the storage closet instead of fighting in the middle of the office. Bennett followed suit, adjusting his collar while Eliza waved to their guest.

The lady looked to be in her later forties or early fifties and smelled of warm sugar cookies. Searching her face, he soon realized her eyes were the same shade of green as Eliza's. The women shared the exact placement of dimples, too. Come to think of it, the chestnut dispersed among the strands of gray resembled the shade of Eliza's hair. *Her mother?*

The woman bypassed Eliza and Hanna as she made a beeline for him. Smiling, she stuck out her hand. "Well, hello there. And who might you be?"

"I'm Bennett, ma'am, with McCoy Railway." Bennett pasted on a smile as he shook. "And you are?"

"Debbie, but you can call me Mama Deb. Everyone does, even though I only gave birth to Jett, Jonah, and Eliza Lee." She dropped the handshake and scooted next to Eliza. With the women side by side, the resemblance was uncanny.

"OK, Mama Deb." Bennett relaxed his smile. "How are you?"

Before she could answer, Hanna rose from her seat and hijacked the conversation. "How dare you walk right by me without hugging me. Get back up here right now."

Mama Deb shuffled over to Hanna. "I was just introducing myself, Love. Come here."

The two embraced, and Bennett dismissed himself from the conversation. He made his way back to his desk. Slinking into his seat, he found Eliza staring.

"In case you missed that, she's our mom, mine and Jett's, and Hanna's mother-in-law." A twinge of annoyance lined her voice, but Bennett couldn't tell if her mother or their argument had put it there.

"So she said." Bennett crossed one leg over the other, holding his ankle as he watched them. How would it feel to fit into a family like that? Longing replaced his earlier anger as he continued to listen.

"What are those on your feet, Miss Priss? Didn't I tell you to stop with the heels while you're carrying my grandbaby?" Mama Deb's scolding filled the office from front to back. Her hands gripped Hanna's shoulders tightly but she stared at the ground. Bennett glanced at the feet in question. Black wedges no less than three inches high jutted out from the hem of her skirt. Trying not to laugh, Bennett turned to his computer screen. Sneak peeks around the monitor kept him tuned in to the show.

"Relax. I've been walking in shoes like these since I was knee-high to a grasshopper. Besides, I go muddin' in these. I promise they're safe." Hanna shifted her gaze to Eliza, a silent plea for help reflecting in her eyes.

In a cool tone entirely opposite of what she'd used minutes prior, Eliza Lee spoke up. "Mom, leave Hanna alone and come tell me where you're off to."

Mouthing "thank you," Hanna Bell wasted no time busying herself as she grabbed a folder.

Mama Deb ambled over to Eliza's desk and leaned against the edge. "I'm heading to the store to get cream cheese for my peanut butter pie. The social's next Wednesday, ain't it? Or is it Sunday after church? Either way, it's got to be bought." Mama Deb shrugged.

With the break in conversation, Bennett raised his pointer in the air to get their attention. "Speaking of church, where is it?"

Both ladies turned their heads. Mama Deb grinned and spoke without hesitation, making Eliza blink at her.

"Why, it's right in town, not far from The B&B Inn. That's where you're staying, right?"

"Yes, ma'am."

"Why don't we meet you at the inn Sunday morning and you can follow us if you want to."

Bennett stifled a laugh as Eliza's mouth fell open. Clearly, the invitation surprised her as much as it did him.

"Thank you, that's very kind." Bennett rocked his chair a couple of times, hoping to give the impression he had to think about his answer. "Are you sure it won't inconvenience you? I'd hate to cause trouble."

"No trouble at all. And after church, you'll have to come to Sunday dinner. Won't he, Eliza Lee?"

Eliza glared at her mother, seemingly making notes to argue about later. She smiled tightly and nodded. "Yes, you will. Unless you've made plans already."

Bennett met her eyes with his. She was giving him an out. Or was she giving herself an out? Either way, he should take it. Pine Valley offered him space from his breakup and a way to win his father back. He needed to remember that and focus on Project Pops, not the green-eyed beauty waiting for his reply.

He should turn down the invitation. Hole up in his hotel room, order food in, and play mindless games on his phone to pass the time. Maybe go for a run or pound out some extra push-ups or take up yoga.

But Bennett didn't feel like doing things as he should. Had Eliza's rebellious streak rubbed off on him? *Maybe.*

Turning back to Mama Deb, Bennett smiled. "No plans. I'd love to join you."

"Great," she said, taking a step forward. "Now that that's settled, tell me a little about yourself."

"Mom, don't you need to get to the store? They open in just a few minutes." The initial frustration Eliza had tried to hide blared full force, making Bennett second guess his decision.

A home-cooked meal sounded nice, but not if he wasn't welcome. Being present but unwanted didn't appeal to him in the least. He'd experienced enough of that in the city.

Mama Deb fished her car keys out of her pocket. "I guess you're right, Eliza Lee. See y'all later." After hugging everyone in the office, even him, Mama Deb headed back out into the cold.

Bennett heard the wind gust upon her departure and shivered, thankful to be inside. He took another sip of coffee and opened his email. Halfway through the first message, Eliza interrupted him.

"Sorry about that." She blew out a deep breath. "My mom is like the welcome wagon. I hope she didn't make you uncomfortable."

"Uncomfortable? Not at all."

You, on the other hand?

Bennett rose from his chair and joined Hanna at her desk. "Let's get back to this scanner, shall we?"

He tapped the power button and looked to Eliza. She nodded, stiff and short. Whipping her head back to her computer monitor, her mouth turned down. Instead of focusing on the frown he felt responsible for, Bennett reveled in the small victory of her acquiescence. He'd won the battle, but the war?

The war was far from over.

Chapter Seven

Eliza Lee inspected her overfilled closet, still madder than a wet hen. *What a way to start the weekend.* She'd barely spoken to her mother since her visit to the office and had no plans on chatting her up anytime soon. Petty? Yes, but Eliza didn't care. A line had been crossed this time.

From the moment Bennett set foot in Pine Valley, the gossip mill had started. It didn't take long to reach her mother. A handsome, unmarried stranger working alongside her still-single-nearing-thirty daughter? That was all her mom needed to hear. Never mind the part about the Appalachian Express being sold or the possible ending to the Santa Run or even her career. That information didn't matter.

Eliza rolled her eyes, partly at her mother's meddling and partly at the closet. The storage container she'd bought on the way home remained empty on the floor behind her. It was time to change that. Eliza scooted the tub closer until the rug stopped it. After declining Jett and Hanna's invitation to be a third wheel for dinner and letting voice mail pick up Jenny, she'd reluctantly decided to clean out her closet. She hoped the task would dispel thoughts of Bennett and the impending church rendezvous.

With more force than necessary, she yanked her summer shirts off the hangers one by one. Still, her thoughts continued to drift to her new boss. No matter how many times she reminded herself to look past the job title, her brain refused to cooperate. Bennett represented the epitome of big business.

Worse, he had corporate power. With a wave of his hand, Bennett could shake up the office or cut her from the railroad or kill the Santa Run. She had to watch herself.

Unfair to the man? Yes, but the mindset remained unshakeable. Though he'd assured her no one's job was in jeopardy, she wasn't convinced. Not with his fancy car, leather shoes, and the loophole he'd left himself.

The crew will remain intact and, if all the changes go according to plan, will stay that way. It wasn't a guarantee, not by a long shot. Pine Valley proved that. Mine owners had given the same kind of assurances only to shut their doors a month later. The sudden closures left their workers without severance pay and little prospect to find new jobs.

Letting her guard down wasn't an option, not when Bennett had the power to take away everything she'd worked so hard for. Not just her day job but her newfound independence. Her paycheck made it possible to live by herself. Without it, she'd be forced to move back in with her parents or into Grandpa Walt's old house. Both choices made her cringe.

For months, she'd tried to stick it out at Grandpa's house, but too many memories hung on the walls, lived in the paneling, creaked in the floors. Memories that ripped the scab of her grief wide open each time the healing process started. She couldn't go back there.

Sensibility urged Eliza Lee to dig in deep and stand her ground. She had every reason to keep a safe distance from Bennett. The problem was she didn't really *want* to keep her distance, which made her mother's invitation all the more frustrating.

After Eliza had gone through her whole closet and a good-sized pile of clothes lay on the bed, she sat down and started folding. Once the summer shirts were neat in the container, she tapped her chin as she looked around the room. *What next?* Shoes?

Eliza Lee gave a "why not" shrug and bent down. As a self-proclaimed shoe enthusiast, her collection, disorganized though it may be, did not disappoint. She picked up one of the numerous flip-flops surrounding her. *How did I end up with all these? No self-control and a shiny plastic card, that's how.*

"I need coffee." Eliza dropped the shoe and strolled into the kitchen. Her favorite mug, a large ceramic cup painted to look like a holly jolly snowman, sat in the sink. After a quick wash and dry, she turned on the Keurig. She placed it underneath the spout and reached for the carousel. Bare holders mocked her.

"You've got to be kidding me." Eliza threw her arms in the air and took a deep breath. Once calm, she talked out a solution. "Know what? It's fine. I'll make a quick run to Country Confections. No big deal."

A glance in the mirror told her to change clothes. Her dingy sweats were not fit for the public and her Mickey Mouse tee had been threadbare for years. But if she didn't hurry, she'd never make it before closing. Eliza chose caffeine over fashion and rushed to the bakery.

An empty parking lot greeted her. The lack of customers echoed the late hour as a gust of wind hurried her along. Despite the brisk pace, her fingers still felt frozen by the time she pushed open the door.

Eliza no sooner stepped through than the scent of chocolate chip cookies and warm donuts engulfed her. She took a deep breath as she read the whiteboard, the verse of the day jumping out at her.

And we know that all things work together for good to them that love God, to them who are the called according to his purpose.

—Romans 8:28

Eliza's heart tightened as she stood staring at the words. The anger she'd been nursing for days waned as forgiveness trickled through her. Mom had meant well enough, matchmaking and all. It wasn't her fault Bennett was a sore spot, his presence forever looming in her mind like an out-of-reach itch. She'd have to call her and patch things up.

Not before coffee. Eliza stepped up to the display case where a friendly face greeted her.

"Hey, darlin'. Are you here for the return of our peppermint mocha? I know it's your favorite." Danny Jo smiled as she wiped her hands on her apron. In half a minute flat, she'd positioned herself between the register and glass case that was purt-near empty with closing sneaking up.

Eliza squealed. "It's back? And Lily Anne didn't text me?"

"Oh, now, don't be too mad at her. You know she's still in that honeymoon phase." Danny Jo chuckled before turning around to grab the largest cup on the counter.

"Does the honeymoon phase last that long? She got married in February." Eliza laughed as the gray-haired lady winked.

"Yup. Sometimes longer." Danny Jo pointed to the cup. "Marshmallow cream?"

"Yes, please." Eliza paused as she scanned the case, eyeing a lone corner-piece brownie topped with caramel and nuts. She couldn't resist. "And the turtle brownie."

Danny Jo carefully grabbed the treat with parchment paper and began wrapping it. "To go?"

"Nah, I think I'll eat in." Pictures of flip-flops flew through her head while she spoke, but she ignored them. The closet had waited this long. A few more minutes wouldn't hurt.

"All right, doll. You've got your pick of tables tonight." Danny Jo gestured to the dining room before putting the finishing touches on her drink.

The window seat looked inviting, so Eliza snaked her way between the display tables, slid in, and gently set her goodies on the end table off to the side. Night had fallen, but the outside lights gave her a view of the cars driving past and the leaves tumbling across the lot. A calm covered her. Reveling in the peace, she discarded the lid of her coffee and breathed in. The scent of peppermint and gooey marshmallow made her toes wiggle inside her shoes. She bowed her head and murmured a quick grace.

When Eliza opened her eyes, she was no longer alone in the shop. A tall man in jeans and a hoodie stood waiting at the counter. In the air, a light woodsy scent floated from his direction. She knew that scent, meaning she should have known the mystery customer, but her brain scrambled for an identity. *Brother Bill?* Nah, way too young. *Pastor Clemens?* No suspenders, so not him either.

Danny Jo appeared from the kitchen and welcomed her guest as sweetly as she had Eliza moments ago. Before the man placed his order, Eliza piped up to give him the skinny on the peppermint mocha. She hoped, too, her interruption might make the man turn around. It did.

"Peppermint mocha? That sounds amazing. Thank y—"

"Bennett!" Eliza cut him off midsentence as his deep brown eyes met hers. "I didn't realize it was you."

He was the last person she'd expected to see. While his gaze swept over her, she wished she'd changed clothes after all. Reacting to his stare, she straightened on the bench before remembering she wasn't at the office. Here, he wasn't her boss.

"You caught me. I confess. I'm Bennett, and I have a donut problem." He laughed, light and hearty.

The sound made Eliza Lee sit up and listen. It was a real laugh, the kind he didn't share often. Of course, he hadn't had much of a reason to, not with their fight and her mother's visit. She'd given him the cold shoulder since. Sunday's invitation wasn't her idea, and she didn't need him thinking it was, so she'd ignored him whenever possible. Disgusted by the memory of her actions, Eliza took a sip from her cup hoping to hide the frown beginning to form.

"The best kind of problem to have," she said, breaking the silence when it passed the point of awkwardness. "Get a glazed with the mocha. Trust me. You won't regret it."

"That does sound tempting." Bennett's eyebrows rose slightly, revealing his lustrous lashes. A five o'clock shadow had sprouted since they last saw each other, adding a ruggedness to his otherwise boyish expression. His voice remained smooth and undeniably charming. *All things for good, right Lord?*

Eliza sipped her drink as Bennett placed his order. One glazed donut and a peppermint mocha. To go.

"I had a late order tonight, so I put a few extra donuts in with it. The batch is getting ready to come up if you wanna wait for a fresh one." Danny Jo's voice carried to Eliza's window seat.

Watching him closely, but not *too* closely, Eliza waited for an answer. Her head listened for a no while her heart prayed for a yes. As if sensing her eyes on him, he cast a look in her direction. *Busted.* In that moment, Eliza had two choices. Let him see her squirm or play it cool. She opted for the second. Snatching her fork, she snared a chunk of brownie and slipped it in her mouth.

Bennett tapped the counter with his knuckles. "Sure, I'll wait."

While he strolled through the dining room, Eliza continued to sneak peeks between bites. She couldn't help noticing his leather shoes had been replaced with lace-ups. Maybe there was hope for him yet. *You're catching on, City Boy.*

Without thinking, she scooted closer to the right and patted to the empty spot she'd made. Surprise colored his features, but Bennett joined her. The light scent from earlier multiplied.

"That smells heavenly." Bennett motioned to the cup she held in her hand, pulling her focus to the drink instead of his cologne.

"It sure does," she agreed, hoping her voice didn't reveal the true meaning behind the remark. Excitement rushed through her veins. It'd been a long time since she'd shared a Saturday night with a man. It felt nice, comfortable even. With the coziness of the bakery and the two of them perched in the cushy window seat, Eliza could almost pretend the outside world—where Bennett was her boss—didn't exist.

She took another drink from her cup. "The mocha tastes even better than it smells."

As she swallowed, she catty-cornered herself to face Bennett better. Eyes sweet as chocolate, rich and delectable, held her captive. She didn't want to break free, but a clang from the kitchen shattered the peaceful moment. Jumbled images of the office tugged at her. Paperwork embossed with McCoy Railway in gold lettering, manila folders, and a makeshift desk skittered through her mind. *Remember what's at stake, Eliza Lee. Don't forget who he is and why he's here.* The internal reminder reconstructed the wall around her heart.

"What are you doing here, anyway?" Bennett widened the distance between them, throwing one arm over the top of the bench. "Isn't Saturday night family night?"

"Usually, but not tonight. I'm taking some 'me' time and reorganizing my closet." Eliza Lee fought back the urge to smack her forehead. *Lame, Eliza. You might as well call yourself Baby and carry a watermelon.*

"Sounds like a wild time." Bennett made them both laugh as he waggled his eyebrows.

"Oh, it is. I needed a coffee before tackling the flip-flops. Danny Jo talked me into this amazing concoction instead, though." Eliza Lee nearly screamed the last part, making sure Danny Jo heard. When she turned her gaze on them, Eliza winked before turning back to Bennett. "Are the weekends crazy for you in the city? Texts like stair steps? Phone ringing off the hook? Dates galore?"

The word *date* made Bennett flinch. "No, to all of the aforementioned. I work most Saturdays, a habit women usually find frustrating."

"I can understand that." Eliza Lee nodded, thinking to herself that the same could be said of men. Austin never voiced his opinion on the late hours she stayed at the office, but Eliza could tell it bothered him. "No one waiting for you back home, then?"

"No." Bennett snapped his fingers, like he'd remembered an important detail. "Not unless you count my houseplants, which I make time to water on Sunday before church. Then, I go to morning service and, afterward, take a jog through the park."

"So, basically, you're trying to perfect your mysterious loner vibe. Am I right?" Placing the cup back on the table, Eliza snuck in a quick once-over of her company. The sweatshirt he wore fit in nicely with her worn-out tee and the jeans washed away the city vibe his slacks emanated at the office. Away from work, he didn't exude the in-it-for-the-money vibe. Had she been wrong about him?

Eliza crossed her legs, cradling her chin in her hand. Bennett had her full attention, and from the look he gave, he knew it. The air around them grew warmer with each bat of those dark lashes of his. Before long, she needed to shed her coat.

Chuckling, Bennett pulled at his sleeve. "Loner vibes are not for me. It's that I haven't found my social circle and my father works even longer hours than I do."

"Seriously? What about your mother? Mom's not my first choice on Saturday night, but she gets me through in a pinch." Eliza tried to stifle her shock with humor as she tacked on the joke.

Bennett twisted his key ring a few times before looking back at her. When he did, his gaze turned tired as the brown of his eyes deepened.

"My mom died when I was in high school. Breast cancer. Now, it's just me and Pops left."

Instinctively, Eliza uncrossed her legs and leaned in, placing a hand over his. "Oh, I'm so sorry."

"Don't be." Bennett covered her hand with his own, keeping his gaze downward. "It was rough, but I made it through by God's grace. It taught me a lot. About contentment, bitterness, thanksgiving. About family."

Eliza winced as his reality came alive to her. The thought of losing a parent as an adult brought her to tears, but as a child it must have been devastating. Yet, Bennett seemed to not only survive his hardships but thrive despite his pain. His perseverance left her awestruck as she waited for him to look up.

When he did, she recognized a desire in his eyes—the desire to grieve and be left alone—the same longing she saw in the mirror on her bad days. Giving him the escape she wished her family would give her, she changed the subject.

"I'm sorry about the blow up at the office too. Sometimes, I let my emotions get the best of me." Eliza looked down and realized they were still holding hands. She slipped her hand free and reached for her cup. "I shouldn't have been so upset about the scanner. Or the phone system. If you think the changes are good for the office, then they will be." *Hopefully.*

Bennett didn't move an inch, keeping his gaze on her as he spoke. "Thank you. That means a lot coming from you."

"Your donut's done." Danny Jo called from the front. "Let me grab your mocha, and you'll be all set." Without so much as glancing their way, she busied herself mixing the various parts of the drink.

"Thank you." Bennett said again, his voice coarse and lower than before. A smile spread across his face, followed by a hint of a laugh. "You're saving a little whipped cream for later."

After pulling a napkin from its holder, Bennett scooted close to Eliza, leaving a pencil width between them. Gently, he wiped her cheek. When he had finished, he let his hand rest along her jawbone, making all the air withdraw from Eliza's lungs. For a moment, she didn't care about the company he represented or her career. The city he called home didn't matter either. As she imagined his lips brushing hers, all she cared about was Bennett.

"There." He gave one final swipe. "Got it." His hand slid from her face, but the place he touched tingled despite its absence.

"Thanks. 'Preciate it."

"Anytime."

Eliza tracked him as he stepped to the counter and paid for his purchase, unable to tear her eyes away until he suddenly turned to face her again. Quickly, she tipped the cup up and pretended to take a drink. She needed a refill, but he didn't know that.

With a smile, Bennett waved goodbye. "See you in the morning."

"See ya," Eliza called, but he was already out the door.

Alone again, she went back to her brownie. The fudgy treat tasted sweeter than before.

Eliza checked the clock, mug in hand. The morning sunlight had woken her much earlier than the screeching alarm she relied on most days. She'd already had time to shower and brew a cup of peppermint tea. The drink didn't provide the caffeine jolt she needed, but she'd have to make do since she'd forgotten to pick up K-Cups on the way home from Country Confections. Other things weighed on her mind, like the hurt she'd seen in Bennett's eyes and the notes of loneliness he hid in his voice. She'd been too busy being defensive to hear them before, but last night they rang as loud as a beaten gong in her ears. Haunting, but mesmerizing, unable to be forgotten.

"Come on, 'Liza Lee. We're gonna be late." The door slammed as her father's yell carried up the stairs. *Right on time, Dad.*

"Go on without me. I'm driving myself today. Might take Lori shopping a little between church and dinner." Eliza shouted down.

Usually, her parents picked her up for church. This morning she wasn't ready, purposely on her part, when the "Dinosaur" pulled up. She'd rightly named the rust bucket Blazer years ago when her daddy threw massive tires on the back, paired with normal ones on the front. The image of a Tyrannosaurus rex had immediately popped in her head, the small tires reminiscent of the extinct animals' tiny arms.

"Hey, Dad." Eliza added, banking on him still lurking downstairs. "Tell Mom I love her."

"Can do," he yelled back. "It's 'bout time the two of you'uns made up."

"I know, Daddio." Eliza Lee hollered. "Love you. Be careful."

"You be careful. Drive like you got eggs to sell."

The door closed and the house fell silent again. Eliza turned to her partially redone closet, giving her outfit of the day more attention than she had in ages. A polka-dot cold-shoulder dress caught her eye. She tried to remember the last time she'd worn it but couldn't. Had she bought it after the breakup? Yes, she had. Emma Lou had insisted on the purchase, calling the dress a get-over-him gown. Eliza held the garment against her, deciding the time had come to give the dress a go.

"That'll do, Eliza Lee. That'll do." With that, she headed for the bathroom, refusing to admit her wardrobe choice had anything to do with her new boss.

Chapter Eight

The blaring of a horn beside him roused Bennett to consciousness in The B&B Inn parking lot. A whiff of cold air trickled in through the crack in his window, speeding his wake-up as he rubbed his eyes. Between the heat blowing on high and his restless night, he'd been lulled to sleep in the driver's seat while waiting on Mama Deb. He hadn't even heard her vehicle pull into the parking spot next to him.

Bennett knew better than to drink caffeine so late, especially adding a donut on top of it. The mocha had left him wired, but thoughts of Eliza deserved much of the blame for keeping him awake. Their impromptu meeting had left him more confused than ever. This woman changed like the wind. One minute, a green gaze sparkled at him and he basked in Eliza's warmth. The next, an icy stare looked through him and the room turned to a meat locker. She didn't make any sense. Not that it mattered. Kentucky was supposed to be about winning his father back, not figuring out a southern beauty with more layers than a lasagna.

Stifling a yawn, Bennett rolled down the driver's side window even farther. The lowered pane allowing the winter chill to sweep through. He shivered from the sudden shift in temperature. In the vehicle next to him, a dark-haired man with eyes the same almond shape as Eliza's rolled down his window.

"Bennett, I'm guessing?" The man waved, choosing to remain in the car instead of getting out for a proper introduction.

"Yes, sir." Bennett waved back.

"Nice to meet you, boy. I'm Luke James, Eliza's father." Luke nodded while Mama Deb waved from the driver's seat. Then, he jerked his head toward the road behind them. "You ready to go?"

"I sure am." Bennett gripped the steering wheel tighter. "Lead on."

"All right, then. Keep up and watch for potholes. Don't wanna drag the bottom out of that purdy car of yours."

In a flash, Luke's window shut again. Bennett watched in the side mirror, annoyed but impressed, as the Elliotts backed onto the two-lane road. He quickly followed suit. It didn't take long to realize the man hadn't been joking as Bennett dodged a hole marring the pavement. The indention rivaled the size of a pizza pan.

A few blocks into town, the Blazer turned into a small lot overfilled with cars. A white brick building stood before him, topped with a tiny steeple. Painted gray steps led to a small stoop and front entrance. A porch wrapped around the side with a ramp to the right for those who needed it. Doors opened and closed as ladies dressed in buttoned floral gowns rushed in. Accompanying men followed close behind, donning suspenders, slacks or jeans, and button-downs with a few blazers snuck in here and there. Watching them, Bennett was glad he'd decided against his sport coat. His argyle sweater screamed "visitor" loud enough.

A few people meandered outside, shaking hands or smoking on the bench. He watched as a blonde in braids, no older than four, tugged a white-haired man's sleeve, held out her hand, and swayed back and forth impatiently. After pulling out a pack of gum, the gentleman bent down beside her and opened his arms wide. The little girl leaped against his chest, and he hugged her tight, dropping the pack of gum into her open palm after she let go. Skipping, she topped the steps and disappeared into the sanctuary.

Quietly, Bennett shut the car door, locking it beforehand so as not to make noise with the key fob. He made his way through the lot and climbed the small set of stairs. There, he rejoined his gracious hosts who stood outside the door waiting for him. Together they found one of the few empty pews left. Bennett slid all the way down to the end.

Sincere greetings, hearty handshakes, and a few hugs eased his anxiety to a manageable level. The tension in his shoulders slipped away as he made himself comfortable, stretching his legs beneath the pew in front of them. To his left sat Mama Deb and Luke James. Perched directly in front of him, Jett sat knee to knee with Hanna. The two looked ready for maternity photos. His arm was draped around her shoulders, her head was tucked under his chin, and the growing baby bump was on proud display. Bennett would have to tease Jett about the pose later.

But where was Eliza Lee?

Skipping church to avoid him seemed out of character. Last night had been the best Saturday night he'd had in months. Waiting on food had never been more enjoyable. There had even been a spark or two. *Maybe?* On his part, yes, despite knowing how wrong it was. But what about for her? The memory of her nearness, the sweet shade of brightened green dancing in her eyes, the playfulness of her voice seemed to echo his sentiments, but Bennett knew better than to assume when it came to Eliza.

Mama Deb poked his forearm with a corner of a songbook and handed it over to him as the front platform filled up with singers. An elder of the church, possibly the pastor, took his place behind the pulpit. He welcomed everyone with a hearty greeting before calling out a page number.

Bennett tried to sing along but lost his place so many times from looking around, he gave up after two verses. Eliza's absence had his attention, not the lyrics. When the last chorus rang, he absentmindedly closed the hymnal. Then he and the rest of the congregation resumed their seats while the singers descended and resituated.

Between heels clacking and feet shuffling, a squeak escaped from the foyer behind them. Bennett exhaled a deep breath and turned, unashamed to be caught looking. Mama Deb looked too. Sashaying in with a smile, Lori entered. Her green glitter bow shimmered when the light hit just right and her dress swished around her legs. A lady favoring her far too much not to be her mother walked alongside her. Gently, she guided Lori. The pair had barely passed him when the door opened a second time. This time, Eliza Lee stepped over the threshold and scanned the room for a seat.

Bennett patted the empty space between him and Mama Deb. As he mimicked her gesture from the night before, he added a wink. Immediately, shame set in, making him wish he hadn't. *Really, Bennie? In church, no less?* Blood rushed his cheeks as he remembered where he was. While he struggled to regain his composure, Lori motioned for Eliza to come to her. Eliza obliged and joined her niece on the other side of the sanctuary.

Lovely didn't do her justice, and he'd but glanced at her. Black knee-high boots met the hem of her dress, light and flowy. White dots in various sizes and patterns splattered the garment from top to bottom. A wide leather belt wrapped around, accentuating her curves in all the right places. One look left him speechless.

Welcoming the reverent silence of Sunday morning as a cover to his reaction, Bennett tore his eyes away from Eliza. He fixed his gaze on the pulpit.

The wood was worn and faded with a cross running almost its height and a songbook propping it level. It had seen better days. Still, quiet beauty, heightened by the aging, emanated from the boards and created a picturesque quality the new-age model of the city lacked despite its cool metal and clear-cut glass. Hard to imagine both served the same purpose.

Yet the longer the service went on, the more evidence proved they did. Verses he'd learned at his home church stirred internally as the familiar words sounded in his ears, reminding him of the ubiquitous presence of God. The Father was with Bennett despite his location, be it in New York or Kentucky. Even without his mother and his father, he was not alone.

The realization of God's omnipotence comforted Bennett leading him to bow his head as he offered a silent word of thanks. The preacher wrapped up the sermon as Bennett prayed. An altar call was given, the invitation hymn sung, and the service dismissed not long after.

As the congregation readied themselves to leave, Eliza Lee joined him. "Well, Bennett, did you like the service?"

"Yes, very much." Bennett stood as he answered. Even in boots, she barely passed his chin and with her head slightly upturned, she exposed full lips painted pale pink, smooth and seemingly soft.

Only one way to know for sure.

"Y'all ready to eat?" Mama Deb's voice shattered the wayward thought as she slid in beside her daughter. "I done got the beans in the slow cooker, and it won't take too long to get the rest of it on the table."

"I am," Eliza said. "But I promised to take Lori shopping in the commons before dinner." At the mention of her name, the little girl appeared and seized Eliza's hand.

"The commons? I don't think I've been there." Bennett skimmed a finger across his jaw as he mentally backtracked through town.

"The commons is our favorite place to go. Family-run shops, down-home cooking, holiday decorations, even a stage for local musicians in the square. I don't know who thought it was a good idea to name the city park The Square, but it stuck. Who am I to argue? Anyway, Lori and I like to walk the commons on Sunday, even though most stores are closed. Window shopping is kind of our thing. Right, sweet girl?"

"Yuh-huh. Come with us, Bennett." Lori twirled a lock of hair as she looked up at him expectantly.

"Lori, don't put Bennett on the spot like that. He may have other plans." Eliza didn't raise her voice, but leveled the child with a you-know-better-than-that look, softened only by the slight smile playing at the corners of her lips. "He's more than welcome to tag along, though."

"It'd be rude not to accept after such a thoughtful invitation." Bennett nodded to Lori but kept his eyes locked on Eliza. "Especially one coming from such a pretty hostess."

The little girl clapped in approval, eyes shining like new pennies. Everyone laughed as the trio exited the church and descended the front steps.

"My car's toward the end, so take your time turning around." Bennett surveyed the parking lot. "Just don't leave me. I'm in the black J—"

"Jaguar." Eliza Lee finished his sentence for him.

Bennett raised an eyebrow and flashed his best touché look. Drawing her lips into a smug smile, Eliza accepted his unspoken praise. Leave it to her to defy female stereotypes through car recognition. *Looks like that in heels and knows a Jag when she sees it? Am I in Kentucky or heaven?* While he contemplated the answer, a voice called out behind him.

"Don't dawdle. Dinner won't be worth a lick if it gets cold." Mama Deb broke in as she joined the group, waving the preacher over to them. "Pastor Clemens, are you sure you can't join us?"

"Thank you kindly, but I've got an anniversary to celebrate. Forty-five years on Tuesday." The preacher adjusted his suspenders and beamed. "Maybe next week."

"Mark it down." Mama Deb patted his shoulder and stopped alongside him at the door of his truck. The beat-up Ford had seen better days. Rust covered the body like spots on a Dalmatian's coat and the dents on the tailgate needed attention in the worst way. The *For Sale* sign that hung in the back window looked to be the most up-to-date part of the vehicle.

"Are you selling this beauty, Pastor?"

"Sure am. None of the grandkids want it, and Sunday's the only day I ever drive it. The rest of the time, we're in the Buick. Automatic and easier to drive when my arthritis acts up. Don't know anyone that's looking to buy, do ya?"

"Not right off, but I'll think on it." Mama turned back to Eliza, who'd been patiently waiting.

Eliza Lee gave a quick wave. "Mom, we're heading out, so we won't be late. I love you."

"Love you, too, Punky," Mama Deb hollered back, loud enough for the whole parking lot to hear.

Despite her mother's volume, Eliza Lee pretended not to hear the pet name. The slight flush of her cheeks betrayed her, though, as she strolled to the car. Bennett didn't understand the embarrassment. If he had a nickname from his father, he'd answer it proudly.

Bennett waited for her to pass before following behind. She smiled as she buckled Lori in her booster and walked around to the driver's side.

"Go," she said, waving him on. "I won't leave you. Lori won't let me."

Bennett followed her instructions, carefully watching for slick spots as he made his way across the lot. The temperature hadn't warmed past freezing with the forecast calling for teens by nightfall. It was unseasonably cold from what he'd gathered from the conversation at church and the weatherman on the news.

His shivering hand slipped the key into the ignition and then he turned the heat on full force. When Eliza's red Pontiac rolled past him onto the two-lane road, he promptly followed. Country roads were not his specialty. If given the chance, he'd be lost down a gravel road in two revs of the engine.

Bare branches stood guard along the hills, pine needles providing pops of color between the grays and browns. Even with the slumbering vegetation, the mountains were as breathtaking as ever. Heavy frost shimmered in the noonday sun, mimicking fresh snow, soft and white. It made the perfect setting for a slow Sunday drive.

Much too soon, Eliza flashed her signal and turned up Main Street. Their cars were parked and emptied in mere minutes with the three of them walking toward city sidewalks.

"Punky?" Bennett raised his eyebrows and waited.

"You heard that, huh?"

"Can't say I didn't. Why Punky?" Bennett laughed as Eliza looked away, blushing when she faced him again.

"Punky Brewster was my favorite television show to watch on the oldies channel at Grandpa Walt's house. And he swore I looked exactly like her." Reining Lori in by the hood of her coat, Eliza pulled her back to wait for a green light to start walking. Without a word, she slipped her hand around Lori's.

"Punky." He repeated it, making plans to do a web search later. He needed a visual to compare with. "It's cute."

Like you.

Bennett bit his tongue before the words ran out. "Is this the infamous commons?"

"Yup," Lori answered, pausing at the next intersection and looking both directions after the walking man flashed on display. Bennett stayed on the other side to keep her between them in case she tried to dart away. Once safely across, Lori loosened her grip and swung her arm wildly back and forth, looking up at Eliza every few seconds. A grin stretched from one ear to the other.

"So, little miss, was school good this week? Did you rock that spelling test?" Eliza looked at the little girl's face, her features softening until her expression matched her tone. Warm, friendly, inviting.

Lori beamed. "Yup, I got them all right. Even the bonus. And we got a letter from Daddy, with pictures. I took it to show-and-tell. Everyone told me I have the coolest dad in the world."

"They did, did they?" Eliza planted her hands on her hips. "Well, don't tell him I said this because I'll deny it 'til my dying day, but he is pretty cool."

Gently, Eliza tugged Lori to her side, bent down, and planted a kiss on her forehead. Holding her tight, she rubbed her arms a few times before releasing her and grabbing the little girl's hand again.

Caught up in the moment, Bennett scooped Lori's free hand into his own, getting a good hold, and began swinging their arms. Eliza joined in. Together they lifted Lori off the sidewalk, swinging her back and forth between them. After two swings, Eliza murmured her concern about Lori's little wrists and called it quits. Lori skipped ahead. When she started to open the door to Bella's Boutique, she looked back for approval. Eliza bobbed her head and the child disappeared into the shop, leaving Bennett and Eliza alone outside.

"Thank you," she said, nearly in a whisper.

"For what?" Bennett searched Eliza's face. Grateful eyes peered up at him, but past the appreciation peeked an achy shadow. The pain caused his chest to tighten.

Eliza gestured toward the store. "For making her day, like her dad used to."

"Of course." Bennett cupped her shoulder and squeezed. "Where is her dad, if you don't mind me asking?"

"Alabama. Jonah's an army mechanic." Eliza drew out each syllable with a heavy southern twang, *Al-uh-bam-uh*, making the name sound more like a country song than a place. Bennett had always preferred classic rock, but if she kept talking like that, he'd soon be converted.

"I thought it might be something like that." Bennett let go of her shoulder and dropped his hand. As he did, his fingertips brushed against hers as they stood side by side. Bennett curled his fingers into a fist. No matter how much he wanted to, he didn't need to do something reckless like try to hold her hand.

"Yeah, it's been hard on all of us. I never bought into the idea of distance bringing hearts together, but I get it now. Even though we're in different states, it seems like we're closer than we've ever been. Of course, it's different with Lori. She's too young for the miles to have that sort of impact."

As much as Bennett wanted to reassure her, to explain about Project Pops and why coming to Kentucky meant as much to the McCoy family as it did to the railroad, he knew better. While her openness deserved the same transparency from him, he needed to find a working identity apart from his father, and he couldn't do that if he revealed the meaning behind his middle initial. He quickly changed the subject. "Can Jenny and Lori join him?"

"They could, but that's not what Jonah wants. He insists they stay here, even though it breaks his heart. Told Jenny it's better to keep Lori here where all of us can help tend to her. It kills him every time he visits and has to leave them behind."

"I can't imagine, but I see where he's coming from. It's important to keep family ties strong. Yours seem unbreakable."

His father's face flashed in his mind. Bennett wanted that with him. The acceptance, the support, the love that the Elliotts tossed around so freely. Maybe he should give Pops a call after dinner. Then again, he'd probably get his voice mail.

Breaking his thoughts, Eliza spoke up. "We have Grandpa Walt to thank for our family bond. He passed nearly a year ago, but instead of drifting apart like so many do, we all banded together, for the most part." Eliza drew a ragged breath and turned away. Fastening her gaze on Lori through the window, she continued. "Grieving made us stronger."

"How nice." Bennett longed to live out that sentiment, but his experience had been the opposite. The loss of his mother had ripped his family apart, leaving Bennett hardened and worn. Knowing he couldn't explain that to Eliza, he chased his reply with a bright smile, teeth and all, to camouflage his bitterness.

"It is nice." Eliza laughed lightly. "Until you want to be alone."

Seeing her glee undeterred by his callousness, Bennett knew his cover-up had worked. Too bad he couldn't hide the truth from himself. Since now was not the time to tackle the heavy topic of family, Bennett shrugged off the uneasiness. He choked down the breath stuck in his throat as Lori slipped into view. Bursting out the shop door, she motioned for them to follow her as she moved to the next store.

"Check out that rack of gummy unicorns. Over there in the corner, see them?" Lori pointed through the window at the display, nudging Eliza closer to the window. Their breath fogged the pane. With her pointer finger, Lori started to draw in the condensation but Eliza Lee caught her wrist.

"Don't do that." Eliza released her and dug a few bills out of her pocket. "Here. Go pick out one, but don't you dare tell your mother or we'll both be in snake-face trouble. And you better eat every bite on your plate too."

Lori was halfway to the display before Eliza's warning passed her lips. After an eye roll, she returned to their previous conversation, elaborating on her answer.

"Until Grandpa died, I didn't know what it was like to be on my own. My brothers joke I was his pet, but there's some truth in that. Actually, I was kind of everyone's pet. No matter what situation I got myself into, someone swooped in and saved the day. Until now."

Bennett moved near, closing the distance between them until her shoulder grazed his arm. "After the scanner episode the other day, I can't imagine you needing a hero, Eliza."

She paused to draw in a breath and lifted her head in his direction, putting those soft lips on display again. The desire to kiss her flared up like a live wire. *Supervisors don't kiss their employees.* He knew he should heed the warning bells going off in his head, but the electricity between them shorted out the alarm. Bennett bent down to whisper in her ear. "Leading ladies save themselves."

Eliza inched in a little closer. "You see me as a leading lady?"

"I do." Bennett laid a hand to her cheek, unable to keep from touching her.

The skin warmed beneath his palm as a pretty pink bloomed, but she didn't shy away. Instead, her stare flamed, emerald and sage burning brightly. Just like that day in the office, Bennett leaned in. This time, a little too close, as he found his lips inches from hers. Flicking his gaze between her mouth and her eyes, he searched for hesitation. He found an invitation instead as Eliza went up on tiptoes.

Somewhere behind them, a chime sounded, snapping Bennett back to reality where Eliza remained his employee and the title of supervisor still separated them. He stepped toward the streetlight and pointed at the hanging lights. "I still can't believe all the decorations the town puts up."

Eliza licked her lips and followed his line of sight. "Really?"

Blinking up at the decorations, she looked unaffected by the moment that had simultaneously thrilled and wrecked Bennett. Her nonchalance punched holes in his ego, and maybe a few in his heart, too, until he noticed her heavy breathing. *I see you, Eliza Lee.*

Bennett smirked, but she missed it. Her eyes remained fixed on the Christmas lights as Lori came running up to them. Immediately, Eliza grabbed the little girl's hand and started walking.

"You're right on time, little girl," Eliza said, glancing at the bank clock across the street. "Mom will skin me alive if we're late."

"Well, let's skedaddle, Skittle." Lori paused and motioned for Bennett to catch up to them. When he did, she offered him her empty hand.

Is this what family feels like?

It had been so long, Bennett wasn't sure he remembered. But when he took hold of Lori's hand, he knew.

"Something smells wonderful." Bennett inhaled an array of tantalizing scents as soon as he stepped through the door. Unlike traditional homes, the Elliotts' kitchen was the first room the house opened into, and it was already filled to the brim with guests. Jett and Hanna sat poised with full plates at the counter, while Luke James stood at the head of the table. Mama Deb leaned over him, placing a plate of cornbread in the only free spot left. Cookers still simmered on the stove to the right, filled with green beans, corn, and glazed baby carrots.

Mama Deb smiled. "Thank you much. You and Eliza Lee make you a plate. You, too, Lori."

As the three of them did as they were told, Mama Deb took a seat to the right of her husband. Bennett followed close behind Eliza. Pulling out the chair next to him before his own, he motioned for her to sit. With a nod, she did, her thank you nearly drowned out by the commotion around the kitchen. After she was settled, he slid into his chair, leaving only Luke James unseated.

Lori clapped her hands from her spot at the table. "Hush up, y'all. Poppy's ready to say grace."

"Thank you, baby girl. Everybody bow." Luke James raised his voice slightly, a mere decibel above soft. His tone grew deeper than at church, but still as kind. Those sitting at the table joined hands, Mama Deb taking Luke's first. Eliza placed her hand in Bennett's palm, lacing their fingers but keeping her eyes downcast.

The room fell silent. As heads dropped, Bennett shut his eyes and tried to focus on the blessing. Words jumbled together in his ears, barely discernable over the thumping in his chest. Eliza's skin was soft as baby's breath, her touch light but electric, completing a circuit inside him he didn't know was broken.

"Amen." Voices echoed the closure around the room, Bennett's voice was breathless and low. Expecting Eliza to withdraw her hand, he loosened his grip. She didn't move. In response, neither did he, until a bouncing little girl called his name.

"Bennett," said Lori. "This is my mom, Jenny. Mom, this is Bennett. He didn't know what the Santa Run was. Can you believe that?" Tiny fingers shoveled a spoonful of beans in her mouth as she finished.

Bennett smiled across the table as Jenny answered. "Nice to meet you. And, yes, sweetheart, I can believe that. The Santa Run is common knowledge for you because you've lived in Pine Valley your whole life, but Bennett's not from around here. Santa may visit the city on the subway or by the ferry, or even in a horse-drawn carriage. I'm sure he has many ways to travel."

Lori cocked her head to the side, mulling over the explanation as she chewed. Eventually, she shrugged and dismissed the conversation altogether.

Bennett held back a groan as he remembered the unsent email on his computer. He'd yet to reveal the Santa Run to Pops. He'd meant to, but his father's most recent instruction for Bennett not to disturb him except for a dire situation had caused him to wait. The brevity of that text had made Bennett pause. The final say had always been his father's. Without Bennett by his side, was his father too busy to worry about the Kentucky office? Maybe his father hadn't realized how many fires Bennett put out before they reached his father's desk. Maybe he missed Bennett.

Mama Deb interrupted his musings with a slap to his shoulder. "Eat up."

Putting his father out of his mind, Bennett smiled and surveyed his plate. The macaroni intrigued him.

"That's the lightest mac-n-cheese I've ever seen. Is it made with Swiss or white American?"

Laughter bounced around the table. Turning from face to face, he tried to find the humor but failed. Accepting defeat, he tapped Eliza's arm and waited for clarification.

"It's not mac-n-cheese. It's buttered macaroni, and it's delicious." Eliza answered over Lori's snickering. "Try it. You'll like it." Adding action to affirm her words, she took a big bite.

Bennett eyed the noodles and picked a couple up with the tines of his fork. After giving them a good sniff, he plopped the pieces into his mouth and chewed. Feeling Eliza's eyes on him, he turned to find her elbows propped up on the table, cradling her chin in her hand the same way as the previous night. Her intense gaze left him hungry for more. More mochas, more walks, more dinners.

"And?" She waited, watching intensely. The look she gave him, like he was the most important person at the table, unraveled him until the rest of the room faded away.

"It's good." He answered and reached for his cup, a recycled Mason jar, filled with milk. According to Mama Deb, dairy and sweet tea were the only acceptable drinks to wash down pinto beans and cornbread.

"Told you." Eliza smiled, then grabbed a generous forkful and shoved it in her mouth.

Not shy around the table either. I could get used to this.

Bennett reached for his chicken leg and lifted it to his mouth, ready to sink his teeth in when his phone vibrated. Reluctantly, he lowered the chicken, set it back down on his plate, and wiped his hands on the paper towel in his lap. After excusing himself, he retreated to the porch and fished his phone from his pants pocket.

Seriously? Bennett shook his head and pressed answer.

"Hey, Pops. If you're calling about the new-hire paperwork, it's already been scanned into the system and the hard copi— What? Slow down. I don't have good service. Did you say a tree? I'm not sure. Hang on. I'll get Jett and call you from the office."

Chapter Nine

"Hanna, are you sure you don't want me to stay with you 'til Jett gets back?" Eliza put the car in park in front of her brother's house. "From the way he was talking, it might be late into the night before he makes it home."

"Positive. I don't need a babysitter. In a few months, I'll *be* the babysitter. Permanently." Her chuckles filled the air as she slid from the passenger seat, steadying her wedges as they hit the pavement of their street.

"If you say so." Eliza handed her one of the covered plates from the back seat, Jett's food safe and secure under the tin foil. She watched as Hanna rounded the car to get to the walkway. "If you need me, just text. I'm heading to the office to see if there's anything I can do to help."

"Help?" Hanna hiked an eyebrow. "Sure."

"Yes, help." Eliza stressed her answer, confident she knew where this was going. Bennett's plate wrapped and sitting in the back practically guaranteed as much.

"OK. Keep telling yourself that." Hanna leaned into the open driver's side window. Her lips pressed together tightly except at the corners where her mouth turned up, revealing the slightest bit of a stifled smile.

"It's the truth. I know what you're thinking. You. And Mom. And Jenny. And everybody else in this town." Eliza furrowed her brows, gluing her eyes to Hanna's. "I don't appreciate it one iota. Are you even listening to me?"

Hanna batted her eyelashes innocently. "Yes, I'm listening. But since you're stuck working with Bennett, it'd be smart to get to know your new boss a little better, right? The boss with the knee-weakening smile. The boss that seems to have a sweet spot for southern women. One in particular, best I can tell."

"Hush up, you ornery little mama." Eliza Lee shook her head and pointed toward the house. "Get yourself inside and put those feet up. Your piggies have gotta be squealing by now."

"Yeah, yeah. Just be careful on the road, doll face. And tell my handsome hubby to bring home a pint of ice cream. The little one wants it." Hanna Bell eyed her belly sweetly.

"Can do. Love you, and you, too, baby boo." Gently, Eliza rubbed Hanna's bump, making kissy sounds she hoped the little one could hear.

Hanna waved with a smile. "Love you."

After watching until Hanna safely made it up the steps, Eliza laid her forehead against the steering wheel. "Back off, Eliza Lee, before you get too close."

Saying the warning aloud did nothing to make it more effective. When it came to Bennett, she was too close already.

As she flipped the headlights on and pushed the gas, Hanna's suggestion replayed on blast, mingling with memories of the earlier walk. That almost kiss at the commons had been hot enough to melt her insides, and Bennett hadn't even sealed the deal. How would she feel if he had?

Eliza switched on the blinker and drove toward the office, not giving herself a chance to entertain the bad idea of kissing her boss. She didn't need that kind of complication at the office, or her personal life, for that matter. There were enough changes happening without throwing romance into the mix.

He's a bad idea.

Eliza wished she believed that as she pulled into her parking spot. She cut the engine and tugged the tops of her gloves under her sleeves. Her reflection in the rearview mirror made her wrinkle her nose. The makeup she'd worn to church had faded and her once wavy locks now lay lifeless on her shoulders.

Oh, well. Good thing you're only here to help.

Eliza climbed out of the car and shut the door, not even bothering to lock it. Straightening herself to the total capacity of her frame, she pushed her shoulders back and headed for the office, Bennett's leftovers in hand. The hinges creaked as she pushed the door open, sending three sets of eyes her way. Neither Jett, Bennett, nor Joe cracked a smile. Intending to lighten the mood, she started to say the cavalry had arrived, but a deep voice stopped her in her tracks.

"How soon can we begin the cleanup?" The words landed cold with a matter-of-fact tone. All the men concentrated on the phone Bennett held between them.

Jett's even voice countered the chill. "Even though we know the cause of the accident, a formal investigation is underway. Once that's done, we can start. I've already texted the crew with the location. This isn't our first derailment. Our guys will have it taken care of in no time. If there's no damage to the railway, and we suspect there isn't, we can resume regular schedule with few delays." Jett's steadiness under pressure continued to amaze her, making him head and shoulders above the rest when it came to his job. He deserved every ounce of respect he'd earned from the men.

"Have you touched base with the conductor? Or the engineer?" Monotone, the hidden face talked on.

"Yes, sir." Jett's voice showed no emotion, but the wrinkles on his forehead revealed his concern. "No major injuries, just a little bruising."

"Glad to hear it. I've only dealt with one derailment on our passenger rails, but it is an experience I've yet to forget, and one I have no desire to repeat."

Lowering his eyes, Jett nodded. "I'd say, sir."

Eliza tightened her grip on the plate as she listened. She made her way to the break room to keep from interrupting.

After putting Bennett's food into the refrigerator, she decided it was time for a fresh pot of coffee. She started the brew and listened as the machine perked.

Waiting for the pot to fill, details of the accident trickled through her mind. The winds from the storm to the west of them had been heavy. A strong gust snapped an old tree and knocked it across the tracks just minutes before the train crossed its path. The trip wire had sensed its presence and the alert gone through to the engineer, but there was no way for him to stop in time. The trunk was too massive for the cow catcher to move. The train's decreasing speed had lessened the impact but not enough to prevent the derailment.

Most of the cargo remained intact, but a few cars had spilled. More important, the boys were safe. Dropping her head, she gave thanks to the Lord for watching over them. Her silent praise was interrupted as heavy footsteps carried a disheveled Bennett through the entry.

"I couldn't hold out any longer." Bennett stood in the doorway, worry deepening his chocolate eyes. The clean shave from earlier had been replaced with short stubble as fine hairs dotted his jaw and chin. His hair, no longer styled, had out-of-place tendrils twisting this way and that.

Unable to look away, Eliza followed him with her eyes. He'd been handsome at church with his seamless, put-together appearance, but the wearing of the day had exposed his rough edges. His vulnerability made him even more attractive.

Stepping away from the counter, Eliza walked his way. "Hold out for what?"

She pushed the possible connotations of his words away, but her cheeks still warmed. *Yes, Eliza. He counted down the minutes until he could see you again. The few hours away have been torture.* She shook her head. *You don't want a love life, remember? Definitely not one with your boss.*

Bennett pointed to the pot. "Coffee. The scent was teasing me."

"Oh. Right." Eliza turned her back to him and opened the door under the sink. "Sit down and let me get it."

Wrapping her fingers around the ceramic handle of the clean cup, she took in a breath. *Here goes nothing.* Carefully, she poured his coffee and handed it to him.

Bennett's hand froze in midair. "That's not my mug, Eliza."

"Yes, it is." Stretching the cup closer toward him, she nodded. "I figured you needed your own while you're here and I hunted this down for you. My college roommate gave it to me after she crashed a vital study session. It didn't change the C minus I got, but the picture made me smile. I figured if you're feeling homesick, this might fix you up. Consider it an early Christmas present."

Because you might be gone by then. Eliza's shoulders dropped at the reminder of his impending goodbye. Hadn't she said that enough to the men in her life? Grandpa, Austin, Jonah. The fact she'd soon add Bennett's name to that list stung, but strengthened her resolve to stay single.

Bennett wrapped his fingers around the handle and took the coffee. As she watched him read the bold "NYC" letters above the silhouette skyline, she wondered if she'd made a mistake, until he held the cup to her in a toast. "This is so thoughtful. Thank you."

"Of course." Feeling too much like a kid handing out valentines for the first time, Eliza pointed to a pile of coffee grounds on the counter. *Thank goodness I'm a hot mess express.* She grabbed a paper towel and swept the heap into her palm.

Voices from the office spilled down the hall as she emptied the coffee into the trash. Bennett cringed. "I better get back out there. I just stole away for a pick-me-up java and to stretch my legs."

Eliza nodded and glanced at the coffee pot. "I'll grab myself a cup and take a seat in the back. Who is that anyway?"

"Po—President, CEO, and owner, Mr. Oliver McCoy."

"That's a lot of hats for one person to wear." Whistling sharply, Eliza turned on the faucet and rinsed her cup. "Impressive."

"He does his fair share of delegating, too, but the acquisition is his baby and he's keeping a tight leash on me."

"Mr. McCoy isn't upset with you, is he?" Eliza searched his face. His eyebrows rose a touch, and his eyes widened ever so slightly, filled with appreciation. A smile followed. Not a fake one, but the kind that crinkled his eyes at the corners. Her heart did a flip-flop. *Stop it, Eliza Lee.*

How had Bennett managed to get under her skin so much in so little time? Maybe it was a blessing dinner had been cut short.

Oblivious to her thoughts, Bennett scratched at his stubble. "No, but he'll be angry if he notices I'm gone."

"Well," said Eliza, jerking her head toward the door. "Ya better get movin' then."

Bennett was gone by the time she had her coffee poured, but the manly scent of him remained. Notes of cedar and spice filled the air. Even from her seat in the back of the office, she could still smell it. The comforting aroma helped alleviate Eliza's worry as she watched the men huddle around the screen.

Jett ran a hand through his hair. "As awful as the accident is, we're fortunate the derailment happened today instead of a few weeks from now during the Santa Run."

Mr. McCoy's voice boomed in the small space, the tone sharp and cutting. "The Santa Run? What is that? Bennett, I will need a detailed agenda for the event sent to me ASAP. As in before tomorrow. I need prospected losses and cost for today's cleanup as well."

"You'll have it as soon as possible." Bennett answered Mr. McCoy. His voice sprung tightly, a stark difference from in the break room. The tone seemed deflated, too, as if the reply had sucked all the life out of him. Tensing, he straightened his shoulders.

Jett hunkered next to him. "I'll help him with that, sir."

"I expect nothing less, Mr. Elliott. Research to improve safety precautions will start tomorrow. We'll have a game plan for you by early next week. In the meantime, I'll be crunching the numbers. This accident cost us, but I need to see how much and find a way to make it back. Starting in the red is not my idea of a successful business."

"I understand, sir. We'll get whatever reports you need. With Thanksgiving this week, it may take a few days, but as soon as I have it, you'll have it."

"I appreciate that." Mr. McCoy's voice softened slightly. "I suspect you need to be at the site of the accident, so I won't keep you. Joe, it was nice to meet you. Bennett, I'll be waiting for an update."

Bennett responded with a small nod at the screen and Mr. McCoy ended the video. No *talk to you soon*, no *have a good night*, not even a goodbye. Did his boss always treat him that way? Though usually not one for hasty judgments, Eliza decided, then and there, she didn't care for Oliver McCoy and his steely demeanor.

Bennett stood from his seat. "Jett, do you need me to come with you? I can't say I'll be much help, but I'm an extra pair of hands at least."

"Joe and I have it covered, but thanks." Jett glanced at the clock and sprung to his feet. "The crew's probably there by now. You go on home and get some rest."

"I hate leaving you to do the dirty work." Bennett snatched his coffee from the desk. His knuckles turned white on the handle as he gripped the cup tighter. "And isn't Hanna home by herself? How close is the due date now?"

"A little more than a month." A lopsided grin spread across Jett's face, cracking his cool facade. Rarely did her brother's gooey side make an appearance, but when it did, she adored him even more. Lori usually reaped the benefits. He constantly snuck her chocolates or suckers before dinner. He was going to spoil his baby so much.

The baby! Eliza Lee gasped and pointed at her brother. "Speaking of Hanna, she needs you to bring home ice cream. For the baby."

"Of course, she does." Chuckling, Jett turned from Eliza to Bennett. "Hanna's craved ice cream since before we found out she was pregnant." Her brother directed his attention back to her. "I'm gonna be tied up for a while longer. Joe has to give the engine a thorough inspection. Can you grab it for h—"

"Consider it done, brother." Eliza cut in. "I'll drop it off on my way."

"And I'll lock up, so you don't have to come back." Bennett walked closer to Jett. His voice had warmed, but the light was gone from his eyes. The absence touched a nerve deep inside of Eliza. The part of her that connected with him and saw past his managerial status longed to return the luminescence, and with it, his joy.

"Thank you, Bennett." Jett nodded and started toward the door. "C'mon, Joe. We'll take my truck."

"Right behind ya." Joe's heavy boots pounded the floor as he stalked from the back. In three long strides, he'd caught up with Jett and Bennett. He yanked his jacket from the coat rack and slipped in his arms. "When y'all leave, be careful."

Eliza Lee circled an arm around his waist and hugged. "Always. You too."

Silently, she said a quick prayer for safety as she watched him march into the parking lot. Before the door shut behind him, Eliza caught a glimpse outside. Night had nearly fallen though it was only six in the evening. The air had grown so much colder too. With the sun resting behind the rolling mountains, the chill ran rampant through the town. This winter had set record lows with its unseasonably frigid conditions, and tonight was no different.

Eliza rushed into her coat. "Well, I guess I better get going. Keeping a pregnant woman waiting on ice cream might be a death sentence." As she stepped toward the door, Bennett's cup streaked across her peripherals.

"The coffee pot. Shoot. I better go turn it off." Eying the mug he still clutched, she reached for it. "I'll take this as I go."

At her exclamation, Bennett relinquished his cup to her waiting hand but barely looked up. The wheels were clearly turning in his head, but about what? The accident? Mr. McCoy? *Me?*

As she walked past, Eliza's shoulder brushed against his solid bicep. A fresh set of shivers snaked down her arms. Rather than admit Bennett's touch had caused the reaction, she blamed the derailment. The accident had left her wired and overstimulated. Nothing more.

Once in the breakroom, Eliza Lee filled a couple of to-go cups and secured the lids. She poured the rest of the coffee down the drain. She flipped the switch on the machine and emptied the coffee grounds before returning to the front of the office.

Smiling, she handed a cup to Bennett. "Thought you might like some for the road."

"Thanks. When Jett and Joe get done, I'll need to prepare a preliminary report for Mr. McCoy, and who knows when that will be." Bennett tapped the side of his cup a few times as he spoke, almost in sync with the ticking of the clock behind her. "Nothing to do but wait."

"It won't take too long. The boys are fast when it comes to this kind of thing, especially Joe. As yardmaster, these trains are his babies, and when one's down, he worries himself sick until it's back in tip-top shape. It's sweet to watch in a weird sort of way."

She wanted to giggle, but one look at Bennett proved her joke had fallen flat. *So much for cheering him up.* Rubbing her lips together, she started toward the door again. "Well, I better head out. Are you locking up now?"

Bennett sat on the corner of a desk. He kept his sights set on the wall as if he were attempting X-ray vision. Eliza Lee hated to leave him, especially when he looked so glum with those puppy dog eyes. Hounds had nothing on him.

Shifting his eyes to hers, he answered. "Yes, in just a few." He blinked a few times, as if remembering where he was, and headed for the door. "Thanks for coming out. And for the coffee. It'll save me a trip to Country Confections."

"No, I saved you from a caffeine headache. Country Confections is closed on Sunday."

"Huh." Bennett tilted his head. "I've heard of closing on Sunday, but never seen it for myself."

"Perks of small-town living." This time, the joke hit pay dirt. Light laughter passed between them and Eliza lost herself in the moment.

Hanna was right. The man's smile needed a warning label. If Eliza didn't watch out, she'd find herself head over feet before she knew it, and that was not an option. Too much was at stake. Her job, her loyalty to Grandpa Walt, her independence. If she took a chance on Bennett, she stood to lose everything she'd worked so hard for since Grandpa's death. *Was it worth it?*

Eliza didn't know. What she did know, however, was that she needed to get home where she could think. "Well, I'll leave you to it, Bennett. See you tomorrow."

"OK. Tell Hanna to eat a bowl for me too." Bennett pushed the door open for her. "Have a good night, Eliza Lee."

She exited and made her way through the parking lot, keys in one hand and her coffee in the other. Disappointment wove its way through her heart as she crossed to her car. Shaking her head, she huffed twice. Little puffs of steam followed each exasperated breath. She wasn't sure who she was more upset with, herself for not sticking around or Bennett for not tagging along. After a mental scolding, she settled on herself, recalling the long list of reasons why it was better she kept her distance. More than halfway through the bullets, a voice broke the silence around her.

"You didn't bring any leftovers, did you?" Bennett leaned against the door frame with his hands cupped around his mouth.

"Maybe." Eliza yelled back. "OK, I did. Your plate is in the fridge."

Bennett raised his hands in the air, seemingly offering thanks to Jesus and her. "I owe you, Eliza Lee. Thank you."

"You're welcome." Waving, Eliza wiggled her fingers at him a few times. "See you tomorrow."

It was hard to tell from where she stood, but his eyes seemed to brighten as he flashed a half grin, the one that made her forget her name. Eliza yanked her car door open and slid into the driver's side. A smile split her face, but she remained eager to put more space than a parking lot between them. One key turn and the engine roared to life, the low rumble replacing the sound of a beating heart in her ears. Out of habit, she checked the mirror, then backed out, not bothering to turn the heat on.

She was warm enough already.

Chapter Ten

Bennett eyed the total, narrowing his gaze until his vision blurred. Even obscured, the sight turned his stomach. The damage from the accident was more costly than he'd expected.

After collecting the data and crunching the numbers, the loss made him squirm. No doubt, the estimate would have the same effect on his father when he opened his email in about an hour or so. Creature of habit as he was, Pops was likely in the downstairs lobby of his building, a newspaper in one hand, blueberry muffin in the other. He swore a relaxing breakfast started the day off right.

Bennett's morning had been anything but relaxing. More like a whirlwind as he gathered the information his father demanded. Bennett had worked into the early morning hours while the sun slept. Around 3:00 a.m., he'd finally lain down. A few hours later, a text had come in from Jett.

HEADING IN EARLY. I'VE GOT THE REPORTS. COME ON IN WHEN YOU WANT.

Having dedicated employees was one thing, but having committed, early-morning employees was another thing entirely. Not that he wasn't grateful. Jett had proved himself integral to the success the Appalachian Express enjoyed and had welcomed McCoy Railway with open arms. But sleep had

When Bennett finished explaining the run, he shared the donor list and what each business had contributed, hoping to highlight the immense support for the event. His father was a humbug, but he understood the importance of community backing, especially for an immigrant company like McCoy Railway.

Pops had been kind enough during their emergency meeting, but he had that look in his eye. Bennett had learned to read between the lines, and he didn't like the message he saw. *This accident cost us. I need to see how much and find a way to make it back.* There was no end to the lengths he'd go to make a buck. Nothing and no one were off-limits.

"You're here early." Eliza's voice tugged his gaze from the computer to the door, now shut behind her. Deep in thought, he'd missed the familiar creak as the hinges swung open, but there was no missing that voice.

"Sadly, yes." Bennett rubbed his eyes and gave a long stretch, extending his arms high above his head. He closed the laptop. Standing from his desk, he decided it was time for a break.

With a smile, Bennett pointed toward the hall. "Coffee's ready. Do you want a cup?"

Eliza Lee nodded as she shuffled to the end table, her arms filled to the brim. Thuds echoed in the office as she released her hold. Her cargo scattered across the tabletop. One metal tin landed on its side while another flipped upside down and a striped tube rolled to the floor.

"Drat." She reached down to grab the fallen item. "Can't lose this. Candy cane lip balm is the best for cold weather."

"Can't say I've tried it. What is all that?" He didn't wait for an answer but headed for the break room. He'd been in Pine Valley long enough to know that walls didn't stop conversation and female voices carried straight through without missing a beat.

"Mom's recipes," Eliza hollered back, raising her volume to the perfect decibel to remain audible. "I have to find a pie to make for the social before Wednesday. I thought Hanna might help me."

Bennett returned to her side and handed her the coffee. Together they surveyed the gaggle of books, magazines, and a couple of recipe tins scattered across the glass.

"Thank yoo-uh." She made the last word two syllables instead of one as she took her cup. "I need this in the worst way."

Bennett nodded, wishing she'd keep talking. He loved her voice. Did the drawl deepen as she grew tired? Linger through her sleepiness? *It might make it cuter.* Feeling heat rise to his face, he skirted behind her to his seat.

"Not as good as mine, but it'll do." Eliza sipped as she walked back and forth, stopping between the front two desks. "Where is Hanna? I'm always the last one in."

"Preach." Jett piped up as he clicked off his headset, following the comment with a chain of chuckles. Bennett joined in, but Eliza mock glared.

With dramatic motions, she crossed her arms over her chest. "Nobody asked for commentary from the peanut gallery, brother."

Jett leaned back in his chair and winked. "Didn't have to. I give it freely. Enjoy."

"Harty, harr, harr." Eliza planted her hands on her hips and wagged her head in rhythm with the words.

At her antics, Bennett laughed harder. The sibling squabbles never ceased to entertain.

Jett raised back up and pointed to Hanna's desk. "She ran to town for some supplies. She'll be back in a bit."

A light on Jett's phone flashed, ending the conversation. He clicked on his headset, immediately switching to his business voice. It was as friendly as before but polished as he held his accent in check.

After hanging her coat up, Eliza Lee turned to Bennett. "Well, Bennie, I guess you're up. Hand me that box, will ya?"

"Bennie?" Hiking an eyebrow, he repeated the name. It had been years since someone had called him that.

"Yup." She popped the *p* at the end of *yup*. "I found the trucker hat—the country version of the Hogwarts sorting hat I told you about—and drew for you. Like your new name?"

"Love it." Bennett grabbed the tin and passed it to her. Rust speckled the outside where the blue and red stripes of paint had begun to peel. It had seen better days, practically guaranteeing the recipes inside to be tested, tried, and tasty.

Eliza raised the lid and grinned. This time the corners of her smile traveled to her eyes, brightening the green. The shade settled somewhere between forest and jade.

To keep from staring, Bennett pulled out a card and waved it in the air. "What kind of pie are you considering? Fruity? Savory? Pizza or pot variety?"

"Definitely a dessert." Eliza squinted as she flipped through the first few cards. "Dinner pies never sell. I usually make peanut butter since it doesn't take too much skill and always turns out. But Joe has requested one from Mom this year, so I need something new." She lowered her head and returned to the hunt.

"Pumpkin?" Bennett offered.

With a shake of her head, she answered, not looking up. "Nope, Brittney makes that for Pastor Clemens."

"Cheesecake?"

Jett pushed off from his desk and rolled his seat closer to them. "No one wants that, Bennett. She can't cook a lick." Jett eyed his sister as he quipped, a smirk plastered on his face.

Eliza Lee scrunched her face into a pretend scowl. "You don't have to rat me out."

More laughter, light and loving, surrounded them. The office was so different from his in New York. Both crews ran efficiently, but in the city, hidden agendas, pushes to get ahead, and cutthroat drama lined the day. The country yard was just the opposite. Friendly conversation and inside jokes fueled the labor, making time pass by quickly.

"Besides," Eliza continued with a wave of her hand. "The Andrews' girls, Shelby Jane and Ruby, make the best cheesecake in town. No way I'm putting one of mine on the auction block beside theirs."

"OK, cheesecake is out." Bennett thought aloud. "Apple?"

Eliza shook her head and kept searching the box. "Sue from Nonnie's has dibs. Mr. Stone buys it every year."

Bennett tilted his head. "I'm confused. If the ladies make the same thing every year only to be bought by the same person, why even have the social?"

Eliza pried her eyes away from the recipes and looked up at him, amused. "Recipes are handed down from grandmas to mothers to daughters to granddaughters and so on. The good ones anyway. The social lets families share their food without giving away their kitchen secrets. That's why it's the Wednesday before Thanksgiving, to add a little something special to the holiday." She waved her hands as she talked. The tradition clearly charmed her. Bennett found himself charmed as well. By Pine Valley and her.

"Hmmm." Bennett considered the explanation and nodded. "That makes sense. Who usually buys your pie?"

Expecting Jett to chime in again, Bennett paused, but instead of joining the conversation, Jett removed his headset. He tipped his empty cup and excused himself to the break room. Quietly. *That's strange.* Eliza sat silent too.

Had he said something wrong?

Eliza started to answer but paused to thumb a note card before following through.

"Depends. I'm sort of a wild card, I guess." Refocusing her attention to the tin, she pushed a recipe back to read the title. "This might work. Lemon Cream Pie. No one makes that."

Bennett nodded. "Anything lemon sounds like a winner to me."

"Me too." She scanned the card again, her face turning serious as she reassessed the recipe. "Hey, what does that say?"

Eliza motioned for him to come near as she squinted at the card. Bennett leaned over her shoulder to get a better look, vanilla and honey bombarding his senses. He took a quick breath and tried to focus on the scribbled letters instead of the sweet aroma.

"A.K.A. The Man Catcher." They read the last three words in unison.

Bennett turned his gaze from the card to Eliza. Her brows furrowed as she angled her head slightly, bringing her face closer to his. Pink lips pursed together, nearly in a pucker, just out of reach. The nearness teased him, stoking an ever-glowing spark. Beneath his sweater, his heart plowed against his chest as sweat beaded the base of his neck. Electricity flowed between them, making it impossible to turn away. He didn't dare. Not when she looked at him like that, inviting, waiting, eager. Stepping away from her in the commons had been a mistake, one he did not plan on making again.

Instead of backing up like before, Bennett closed the gap between them. His gaze never moved from hers. Abruptly, she stilled. From second thoughts? Maybe, but they must've disappeared as suddenly as they had manifested, for she leaned closer. Her eyelids fluttered shut and Bennett let his do the same as their lips met. Sparks burst into flames as his mouth moved against hers, warm currents heating his skin with every heartbeat.

"You guys won't believe what I found on clearance at the Stop-N-Save." Hanna's voice mingled with the sound of a slamming door. A short gasp followed. "Uh, never mind. I'll just go put this stuff away. Carry on."

Bennett broke their connection, but didn't raise up. His face hovered close enough to feel Eliza's breath rush against his lips and he nearly went in for seconds. Instead, he listened for Hanna's heels. When he was certain she'd gone down the hall, he pulled away.

"I think the recipe works." Bennet breathed the words, low but steadier than he'd anticipated with his heart stuttering in his chest.

"Maybe." Her voice, sweet and sultry, drawled out the word and his pulse flew faster. Looking toward the breakroom, she stood and bit her lip. *Was she upset?* Despite his most recent breakup, Bennett prided himself on his ability to read signals. Still, he could've been wrong. Perhaps the second thoughts hadn't disappeared like he'd assumed. Apprehension tugged at him until Eliza smiled, dimples and all, cheeks boldly blushing. "I better do damage control. Excuse me."

"Of course." Bennett followed her with his eyes until she walked out of view. He turned to the computer, licking his lips. Peppermint and coffee—a perfect pair.

A new message in his in-box snared his attention. At the sender's name, he held back an eye roll. *Couldn't let me enjoy the moment, could you, Pops?* Bennett's jaw clenched as he pushed the mouse. His face drew tighter with each word he read. By the time he'd finished the email, his frown might as well have been carved into his skin.

Forever a man of your word.

Before he could close out the email, Eliza stood in front of his desk. "Bennett? Are you OK? You're white as a sheet."

"What?" Bennett kept his eyes on the screen, reading his father's message a second time.

"Are you OK?" The worry in Eliza's voice wrenched his gaze from the computer to her fidgeting form.

She stood tapping her toe at the corner of her desk, waiting for him to speak. He wanted to answer, but his mouth dried like the Sahara. Desperate, he swigged the remainder of his coffee. The cold and bitter liquid offered a stark contrast from the kiss they'd just shared. The taste fit the email perfectly, though.

Bennett shook his head. "Can you get Jett and Hanna? We need to talk."

With furrowed brows, she positioned herself directly in front of his desk. "I'm not going anywhere until you tell me what's wrong. It's not *me*, is it?"

"You?" Bennett blinked back his shock. "No. The announcement affects the whole office, so I need them in here too."

Before he could explain further, heels clicked in the hall and Hanna appeared. "Need us for what?" Hanna stopped in front of the door and Jett followed. The two shared a quick look before turning first to Eliza, then to him.

"I'm sorry to tell you this." Bennett paused, long enough to silently pray for wisdom before continuing. "But the Santa Run is canceled."

Chapter Eleven

"Y ou said the run might need to be reworked, not canceled." Eliza's knees buckled under the weight of the word *canceled*, sending her hand searching for the wall. She needed to brace herself. Either her ears had deceived her or Bennett suffered from a sick sense of humor. The run couldn't be canceled. The town needed hope.

And I do, too, Lord.

Bennett took a slow step toward her. "I know what I said, but the accident changed things. After I sent the preliminary report detailing the loss from the derailment, Mr. McCoy made the decision to cut the event. The cancellation is his first attempt to make up the deficit."

To keep from balling her fists, Eliza slipped her hands in her pocket, a feeble attempt to retain appropriate office etiquette. She didn't need a repeat fight with her boss. Especially if he could help reverse the decision like she thought he could.

If news like this had come last year, she would have already been crying her eyes out on Jett's shoulder or pacing around the room or shrieking frantically at no one in particular. But the sorrow she'd faced through Grandpa's death had toughened her up. Not enough to keep tears from filling her eyes as she scanned the room, though.

Despite her best efforts to control her emotions, a huff slipped past her lips. "He can't do that."

"Yes, Eliza Lee, he can." Jett touched her shoulder gently. The way he did before Jonah left for basic. The way he did before sharing the news of Hanna's miscarriage.

The way he did before leading her to the casket at Grandpa Walt's funeral.

"He can and he did." Bennett's words struck her like an arrow to the heart, straight through to the place he'd touched with a single brush of his lips. How were those same lips telling her the Santa Run was over?

Eliza swallowed hard. "But you got those results hours ago. Mr. McCoy hasn't had time to even look for the money elsewhere. Maybe our expense account? Or the emergency fund? There has to be something we can do."

Reining in her desire to scream, Eliza took a deep breath as she paced back and forth. The caffeine from her coffee picked now of all times to kick in. Standing still was not an option, but she had to maintain some semblance of a put-together appearance—for the sake of her job and her family. She didn't need to give them more reason to worry. They did that enough already.

Eliza turned to Bennett. "What if we explain the tradition of the run? How long it's been around? Why it's so important to Pine Valley?"

Why it's so important to me?

All the hours she spent rounding up volunteers, calling for supplies, and organizing the stop schedule demonstrated more than dedication to her job or the need for a distraction from depression. Her role with the Santa Run gave her purpose, a focus, a way to channel her grief into a cause, one not only beneficial to the community but significant to her personally. Through Eliza's contribution, she kept her grandfather alive in action rather than mere memory.

"Why don't you call Mr. McCoy and let me explain?" Laying a hand on Bennett's forearm, Eliza pleaded.

Surely, he would understand. The owner had been cold and distant with Bennett, but the man had to have a conscience. Even if he didn't, Mr. McCoy wouldn't let the planning end in vain. Wasted time equaled wasted money. Such a savvy businessman like himself understood that.

Bennett shook his head. "Eliza Lee, while I know you mean well, explanations won't make up the deficit this railroad is facing."

Jett moved closer, pinning her with a concerned gaze. "As much as it pains me to say this, Bennett's right. I know how much this hurts, sis, and I'm sorry. Maybe you should take a walk around the lot and clear your head."

Giving in to her brother's advice, Eliza Lee nodded. She let her frustration carry her out the door and down the steps. The panic she'd successfully fended off indoors pulled her forward to the gate while common sense and the memory of Grandpa stopped her just shy of walking through it.

Think, Eliza Lee. Think. How had this happened mere weeks before Santa was scheduled to arrive?

Eliza walked faster even as her legs begged her to slow down. Instead, she ran her hand against the chain link fence on the river side of the lot, letting the tips of her fingers absorb the cold from the metal. The bite stung the sensitive skin. With closed eyes, she raised her face from the gravel to the stirring breeze. A chill started at her nose and spiraled out, filling her cheeks, caressing her forehead, and ending at her ears, causing her jingle bell earrings to sway softly. The wind smelled as cold as it felt and as fresh. It soothed her, stealing the pent-up tension and replacing it with a memory of scripture.

Trust in the LORD with all thine heart; and lean not unto thine own understanding.

Her heart rate steadied as she recited the verse, letting the words clear her head. Shame surged through her. Jett was right to send her outside. She'd been acting like a brat, but she wasn't going to admit that to him.

In the distance, a whistle blew. Eliza focused on the sound, nodding her head in time with the melody it made, stilling when silence rebounded. She didn't understand how people only heard noise instead of the beautiful music that filled her heart.

"Hey. Are you OK?" Startled, she turned to find Bennett a few feet away.

"Um, yeah. The Lord straightened me out." Eliza headed toward him, remembering midway the fit he'd witnessed. A fresh wave of heat filled her face. "I owe you an apology. Like I told you the other night, I tend to overreact. I've actually gotten better at handling my emotions since last year, if you can believe that. Looks like I still have more work to do, huh?"

Bennett flipped up the collar of his coat. "Not necessarily. Your reaction shows how much you care."

Now she was sure she was hearing things, but his smile supported the outlandish declaration. She expected Bennett to display the same type of aggravation she felt toward herself. But none appeared. Rather, adoration beamed back at her.

How, Lord? In awe, she stepped forward and tried to make sense of the morning. The kiss and cancellation collided, joy and panic warring inside her. The contrast left her reeling, as if she was in a wheel slip with no way out. Unnerved, she blurted an uncensored response.

"I do care. So much. But do you?" Part of her longed to take the words back as soon as they were out, but a deeper part needed to know.

Bennett tensed, his muscles tightening. "Of course, I do, Eliza Lee. You know that." A warm hand cupped her cheek, sending a fresh shiver down her spine. Heat spread beneath his palm. The sensation almost melted her fear. *Almost.*

"No, I don't know." She drew in an uneasy breath before continuing. "But I think you do."

"Nice to know where I'm starting." Bennett slid his hand to her shoulder and down her arm. Lacing his fingers with hers, he gave a gentle squeeze.

Eliza squeezed back and weighed her options. She could overthink the situation and keep herself closed off—the way she refused to call Jett on the nights Grandpa's absence kept her awake—or she could dare to open her heart and ask Bennett for help. With the run on the line, she decided on option number two.

"Do you have time to take a drive with me?" Eliza's words came out as a whisper, but she stood up straighter all the same. Quiet bravery deserved praise, too, especially in the face of vulnerability.

A grin stretched across Bennett's face. "I'll make time. Let me tell the others we'll be back in a few. Want me to bring your coat?"

"Yes." Eliza slipped her hand free from Bennett's and hugged herself. "Please."

"Be right back."

As Bennett trekked back to the office, the teeth chattering commenced. With her adrenaline fading, the cold snuck through Eliza's sleeves like a stowaway moving through freight cars. Had she been the levelheaded, responsible woman she pretended to be, she'd have grabbed the jacket straightaway, but her driving emotions cared little about comfort.

The whistle blew again, one long, two short, followed by one longer than them all. Distracted by the sound, she missed Bennett's footsteps behind her as he draped her coat around her shoulders. She slipped her arms in, dug out her keys, and jangled them loudly.

"Ready?" He stood behind her, his voice carrying on the wind.

"Yup, let's go, City Boy." Eliza gave the keys one more shake before unlocking the doors.

Bennett held up two fingers. "Two questions. One, do you drive as bad as I hear you cook?"

"No." Eliza deadpanned as he caught up with her. Then, punched his arm before resuming her previous pace.

"Good. Two, did you call me City Boy?"

She knew by his voice there'd been no offense, but she'd earned herself a good teasing.

"Did I forget to mention it? Your slip I drew from the hat had two names, one on front and one on the back." Quickening her steps, she opened her door and slid in. The small lead she had on him gave her time to check her reflection in the mirror. Her bangs had blown every which way in the wind, making her appearance match the disheveled state of her nerves. Eliza smoothed them as best she could and started the car.

While she cranked up the heat, Bennett took his place in the passenger seat. "For the record, I like Bennie better."

"For the record, City Boy is a term of endearment."

"It didn't sound that way to me." Bennett widened his grin, a glimmer of mischief peeking out from the crooked smile.

"You didn't hear me right, then, *City Boy*." Laughing, she pushed the gas and rolled out of the yard.

Christmas carols hummed through the speakers. The music rang loud enough to keep the silence at bay but soft enough to allow friendly conversation. Like at the bakery, comfort surrounded the two of them. She didn't understand the effect he had on her, but she didn't hate it. *Not even a little bit.*

Bennett folded his hands in his lap and looked out the window. "Are you going to tell me where we're going?"

"Nope," Eliza answered, popping the *p* and shaking her head. "You don't get car sick, do you?"

Bennett side-eyed her. "Not usually. Why?"

"The roads aren't exactly straight from here on out. Just let me know if I need to pull over. I can't let you ruin those leather shoes."

Bennett laughed, louder than she'd heard him before, the sound drowning out the music. After years of practice with her brothers, she'd never mastered the art of comebacks, but with her get-them-before-they-get-you philosophy, it didn't matter.

"Just concentrate on driving, Eliza Lee, and I'll worry about my wardrobe."

She steered around the mountain curves, evergreen pines standing tall among the hibernating redbud and poplar. Faded leaves filled in the ditch with a few vibrant oranges and yellows peeking out. To some, the forest might have looked dead. But not to Eliza. On the hillside, she saw rest. A winter's sleep that would bring the spring flowers when the time was right. The scene gave her hope.

After driving a little over an hour, Eliza pulled over to the side of the road and parked. The view took her breath away, same as it always did regardless the season. She smiled at the sun-kissed mountains.

"It's not much to look at now, just a bunch of bare trees and evergreens. But when the snow falls? It'll rival the cityscape at midnight." Eliza pointed out the window. "There's another sight for sore eyes. Look over there and tell me what you see."

Bennett followed her instructions, leaning forward to get a better look. "Old houses. A school that looks closed. What used to be a grocery store. A run-down park." He nodded toward the swings. "The kids don't mind, though. They're having a blast."

"You're right; they are. They make do with what they've got and are thankful to have it. The further out in the county you go, away from Pine Valley and the center of town, the harder life is. You can practically see financial struggles." Eliza took a breath at the same time a little girl jumped from the monkey bars. Seeing the child's bravery stoked her own and she continued.

"That's why the Santa Run is vital to the Christmas season. Some of these kids have coats only because of the donations we hand out. Gloves, hats, fuzzy socks to keep their feet dry. Those too. This is why I care."

Eliza watched as Bennett surveyed the surroundings. The Santa Run looked nice on paper, but seeing it firsthand changed lives. It certainly had for her family. Grandpa Walt started the domino, and the effects were still trickling down the family tree.

Bennett nodded but remained quiet. Not the response she was expecting. Maybe he was overwhelmed or caught off guard. Or maybe she had read him wrong. Bennett seemed like a man she could open up to and ask for help. Their country drive was her asking for help the only way she knew how. As she turned the car and headed back down the mountain, she feared her plea had fallen on deaf ears.

The drive back to the office was solemn. Light chit-chat bounced between them, along with the chorus of "Rudolph" and "Mary Did You Know," but something had shifted since they'd left. Bennett wasn't the same. He'd barely looked her way, and the light drumming of his fingers against the door panel made her nervous.

Pulling into the parking lot, she swallowed and tried to untie the knot around her vocal cords. Her earlier fears sloshed through her mind as the gravity of the day crashed inside her heart. She was so sure if Bennett saw the good the Santa Run did for the community, he'd offer to talk to Mr. McCoy on their behalf. Instead, he'd distanced himself from the event.

And from her.

Bennett wiped his palms up and down his thighs before unbuckling. "Well, better get back inside." Without another word, he opened the door and got out.

Eliza didn't move, staring in disbelief. Earlier, he'd been so reassuring, comforting, a safe place to land when her world was falling apart. But now, after she'd shown him her heart, he seemed to shut down. The change didn't make sense.

As she continued to rack her brain, the driver's side door popped open.

"Th-thanks," she said, making quick work of the seat belt while Bennett held open the door.

Eliza clambered out of the car and stood nervously beside him. What was going on? Unsure, she reached for Bennett's hand, searching for a sign. He didn't move but didn't take hold either.

Though she hated to ask, Eliza forced herself. "Did I do something wrong?"

Bennett's eyes met hers and the answer surfaced from the deepening brown like a shaken Magic 8 Ball. He blinked, but it was too late to hide the truth.

"No, you didn't. I'm glad you showed me around today, but . . ." When he paused, she continued for him, sparing him the trouble.

"You're not going to talk to Mr. McCoy, are you?"

Silence.

Eliza dropped her hand to her side and walked toward the steps. No, not walked, ran. Bennett caught up with her on the second stair. Grabbing her arm gently, he turned her toward him.

"I want to help, but you don't know Mr. McCoy the way I do. Talking to him will only make matters worse. Men like him are all about the bottom line. Making money is their top priority."

"Money is just like a bunch of rocks if you can't use it, Bennett." She had so much more she wanted to say, but fresh tears filled her eyes. The threat of crying increased with every second she stayed in his presence. She needed space. With a jerk, she broke free from his hold and bolted toward the door.

"Eliza Lee, can't we discuss this?"

"No, we can't," Eliza hollered back, keeping her pace up the stairs.

If the road trip hadn't changed his mind, talking was a lost cause. She'd been fooled by his charm long enough. Her first instinct to stay far away from the city boy had been right. A man like him was incapable of caring about the Santa Run, or the town for that matter. She didn't expect Bennett to love Pine Valley like she did. There was no way he could. It wasn't his home. But she'd thought seeing the run through her eyes might convince him to fight for it. Apparently, she'd been wrong.

When Eliza Lee reached the top of the steps, she took a deep breath, reminding herself she could do hard things. Alone. She'd weathered the storm of Grandpa's passing by herself and she'd make it through this the same way. She didn't need Bennett's assistance, especially if she had to beg for it. Allowing that realization to sink in, Eliza opened the door and slammed it behind her. The oak could do the talking for her.

Chapter Twelve

ennett stood with his hand on the knob, glaring at the door. A single twist stood between him and Eliza. Her storming away had been a godsend, keeping him from explaining the strained relationship between him and his father. The past was messy and not worth diving into, not even to save face in front of her.

Did it bother him to hide himself away? Yes. The more time he spent with her, the harder it became. And the guiltier he felt. But the truth would complicate matters even further. She might expect him to go to bat for the run, which he couldn't. Trying to change his father's mind under normal circumstances was an uphill battle. Attempting to persuade him to save Christmas? A death wish.

If all went according to plan, Bennett would be back in New York catching up with Pops in a few weeks. Repairing their relationship was the goal, a major factor in his trip to Pine Valley in the first place. He'd tried and failed for years in the city. The time had come for a new approach, and a trip down south offered that. Maryland had proved the method after Bennett ran away. Distance had worked before and it could work again.

Blowing out a loud breath, Bennett descended the steps and tried to untangle the situation. Perhaps the loneliness of a new town had resulted in an immediate attachment with Eliza to suppress the solitude. Maybe the breakup with Janet had bruised his ego more than he wanted to admit, causing him to seek female attention subconsciously. Or maybe that hard-to-breathe sensation around Eliza Lee proved the connection meant something. His thoughts squeezed together like an accordion, making it impossible to distinguish the rational from the emotional.

Except for the fear she might find out who his father was. The man responsible for canceling the Santa Run had no place in Eliza's heart. Surely, his son didn't either.

As Bennett's feet hit the gravel, the desire to run surged within him. An old friend from childhood returning to say hello. He wasn't a boy this time, running away from grief and a hurting father. He was a man with responsibilities and a God who loved him, a survivor of the streets who'd promised himself never to go back there again.

Too, he was a man who knew standing in the parking lot in the cold November air did nothing to better the situation. A trip around the block, or the mountain, might not be such a bad idea. He'd earned a break. Besides, as the closest thing to a CEO on the premises, Bennett could come and go as he pleased. Right now, he wanted to be anywhere except in a room with Eliza Lee Elliott.

Bennett grimaced at the peppermint mocha. The whipped cream and chocolate curls invited him to drink while the mingling scents hugged him. Temptation mounted until he caved. As he swallowed, he wished he had picked something different. The mocha wasn't near as good as he remembered. Then again, he wasn't with Eliza either.

Setting the cup aside, Bennett nibbled at the donut he barely tasted while Danny Jo's eyes wandered to him. She hummed as she made her way from the counter to beside him. Gesturing to his plate, she smiled. "Can I getcha' anything else?"

Bennett looked up from the empty saucer. He didn't even remember finishing the pastry, but the evidence didn't lie. Dazed, he shook his head and Danny Jo moved on.

Country Confections had quieted now that the breakfast rush was over. Man, had the place been hopping! If he hadn't seen a hundred donuts walk out the door, he hadn't seen one. Not to mention the cinnamon rolls, honey buns, and scones that had rolled out. Bennett enjoyed seeing a local business thrive instead of survive the way most did in the city.

In silence, he replayed the morning, scrutinizing each scene. The kiss. The email. The drive. The door slamming in his face. Each time he wound up at the same table by himself with no easy way out.

Danny Jo emerged again, gripping green chalk in one hand and a wet dishcloth in the other. While she worked to scrawl the new verse, Bennett closed his eyes in a word of prayer.

As he raised his head, the weight he'd been carrying since he left the yard dropped at the Master's feet. Peace wrapped around him, calming his mind. He still didn't have the answer, but he had a God who did. That reassurance, in and of itself, would be enough to get him through the day, but when he looked at the board, his heart overflowed.

> *Fear thou not; for I am with thee: be not dismayed; for I am thy God: I will strengthen thee; yea, I will help thee; yea, I will uphold thee with the right hand of my righteousness.*
>
> —Isaiah 41:10

Bennett finished his drink and had another donut, one he actually tasted, before ordering a peppermint mocha to go. The treat would make for a perfect peace offering now that it was time to head back to the office. While he couldn't give Eliza the truth she deserved, he could try to salvage their relationship.

Explaining his reaction to the road trip made it impossible to keep his identity as the owner's son hidden, and Bennett wasn't ready for the repercussions of such a reveal. The crew would no longer respect him for his own skill but instead for his father's name. People would tiptoe around him like in the city. That was the last thing he wanted. In Kentucky, he had created an open environment where employees could come to him with issues, concerns, or ideas for the future because they considered Bennett one of them, not a high man on the corporate ladder. He wasn't ready to lose the rapport he'd worked so hard to build.

Or his friendship with Eliza Lee.

Friendship? The lie didn't hold water even in his own mind as Bennett licked his lips. The slightest hint of peppermint lingered. Whether from the mocha or her lip balm, he couldn't be sure.

Before the run had been canceled, Bennett worried about a workplace mutiny if she knew about his parentage. He had professional concerns. Now that he'd kissed Eliza, he stood to lose much more than office morale.

Bennett knew better than an office romance, especially with Eliza and the hot-and-cold act she'd perfected. She was infuriating but captivating. Untamed but enchanting. She behaved like a magnet, drawing him near even when she pushed him away with her words. The closer he came, the stronger her pull grew until his lips found their way to hers. He should be ashamed of himself.

But her defiance had inspired him to resistance. Truth be told, she inspired him in more ways than one. *Exactly why you have to keep your mouth shut.*

By the time Bennett left Country Confections, lunchtime was closing in. Pizza had never once disappointed, so he picked up a stack of pies from Nonnie's, the diner next to the bakery. He steered the Jag toward the office and drove. All the while, he rehearsed an apology. The further he went, the more worried he became. How would the crew take it? More specifically, how would Eliza Lee take it? This morning, she'd walked a tightrope between a picture of grace and a wave of fury—passion lining both. Which side of her would he receive?

Suck it up, Bennie, and get back in the game.

Heeding the words of wisdom, he parked, rushed through the lot, and pushed open the front door. The office scene made Bennett blink. To his pleasant surprise, everyone sat in their respective places, working away as if nothing had happened. No one even noticed he'd returned until the door squeaked behind him. Hanna spotted the pizza first.

"Do I smell pepperoni?" She stood as quick as her heels and belly allowed, snatching the food from his hands. "I'll just set this here. Me and Jett can share." Carefully, she lowered the top box, opening the lid for a quick sniff. Then, she carried the others to the break room. Within minutes, she returned, paper plates in tow.

"Thank you for lunch. That's very nice of you, considering." Hanna glared at Eliza Lee while Jett mouthed a "sorry" to Bennett.

"No problem at all." Dismissing the tension, Bennett smiled wide before letting the couple get back to their food and heading to the break room. He slapped a slice of combination onto his plate, dropped a handful of quarters in the machine, and grabbed a soda to round out the meal. Not quite ready to rejoin the group, he sank into the empty chair catty-cornered against the wall. He said grace and sized up the pizza. In seconds, he realized the donuts had filled him up. It may have seemed like he only had one, but his stomach knew the truth.

"Mind if I join you?" Eliza leaned against the door facing, twirling a strand of hair that had fallen from her ponytail. Red lined her eyes and stained the tip of her nose, a sharp contrast to her pale face. Bennett's gut twisted at the evidence of her tears.

"Please." He sprang to his feet and swiped the mocha off the counter. "I come in peace."

With a sad smile, she took the drink and mumbled her thanks. Bennett nodded and pulled her chair away from the table, more out of guilt than duty. She may have overreacted, but he'd been the one who had left.

Eliza collapsed in the chair. Without looking at him, she began to wring her hands. "I'm sorry. Putting you on the spot like that was wrong. You're here to supervise the transition, not coddle me when things don't go my way. I'm a big girl and it's high time I act like it." She paused and took a breath, steadying her tone that had begun to waver. "That's why I've thought up a plan to save the Santa Run myself."

Looking up, Eliza fixed her sights on the wall past his shoulder instead of his face. Her lack of eye contact hurt.

What have I done, Lord?

Bennett opened his mouth to pledge his allegiance to the cause—as long as he didn't have to approach his father—but she went on like he'd never moved.

"Mr. McCoy . . ." Eliza scrunched her nose like the name soured her stomach. "Wants to make up the money we lost so I'm going to make that happen." She crossed her legs. "I spoke to Pastor Clemens an hour or so ago. All the proceeds from the pie social are going toward the loss and there will be a special collection plate passed around for donations every Sunday from now until the Santa Run." When she finished speaking, she propped her elbow on the table and cradled her chin.

Bennett sat still. Though stunned by the support she'd already rallied, her plan was a long shot. He needed her to be realistic. High hopes led to big heartbreak, and that was the last thing he wanted for her.

"That's a great start." Bennett smiled tightly. "But it's going to take more than some pies and a collection plate to cover the deficit."

She held up her hand, silencing him. "I'm not done, yet. The construction crew is heading home for the holidays. They're based out of Tennessee and their services are contracted to us. The men saved enough paid time off to cover from Thanksgiving until the week after Christmas. Their time off wasn't in our agreement, though, so the crew's salaries were budgeted already. That allotted pay can now go toward balancing the books. I laid the figures on your desk."

Bennett's eyebrows shot up. He'd called Eliza a leading lady before, but he'd never expected her to go hero-mode after the cancellation. He should have. "You've done your homework, Eliza Lee. I'm impressed."

Without acknowledging the compliment, Eliza dove right back into her pitch. "I don't do anything half-hearted. I told you earlier I care, and I meant what I said. I can't let the town down when so many people depend on me. If there's a way to save the Run, I'll find it."

Bennett smiled at her determination. "I hope you do."

This time, Eliza nodded in response to his encouragement. She pushed back the chair and stood abruptly. "On your desk, you'll also find a proposal ready to be sent to Mr. McCoy detailing our efforts. Out of respect, I didn't want to send it without your approval. I've instructed him to send all questions directly to me. I won't rope you into this. You have my word."

Bennett cringed at her no-nonsense tone. The playfulness and warmth she usually directed toward him had fallen by the wayside, leaving her voice polite but distant. What did he expect? She'd come to him first, practically begging for help, and he had not only turned her away but offered no explanation for his refusal.

Standing slowly, Bennett considered his next move. Despite all the reasons he shouldn't disclose his identity, he could share his past with her. Reveal his current attempt to connect with his father and his real ties to McCoy Railway. Or he could go along with her plan to the letter and forget the morning mountain drive altogether.

Neither option sounded appealing, so he decided to meet somewhere in the middle. "I'll look over the proposal as soon as I'm done here. About this morning." Bennett reached for her hand.

Turning her eyes to him for the first time during their conversation, Eliza pulled her arm away, and picked up the drink he'd brought her. "Don't worry about it. Things happen."

Was she talking about the kiss? A lump formed in his throat as she rattled on.

"No biggie." She sipped her mocha. "The recipe just lived up to its name."

She *was* talking about the kiss. *Did she regret it? Did she think he did?* Bennett shut his eyes tight as she turned her back to him, directing her attention to the stack of pizza on the counter.

"I have to get back to work. Let me know about the proposal as quickly as you can. And thanks again, for the mocha and for the lunch." She slipped a single slice of combination on a plate and kept walking.

Bennett remained stunned, unable to reply with his arm outstretched to the spot where she'd stood. His rejected attempt at a handhold spoiled his appetite more than the donuts. He picked up his untouched plate and tossed it into the trash. As he did, neurons fired to his mouth again.

"Well, Bennie. It looks like your work's cut out for you too."

Chapter Thirteen

———— ❧❧❧ ————

Eliza gripped the buggy with white knuckles, a woman on a mission. She glanced at her watch then to the cashier ringing up the blonde at the front of the line. At least she was next. To celebrate, she grabbed a king-size chocolate bar and threw it on the conveyor belt.

"Eliza Lee, so good to see you. How's Mama Deb and L. J.?" Eliza looked behind her to find Mrs. Bannerman from down the street. A silver bun shone under the harsh lights of the supermarket and her voice was honeyed, the same as when she sang "Jesus Loves Me" all those years ago in the church basement.

"Blessed, ma'am. And you?"

"The same, but a little lost without Edmond. It's hard livin' without him. He's a-waitin' for me at the gates, though, so I'll just keep on keepin' on. Are you making a cartload of pies, young lady?" Mrs. Bannerman peeked past Eliza to the register and smiled.

"Yes, ma'am, with Mom's help. I figure with her supervision, they might turn out OK."

"I'm sure they'll be delicious." Mrs. Bannerman patted Eliza's forearm. "Say, 'Liza? Will there be turkey certificates on the train again this year?"

The words barreled to the bottom of Eliza's stomach. She nodded and slapped a smile on her face that made both her cheeks—and her heart—hurt. "Why, you know it. We've got more vouchers than last year."

"Is it against the rules for ya to save me one? The cold makes my bones ache summin' fierce, and it'll be freezing at the yard. But if I have to, I'll be there. Can't let them grandbabies down. They're all coming home for Christmas this year. I guess they're afraid to leave this ol' woman alone."

"Don't you even think about getting out in the cold. I'll drop you off a voucher as soon as the run is over."

"Much obliged, 'Liza Lee."

"Of course. You have a good evening, ma'am." After a quick hug, Eliza Lee swiped her card, hung the bags on her arms, and headed out. The whole way to Mom's, her thoughts centered on Mrs. Bannerman. The dear lady continued to be a staple of the community, still teaching Sunday school and singing in the choir every week. She wasn't about to let her down.

Squaring her shoulders, Eliza said a quick prayer not to drop the eggs and sprinted to the kitchen. It was time to get busy. After securing the groceries on the counter, though, she realized she was the only one ready to start.

"What are y'all doing? We've got work to do. Is this even preheated?" Eliza yanked the oven door down, getting a face full of hot air as she did. *Guess it is.* She turned to her mother as her cheeks continued to burn. "Mom, I told you I'd be here straight after work and we'd get started."

"Punky, sit down." Her mother pointed a wooden spoon at the food on the table. "Lori wanted breakfast for dinner, so we cooked some for her. Grab a biscuit and sop up what's left of the gravy. You'll be less cranky with a full belly."

"Mom," Eliza whined. "Gravy ain't gonna save the Santa Run. Money will, and these pies will make money. I hope."

"Jenny already cleaned her plate." Her mother took Eliza by the shoulders and guided her over to Jen. "Give her that first recipe and she can get started while you eat a bite."

Eliza did as she was told, handing off the recipe card to her sister-in-law. "Here, Jen. Thank you so much for helping.

My reputation as a cook precedes me. The pies will sell better if word gets out y'all helped me."

"Sure, sister. Anytime." Jenny tied an apron around her waist as Lori bounced across the threshold dressed in a junior chef jacket and hat to match. She scooted her step stool over and climbed on.

After Eliza finished off the gravy and biscuits, she stood. "OK, girls. I'm moving this skillet off the table so I can start on the lemon pie. Hand me a bowl from under the sink, Lori." Lori hopped from the top step of the stool and swung open the cabinet door. Shuffling echoed behind Eliza until a yellow bowl dropped in front of her.

"Thank you, Love." Eliza squinted at the recipe, making sure not to miss a single word. There was no time for do-overs.

"Did I ever tell ya the story behind that pie you're working on?" Her mother rummaged for a cooker, eventually giving up and pulling one from the overstock shelf along the back wall.

"Nope, but I'm dying to know about that nickname." Eliza forced a laugh as her thoughts drifted to Bennett. His woodsy scent, those to-die-for lashes, the warmth of his lips against hers. His shutdown after their trip up the mountain. Resisting the urge to tap her toes, Eliza centered her attention on her mother.

"Well, the night I made that for your daddy is the night he asked me to marry him. He took one bite and went down on a knee. The poor man didn't even have a ring."

Eliza covered her heart with her hands. "Awww. That's adorable, but the pie didn't make Daddy love you."

"Maybe not." Tapping her wooden spoon on the side of the kettle, her mother grinned. "But it sure helped move love along."

Love or lust?

Eliza kept the question to herself as she reread the recipe, more determined than ever to get it right. In no time flat, her crust boasted a beautiful golden brown. She poured the filling and stood back to study the dessert. *Looks good.* She leaned close and breathed in. *Smells good too. All right, Eliza Lee. Time to kick it up a notch.* Steadying her hands, she slowly added a whipped topping border. She secured the lid and slipped the pie into the fridge before moving over to where Jenny worked.

Eliza gasped. "That looks downright delicious, girls. If I liked strawberry, I'd buy it for myself."

"Thank you," said Jenny. "Lori did most of it. She's getting to be quite the little helper in the kitchen."

"Takes after me." Mama Deb winked at them both.

A few minutes later, Eliza cleared her throat as all the girls huddled around the table. "All right, ladies. We need to think of some other fundraisers. The social is a great start, but I need more. Got any ideas?"

Cradling her chin in her hand, Eliza looked from face to face. Jenny sat across from her with Lori wiggling in her lap. After several minutes, Jenny patted the empty chair beside her and let her down. "You're wallerin' me like a wooly worm, baby. Are you bored?"

Dramatically, Lori nodded.

Jenny pulled her phone out of her pocket and handed it to her. "Well, go snap some pictures of the pies for your daddy."

"Yes, ma'am." She snatched the phone and headed toward the counter where Mama Deb was pouring the filling for the chocolate dream pie. She aimed and snapped, the sound of a closing shutter chiming from the phone.

"Lori, you sneaky snake." Mama banged the spoon against the counter. "Delete that right now."

"Why, Granny?" Blinking, Lori hid the phone behind her back. "You look so pretty."

"Don't you know it's a sin to lie?" Planting her hands on her hips, Mama Deb scowled. "With my hair pulled back and these big ears, I'm like that dwarf from Snow White. What's his name? Dopey. Delete it, lil' girl."

"Don't you dare, Lori." Eliza folded her arms across the table. "Mom's just being silly. Besides, we've got bigger problems than ears and dwarves. I need to make money, and a lot of it."

Jenny cracked a walnut and handed the insides to Lori. "Too bad it's not summer. We could have a walkathon, like they do for the cancer center."

At the word *walkathon*, Eliza sat up like a dead man awakened seconds before the coffin closed. "You're a genius, sister. Not a walkathon, but a dance-a-thon. We can get sponsors to pledge so much money for every hour a person stays on the dance floor. Can you call tomorrow and check on using the high school gym?"

"Sure will." Jenny nodded and crossed her legs. "Eliza, what about the night market? Vendors are already signed up. I bet if you ask them, they'll donate the proceeds to the Santa Run."

"That's a great idea." Cracking herself a walnut, Eliza pondered the possibility. "But holidays are hard and I don't want to make them harder." A vision of Mrs. Bannerman flashed in Eliza's mind. It was her first year without her husband. How many more were in the same situation? Or worse?

"You're not alone in this, Punky. Give people a chance a to help." Her mother turned on the faucet, catching Eliza's gaze as she started washing her hands. "Why don't you set up some games too? Like the dollar duck ponds for the kids? And ring toss? Some horseshoes for the adults?"

"Oooh. And the pop-the-balloon game." Lori chimed in as she snapped a picture of Mama Deb's finished pie. She held it up for the rest of the group to see, getting a seal of approval from all.

"We can do that." Eliza nodded, mainly to herself as she talked out her thoughts. "There's a box full of prizes and games left over from vacation Bible school in my closet, so we don't have to spend a cent." Maybe there was a chance to pull it off. They still had three weeks, give or take a few days.

"I got plenty of spare time on my hands, 'Liza Lee. Find me something worth making and I'll set up a booth too." Mama Deb wiped her hands dry with a dish towel and untied her apron. After hanging it in the corner, she slid into the seat closest to Eliza.

"All right, Mom, I'll research and see what I can come up with." Eliza looked at the clock on the stove. "Y'all, I got to get to bed. Jett and Hanna have a check-up tomorrow, so I'll be opening in the morning."

"We gotta go too." Jenny helped Lori to her feet and retrieved the small coat from the back of the chair. She held it open while Lori worked her way in. "It's past this one's bedtime."

"Thank you, guys, so much. You, too, Mom." Eliza planted a kiss on her mother's cheek. *She may be a meddler, but she's my meddler.*

"That's my job, Punky." Mama Deb stole one more hug before Eliza rushed over to the door.

"I'll see you ladies tomorrow night at the church. Don't forget my pies." Eliza exited her childhood home and walked the few steps to the car. She shivered as she slid in. *Why didn't I let it warm up?* With a huff, she pulled onto the two-lane road. The cold settled deep in her bones by the time she parked in her driveway. Chilled but hopeful now that she had a plan in place, Eliza rushed inside.

"You coming to the social tonight, Bennett?"

Eliza looked up at the sound of his name, wishing it was her asking instead of Hanna. After a successful pie-making session and a good night's sleep, she remained optimistic about the Run. But positive thoughts and uplifted spirits couldn't change Mr. McCoy's mind. *Not like Bennett could.* She didn't understand his reluctance. Or her feelings for him. Since their break room discussion, she'd pretended not to feel his eyes on her as she typed and dismissed the sudden spike in her pulse whenever he walked in. There was no going back to before, despite Eliza's longing to.

Bennett tapped the top folder on the pile. "If I can finish these files between now and then, I'll be there."

Breaking her silent treatment, Eliza threw her two cents in. "Not looking good for you." The words ushered an instant heat up the back of her neck and across her cheeks. Hanna didn't crack a smile, just snapped her head back to the invoices she'd been sorting. Eliza refused to backtrack, though. The office belonged to her well before it did him and she was tired of walking on eggshells. Casting her best yeah-I-said-it look, Eliza braced herself for the backlash.

Sarcasm came instead. Jett raised both arms in celebration. "She speaks."

Bennett laughed but wasted no time turning his attention back to his desk. His lips drew tight as he squinted at the computer screen.

Eliza stood and grabbed her jacket from the coatrack, quite pleased with herself for ignoring her brother's jab. Keeping the peace was important. While Jett had forgiven her outburst from the other day, he'd made it crystal clear he didn't want to be involved. If the Santa Run were put back on the calendar, he'd resume his role as Santa. That was the extent of it. Bennett had offered his services to the cause, though. The gesture confused her even more. His initial refusal still stung like a hornet. The pain kept her from including him in any of the fundraiser planning.

Standing at the door, Eliza chanced a final peek at Bennett. His face was soft again, deep in thought with his chin tilted toward the light. A strand of hair fell over one eyebrow, the only part of him not styled to perfection.

Even though Bennett didn't question her departure, Eliza felt the need to explain. "In case you were wondering, I'm helping set up at the church tonight and Mom made me promise not to be late. So, I gotta scoot."

Looking up from his work, Bennett met her gaze and nodded. She answered with a single head bob and turned to face her sister-in-law. "Jett bringing you, Hanna?"

"Supposed to, but he's barely looked up from his desk all day." Hanna gestured toward Jett talking away on the headset. "We might have to sneak in during a break, but we'll be there."

"Well, be careful when you do come." Eliza cracked the door open as she spoke. The smell of fresh rain rushed the stoop. "It's starting to sprinkle." Before talking herself out of it, she added, "You be careful, too, Bennett."

Afraid to find three sets of eyes glued to her, she rushed down the steps and through the parking lot without looking back. Why couldn't she let a sleeping dog lie? *'Cause you care too much, girl. That's why.*

As Eliza unlocked her car, the truth of her answer taunted her. Regardless how many times she lied and told herself otherwise, she'd grown to care about a certain New Yorker with puppy dog eyes and brown loafers to match.

But did he care about her?

Chapter Fourteen

"Jett still not finished?" Bennett did a double take as his eyes centered on Hanna. He was sure she'd snuck out during his last coffee run, but no. There she sat, rubbing her belly and glaring at the clock. If she didn't leave soon, she'd be late for the social.

"Nope. He's had to reschedule a couple of trains and reroute a few others because of the storm down south." Hanna turned to Jett, but he didn't even look up until she rapped her nails against her desk. Then, his glance lasted only long enough to offer an unspoken apology.

Bennett nodded and blew on his coffee. There were at least two hours left of work for him, maybe more, but the disappointment on Hanna's face plagued him. She'd stayed out of the whole Santa Run debacle, but it wasn't hard to figure out whose side she was on. No doubt, she wanted to show her support for Eliza's first fundraiser. After a quick sip of coffee, he grabbed their coats from the corner and set the cup on the edge of the desk.

"I can't stand to see a pregnant woman sad." Bennett reached out his hand to help her up and waited. "Come on. Let's go to the church."

"That's very kind, but I can wait."

"The files won't spoil, but your sweet potato pie will." Bennett smiled as she pushed her chair back, relieved she'd accepted his offer. Too bad it wasn't solely out of the kindness of his heart. It gave him the excuse he'd been looking for to go to the social without seeming desperate. No matter what Eliza Lee thought, he wanted to see her defy the odds, and he was more than happy to cash in on some sweets to help her along. *But not lemon.* Not because he didn't like lemon pie. He did—almost as much as the woman who made it. But because Eliza Lee wouldn't want his help.

"Are you sure? It won't hurt if I'm a little late." Hanna waved at Jett. When she had his attention, she pointed to the clock. He bounced his eyes from the clock to Hanna to Bennett as he pieced together what was happening. Then, he motioned toward the door, and mouthed the word *go*, hurrying them on their way.

Despite their late arrival, Bennett managed to snag a semiclose space in the church parking lot and the two of them scrambled out of the car. Hanna hustled to beat ninety with a protruding pregnant belly out in front and sharp heels for a foundation. The sight made him question the laws of physics and his sense of humor as he started to laugh. Midchuckle, science caught up to Hanna. The too-high-for-its-own-good heel slipped, her ankle turned, and down she started to go. Bennett slid an arm around her waist with barely enough time to keep her from hitting the ground. Unfortunately, the tray he'd been carrying wasn't so lucky. As Hanna was on her way back up, the pies were on the way down, each landing with a splat.

Blood rushed to Bennett's cheeks as he examined the broken crusts and upside-down tins. *Way to go, Bennie.* He sighed and shifted his gaze to Hanna. "I'll pay for them, I promise. We can average what a pie goes for tonight and I'll double it for each of the ones I ruined. I am so sorry."

"Sorry? For what? Keeping my heinie from kissing the curb?" Hanna smiled and looped her arm with his. "Stop being silly. Now, help me up the steps and don't breathe a word of this to Mama Deb."

Bennett nodded in agreement. "I wouldn't dream of it."

Down in the basement, Hanna cornered a bored-looking teenage couple and sweet-talked them into cleaning up the mess outside. Her persuasion skills were on point. With prowess like that, she'd be a force in sales. Maybe marketing too.

Making a mental note to see if she'd be interested in that type of work, Bennett helped Hanna to a seat. He then took off to survey the room—and the dessert selection. Pies stretched from one end of the buffet counter to the other and it ran the length of the room. There were so many to choose from. After much deliberation, he decided to bid on the classic cherry with a lattice crust. Wasn't that his father's favorite? Bennett searched his memories until an image of his parents surfaced. A singular piece of cherry pie placed on the table between them. *Cherry, it is.* Smiling at his decision, Bennett made his way back over to the crowd and took the empty chair beside Hanna.

At six on the dot, Mama Deb stood up and took her place behind the counter as auctioneer. She clapped her hands, demanding attention. Those standing found a seat or shuffled against the wall. The voices lulled to a whisper, except for the occasional infant crying or toddler laughing. Bidding got underway.

Sue's apple pie went first to Mr. Stone, just like Eliza said. Then, the cheesecake. There had been no exaggeration about the Andrews sisters' baking ability. The dessert looked scrumptious and every bit worthy of the $60.00 it brought in after a bidding war.

Dish after dish went by until there were only three pies left: lemon, peanut butter, and cherry. The lemon was up next. Bennett tucked his hands under his thighs, just in case temptation to drive the price up reared its ugly head.

Mama Deb called out the description of the pie on the auction block, and Eliza Lee stood up. Amazingly, she'd found time to change between the office and the church, exchanging her hoodie and jeans for a yellow dress, a black cardigan, leggings, and knee-high boots. The ponytail from earlier had been restyled, too, into a loose side braid falling over her shoulder. He wondered if she'd matched her wardrobe to the color of her pie. Leave it to her to pull a trick like that.

Well done, Eliza Lee. Props.

As the bidding started, he tried to find a focal point. A flower arrangement, a framed photo, a decorative cross. Anything to distract him from the auction. After a few seconds of scanning, he spotted Lori and a little boy playing checkers in the corner. Lori was down to two checkers when a sharp elbow rammed his ribcage.

"Bid." Hanna tried to whisper, but her excited state made it sound closer to a squeal. When he didn't answer right away, she elbowed him again. "Bid, now."

"What? Why?" Rubbing his side, he looked back at Eliza Lee, finding her ram-rod straight and pale.

"Just bid. I'll give you the money back. Please." Hanna answered, her eyes pleading louder than the words.

"I can't." He shook his head and angled himself away from her in case she decided to throw another elbow. "You know how tense things have been lately. If I bid, she'll hate me."

If she doesn't already.

Instead of another dig with her elbow, Hanna smacked his arm. "If you don't bid, I'll hate you."

"I'm not bidding unless you tell me what's going on." Bennett waited while Hanna pointed to a face he'd never seen before.

"See that guy over there against the wall? Blond hair, baby blues, and a winning smile? He's winning Eliza's pie right now too."

"Going once." Mama Deb rushed the bids along, but her voiced held an edge that hadn't been there at the start of the auction.

"And?" Bennett raised his brows and shook his head, tired of guessing. They were running out of time.

"And that's Austin Stone, Eliza's ex—"

"Going twice—"

"*Fiancé.*"

Mama Deb and Hanna continued, battling for his attention. Their voices meshed together in his ears as Bennett's eyes went wide. *Ex-fiancé?* While he'd had time to make peace with his relationship misgivings, Eliza's past romantic endeavors hadn't crossed his mind. Why had the two of them broken up? Had Austin hurt her? Bennett's teeth clenched at the thought. She didn't deserve heartbreak any more than the man responsible deserved that lemon pie.

What was the bid at? Fifty bucks? One hundred?

Bennett couldn't remember. Better question. How much cash did he have on him? Unsure, he decided he'd go to the atm if need be and yelled over the crowd.

"Two hundred dollars." Bennett's hand flew in the air as quick as the words left his mouth. Mama Deb smiled but kept the auction going to be fair. Like a deer in headlights, Eliza stood wide-eyed. Her toes tapped furiously on the cement floor. When she composed herself enough to look around, she darted her gaze from Hanna to Mama Deb and finally to him. The hurt he saw there made his chest ache.

"Sold." With a slam of the gavel, Mama Deb closed the bidding

Eliza sat down as the sale concluded, dropping her gaze to the floor until the social ended. She stayed still as the congregation moved upstairs. Except the toe-tapping. That particular motion she'd kept up since her pie had been sold. Bennett weaved his way through the empty chairs and slid in beside her.

"You didn't have to do that." Eliza sprang from her seat and crossed the room. Pink stains shone on her cheeks, but the color had lightened since the auction.

Letting a trail of vanilla and honey guide his steps, Bennett followed her to the window. "I like lemon. I told you so, remember?"

"Just stop it, City Boy." She touched her forehead to the windowpane. "Stop trying to take care of me. I don't need your help and I certainly don't want it. Not anymore."

Bennett stepped forward, close enough to see her lip quivering. An overwhelming desire to kiss those lips shot through him like lightning, but he knew better than to act on the impulse. She'd made it clear where she stood.

Mustering all his nerve, he placed a hand on her shoulder and squeezed. "Eliza Lee, please let me explain." Instead of leaning into his touch like he'd hoped, she spun on her heels. She knocked his arm away and faced him.

"Explain what?" A single tear spilled out, but she pressed on. "Why you didn't fight Mr. McCoy on the cancellation, even after I showed you the value of the Run? Why you didn't give me a reason? Why you kissed me?"

Bennett glanced at the ceiling, praying for the right words. He couldn't account for his silence or reluctance regarding the Run without exposing himself as McCoy Railway royalty and son of the man responsible for the cancellation. Such information would destroy every relationship he'd built in Kentucky. He wasn't prepared to face that sort of backlash. Nor was he ready to step back into his father's shadow. Not yet.

Picking his words like steps in a minefield, Bennett answered. "It's complicated. Mr. McCoy is difficult to deal with, but now that he's signed off on the fundraising, I can help. If you'll let me."

"Because you care so much, right?" Her green eyes darkened, the sparkle that starred in his dreams transforming to a sizzle.

"Yes, I do." Bennett drew as close to her as possible. He stood up straighter, resisting the urge to wrap his arms around her.

Eliza met his gaze head on. "You're just like Mr. McCoy. All you care about is the profit. The bottom line. About mo—"

"*You.* That's why . . ." His voice faltered. As her supervisor, he shouldn't admit to his feelings for her. But Eliza was more than a personnel file in a desk drawer. She deserved to know that.

"Why what, Bennett?" Daring him to continue, Eliza hiked a brow. "Cat got your tongue?"

All right. Fine. Two can play that game.

He stepped forward one last time and took her by the shoulders, refusing to let her look away. Instead, she closed her eyes, but he wasn't giving up that easily. He'd stand there all night if he had to.

When she opened her eyes again, he pulled his voice out from hiding. She needed to hear the words. Loud and clear.

"That's why I kissed you. Because I care about you—more than I should. Watching Austin bid on your pie made me see red." Bennett rubbed her arms gently before releasing his hold. "I can't stop my feelings, but I won't act on them again, Eliza Lee."

As if on cue, her lips parted, mocking him. He stepped back. Refusing to be made a liar, Bennett took another breath followed by a final step before he spoke again.

"If there's any more kissing to be done, it'll be by you, not me."

Turning around, he made his way to the buffet counter on wobbly legs. The flames that'd passed between them left him jittery in all the best possible ways. She had to feel it too. Did she honestly not see how much he cared?

Right away, he spotted the lemon pie but stood there pretending he didn't. He needed a minute to collect himself. When his breathing had calmed, he retrieved the tin and started for the sanctuary. The chill of the pan soaked into his palms and Bennett welcomed it.

He turned back to Eliza to say his goodbye. She was tapping her toes against the floor with a vengeance but stopped as his eyes caught hers.

Show her I care, Lord. Let her see that.

Pausing at the bottom of the stairs, Bennett held up the tin. "Thanks for the pie. It looks delicious." He grinned and winked before mounting the first step. "Have a good Thanksgiving, Eliza Lee."

Taking the stairs two at a time, he sprinted up to the main floor and sunk into a back pew. He faded happily into the congregation while Pastor Clemens wrapped up prayer requests. Bennett had plenty to pray about but none he was willing to share. Before they knelt, though, Pastor asked anyone with an unspoken prayer to let it be known with a slip of the hand. Bennett raised his arm high.

SORRY, POPS. CAN'T MAKE IT BACK. HAPPY THANKSGIVING.

Morning light fluttered through the blinds of the office as Bennett hit send and shut the front door. After seconds of searching, he found the switch he'd been fumbling for. Fluorescence flooded the space, overshadowing the sun rays from the window instantly. He shrugged off his coat and threw it in the open chair near the doorway instead of bothering to hang it up. It was a one-man crew today and that man wasn't in the mood to be tidy.

Before resuming his position behind the stack of folders, he started a pot of coffee. A flip of the wrist and last month's accounting report lay open in front of him. Thumbing through once, he ensured the pages were accounted for and in the correct order, ready to analyze.

As he started the first page, a new text came through.

IS THIS ABOUT JANET?

Bennett rolled his eyes and laid aside the report. His father picked now of all times to be interested in his love life? Why? Did he feel sorry for Bennett? *Doubtful.* Bennett typed out a response.

> STAYING HERE HAS NOTHING TO DO WITH HER. THERE'S JUST TOO MUCH WORK LEFT TO BE DONE.

Immediately, a response came through.

> IN THAT CASE, GOOD JOB.

Good job? That was all he got on Thanksgiving. No mention of missing him, no plans to share a meal later, not even a thank-you. Bennett shook his head and locked the screen.

Fonder, huh? Fonder, my butt. It was typical Pops behavior, but he'd hoped for more this year after his willingness to travel to another state for the sake of business. The two of them hadn't celebrated for years, unless a half-day at the office and dinner from a drive-thru counted.

Still, he'd expected something—a morning call, a friendly voice mail, even a funny e-card—especially after all the emails he'd sent his father recently.

Bennett opened his inbox and counted. Eleven messages in the last two days. Opening the first email, he read it to himself. Not finding what he thought he would, Bennett opened the next one. When he'd finished it, he frowned and clicked on the third. A growl escaped him as he realized he was no better than his father. The emails he'd sent? Impersonal and meaningless. Bennett hadn't even bothered to ask about holiday plans. Maybe Eliza was right.

Despite the adoption of his mother's name, maybe he was just like *Mr. McCoy.*

A gust of wind blew outside and crept in under the door, stirring the scent of fresh coffee around him. He stood and stretched. Caffeine was just what he needed, a constant friend that never let him down, no matter the time or place.

With a fresh cup cooling, he rummaged the cupboards for breakfast, or at least something resembling it. He laid the spoils on the table. A Twinkie, a pack of blueberry Pop-Tarts, and a granola bar. Not the breakfast of champions, but he'd make do. Scooping the lot against his chest, he grabbed the cup and returned to the front. A ringing phone welcomed him back.

"McCoy Railway, Bennett speaking."

"Hey, man." Jett's voice sounded in his ear. "Sure you don't need some help? The girls won't let me near the kitchen, so I'm free until dinner gets done."

"I'm good. Promise. Go enjoy the day with your family."

"I appreciate that, but I hate for you to be alone on Thanksgiving." Somewhere in the distance, Lori giggled. The remnants of it carried through the line.

"I'm not alone. There's work galore to keep me company." Bennett forced a laugh and prayed the background noise kept Jett from hearing how fake it sounded.

"All right. But if you change your mind, holler at me."

"Will do. Tell everyone Happy Thanksgiving for me." Bennett pressed his lips together to keep himself from adding, "especially Eliza."

"I will, buddy."

"Thanks." Bennett hung up and found himself no longer in the mood to work but to brood. Jett was a lucky man to have so many people to share his life with. Proud parents, a loving wife, a little one on the way, a brother and sister to lean on despite their differences.

No, not lucky. Blessed.

For the first time since leaving the city, Bennett second-guessed his decision. He would have gotten used to seeing Janet in the building. Besides, neither of them had been crushed by the breakup. Then, there was Pops. Did Bennett honestly think distance might mend his relationship with his father when working side by side for years had failed? It wasn't the cure-all, not even close. Was he grasping at straws?

Bennett squared his shoulders and plucked the sprig of bitterness trying to bloom. Today was not the day to sulk but to give thanks, and he had plenty to be grateful for. Blessings disguised as pastrami sandwiches on rye, a regifted coffee mug, and a well-timed phone call. Yes, he had much to be thankful for.

By noon the clock on the wall had almost lulled him to sleep with its soothing tick-tock rhythm. Usually, the phone rang off the hook, but not today. With nothing to listen to, save his thoughts and the shuffling pages, Bennett found the silence maddening. Maybe a walk on the porch would wake him up. A wide yawn made up his mind, but the door creaked open before he reached it.

As he stood from his chair, Eliza Lee strolled through the entrance.

"Eliza?" Bennett stood and rounded his desk. Beneath his chest, his heart went to war with his ribcage. The wild beating resounded in his ears. What was she doing with him instead of her family?

She held up a hand. "Please don't make this more than it is. I couldn't stand the thought of you not having a proper meal. So, here."

Eliza Lee pushed the food toward him. Two butter bowls and a foil-covered plate bursting at the seams.

Bennett licked his lips and took the meal from her, wondering if his appetite centered around the food or the woman carrying it. "You didn't have to do that. I had leftovers from last night."

"Well, if you don't want it, I can take it back." Eliza reached for one of the bowls.

"Don't even think about it. My mouth's watering at the smell." Bennett pulled the plate away from her reach. "Thank you."

"You're welcome." Taking a step back, she nodded. "Anyway, I gotta get back. I promised Lori a game of checkers. See you tomorrow."

"Count on it." Bennett grinned, not even trying to hide his amusement.

A spark flashed in her eyes. Without another word, she waved goodbye and shut the door behind her.

At least she didn't slam it this time.

When Bennett was sure she was out of earshot, he laughed until he was short of breath. The fact that Eliza made a special trip to bring him Thanksgiving dinner proved she thought about him outside of work. Knowing that pleased him more than it should have. Acting on his emotions for Eliza may have been off the table, but their game of cat and mouse was fun.

Especially when he was the cat.

Chapter Fifteen

"Ugh!" Halfway through her scream, Eliza attempted to overlay a more office-acceptable volume to her voice, but it was too late.

I hate Black Friday.

As soon as she had lifted her head from the pillow, grief rose to meet her. Cold descended like a cloud blocking the sun. The chill, heightening the sorrow scratching her nerves, settled deep in her soul.

One year.

How had it been twelve months since she'd laid Grandpa in the ground? Had she really lasted three hundred sixty-five days without his goodnight hugs and morning pancakes? Did 525,600 minutes truly slip by without the smile that lit up her world?

It had taken everything in her to drag herself to work. Now, she was frazzled, emotionally spent, and lonely. *Oh, so lonely.* Eliza closed her eyes and prayed. *Father, I need help. Making it through today, moving past the pain, saving the Run. I can't do this by myself. Please, be with me.*

After whispering amen, Eliza focused on the counter in front of her. The sight of the speckled granite placed her firmly in the Appalachian Express break room instead of the past Grandpa Walt's death seemed to define. Sorrow slipped into annoyance as she glared at the broken coffee machine. Seeing an empty pot, she wanted to scream again.

Eliza composed herself before a second shriek broke free. When Bennett appeared in front of her, though, she realized her self-control was too little, too late.

"What is it?" Bennett's warm eyes searched her face. "Are you OK?"

"Oh, no. I mean, yes, I'm fine. It's just . . ." Eliza smiled sheepishly, ashamed of the alarm she'd caused. Giving him the cold shoulder was one thing but giving him a heart attack was another. "Sorry I scared you, but I really, *really* need caffeine and the coffee machine won't work. For it to break today of all days . . ."

"Today of all days?" His brows peaked, giving those long lashes room to breathe. "What's so special about tod—"

Midquestion, a familiar and welcome voice began singing "Happy Birthday," the off-key notes floating into the break room.

Eliza froze. She knew who that was. The song made her forget about the coffeepot, the awkwardness surrounding her and Bennett, even the date on the calendar.

With a mumbled "excuse me" and newfound energy, she ran past him. Just clearing the hall, the final line rang out. "Happy Birthday, Dear Eliza. Happy Birthday to you."

Squeals filled the air as she flung her arms around the songstress waiting by her desk. Leave it to Emma Lou to save the day. Hugging her tight, Eliza swayed her best friend back and forth. "Emma Lou, what are you doing here?"

"Stealing you away." Emma broke the embrace and jabbed a thumb toward the door. "Now, let's go."

"Oh, that's so sweet," Eliza looked to the balloon bouquet on the desk and back again, searching for the words to let Emma down gently. "But I can't."

"Yes, you can. I know trains never stop, not even on Black Friday, but the kidnapping is preapproved."

Eliza scanned the room. "By Jett?"

"By all management." Emma Lou glanced over Eliza's shoulder to Bennett and grinned. "Get your coat and meet me at the car."

"You don't gotta tell me twice." In her excitement, she hurried a little too much and knocked the coatrack down, right at Bennett's feet. "Shoot."

"Go on, I got this," Bennett reassured her as he knelt near the rack.

For a split second, Eliza opened her mouth to refuse his assistance, to tell him he'd already done enough by agreeing to the impromptu day off, but his expression stopped her cold turkey. It was the same look he'd given her after swinging Lori that Sunday in the commons and the one from the parking lot after the Santa Run had been canceled.

Why did he have to look at her like he wanted to save her? Eliza had made up her mind to be her own Prince Charming and she meant to do just that. Raise the money. Save the Run. Honor Grandpa. *Without Bennett's help.*

The day off, though? She'd take that.

"Thank you." She threw a hand against the wall to push herself back up. "For the stand and the day off."

Bennett nodded and the warmth of his gaze tugged at her heart. Feeling her defenses start to crumble, Eliza dismissed herself. "I better not keep her waiting."

Before heading out, she skipped between the desks to where Jett sat working away. She wrapped both arms around his shoulders and squeezed with all her might. "Thank you, brother."

Jett patted her arm still around his neck. "Just remember this day when I ask you to babysit."

"I'll be at your beck and call." She planted a light peck on his cheek before bolting out the door. Then, she skipped down the steps. She didn't slow down until she was in the car, buckled and ready to go.

✳

"So, Birthday Girl, what'll it be?" Emma Lou chirped while she opened her menu across from Eliza.

"Em, you know it's not my birthday. Have those kindergarteners made you senile?"

Emma Lou held up a finger. "Once a year is not enough for cake and ice cream, so I dub today your pretend birthday. We shall celebrate it from here on out. I actually started the festivities early by adopting the most adorable pair of kittens. You have to come see them."

"Cats?" Eliza shook her head. "Really?"

Emma Lou simply shrugged. "Most of Pine Valley thinks I'll turn into a cat lady eventually. I figured why not start now?"

"If you say so." Eliza Lee laughed as she looked around. The dining room was surprisingly calm for Nonnie's. From behind the counter, Sue waved, wearing the same smile she donned after reading *Where the Red Fern Grows* to their fifth-grade class. The teacher-turned-entrepreneur after retirement was a sight for sore eyes. Whenever Eliza needed encouragement, she dropped by. Never once had she left disappointed.

"I do say so." Emma Lou smiled. "I figured you needed some cheering up, and making it your birthday was the best thing I could think of."

"Thanks." Staring at the list of lunch combos, Eliza blinked her tears away before switching the subject. "Work has been crazy lately."

Emma Lou reached across the table and grabbed Eliza's hand. "That was some slick diversion tactics and, because I love you, I'll allow it. The changes at the railroad will get easier. Give it time."

"I can't lose the Santa Run. It's all I've got left of Grandpa."

"You won't lose the Run, Eliza. I've seen you hustling around town, kicking butt and taking names." Emma Lou squeezed her hand as an elderly couple walked by. "You're looking mighty pretty doing it, too, I might add. Pretty enough to catch the eye of that cutie in the office."

While Eliza Lee tried to think up a believable retort, the waitress appeared. Eliza pointed to the menu as she gave her order. Emma Lou did the same, giving Eliza time to map out what she wanted to share about her and Bennett. No lying but no details. She'd spill the bare minimum. Eliza opened her mouth to put her plan in action but lost the ability to speak. The door swung open, ushering in Austin Stone. *Today? C'mon. You've got to be kidding me.*

Grinning wide, Emma Lou waved toward the entrance. "Look what the cat dragged in."

Look, indeed.

Eliza had no desire to see her ex-fiancé, so she shut her eyes tight. Realizing how rude she was being, she reopened them and found Emma Lou hugging their uninvited male companion. She mustered a fake grin while the pleasantries unfolded.

"Austin Stone. How are you?" Emma Lou used her singsong voice she sometimes used on Lori when still in teacher mode. "Is Boston treating you good?"

When Emma Lou released him, Austin blew out a long breath. "Decent. How are you?"

"Right as rain." Emma Lou giggled as Eliza ground her teeth behind a forced smile.

Austin lifted his chin to her. "Hey, Eliza Lee." His voice was smooth and light, like freshly fallen snow on a cold winter's day. The smile he wore was sincere, opposite of the imitation Eliza scrawled across her face. She nodded curtly and darted her eyes to Emma Lou, a silent scream for help.

Somehow, Emma Lou heard the plea as she seated herself and took control of the conversation. "Your dad already put you to work?"

"He has. You know that man never stops." Austin appraised his mud-stained jeans before eyeing the register. "I hate to run, but everyone's waiting on the grub. Eliza, I saw the sign-up for the dance-a-thon. It's doubtful I'll be in town, but my firm has some end-of-the-year donation money unaccounted for. Do you still need a sponsor?"

"Oh, I'm the planner, not a dancer. You know I have two left feet." Prom memories marched through her mind. Austin in his black tux with a blue rose in his lapel, the same shade as her dress. The limo ride to the school. The heels his rented shoes squashed a dozen times during the first two songs. She'd blamed herself to save him from the embarrassment and taken them off.

"As I recall, it was me with the left feet, not you. You were the portrait of grace." Austin widened his smile.

When he did, Eliza felt the tension in her shoulders fade. How often had she seen that smile? On the story rug in grade school, after dodgeball in seventh grade, at the homecoming football game when he held her hand for the first time, while the graduation march played. Most recently? When he tried to buy her pie at the church. She knew that smile almost as well as her own. Even though it didn't light up her life the way it once did, she was thankful to see Austin happy again.

The hostility she'd been trying to hide waned. Sitting in a booth at Nonnie's during the darkest day of the year, she let go of the pain and guilt she'd been harboring. The part of her that recognized Austin as a forever friend clicked into place and Eliza returned the smile.

"You've been gone too long, Austin. Time must've messed with your memory." She chuckled, and they all joined in, Emma Lou milking it for all it was worth.

"Maybe," he said. "Well, I can sponsor someone else, then, whoever you think will last the longest. I'll stop by on my way out of town. You still work half a day on Saturday?"

Eliza nodded, surprised he remembered her work schedule.

"I'll be coming through around nine." The blue in Austin's eyes brightened a shade as he spoke. "Is it all right to drop in?"

"Of course. It'll just be Hanna and me, and I'm sure she'd love to see you."

"Sounds good. See you then." Austin tipped his hat to each of the women. "Emma Lou, try to be good."

With that, he turned and headed toward the counter. Eliza watched him walk away feeling none of the sadness she expected she would. Instead, she felt free. The emotion shocked her so much she giggled. Never one to be left out, Emma Lou joined in, a little louder than necessary. Eliza tried to shush her, but the look on her face made Eliza laugh that much harder. They were still laughing when their food came out.

"I did not expect today to be like this." Eliza said, opening her silverware. "A pretend birthday and an ex-fiancé."

"And an office hottie you were getting ready to dish about." Emma Lou popped a fry into her mouth like popcorn before the show. "Bennett, is it?"

Drat. Thanks to Emma Lou's romance-obsessed brain, Eliza wasn't out of the woods yet.

"There's nothing to tell." Eliza pushed a piece of lettuce around her plate, trying to keep from meeting the glare she knew Emma Lou had turned on her.

"Really? Because while I was there, he made eyes at you at least five times."

"He did not. Did he?"

Emma Lou didn't speak. Instead, she crossed her arms and blinked slowly. Knowing she'd been had, Eliza went on.

"OK, so I like him. But he's infuriating. A-a-and my boss." She took a sip of water and tried to wash down the truth with it. "It's complicated."

"The best things in life are complicated, honey. That's what makes it interesting." Emma Lou paused, wagging a finger at her. "Don't let Austin Stone keep the key to your heart. It's time to move on."

"You're one to talk." Eliza leaned across the table and pushed her shoulder lightly. "What about you moving on from Clay?"

"I've dated plenty since Clay. No one sticks. I chase them off after the first night." Emma Lou shrugged. "Besides, we're not talking about me. We're talking about you."

Classic Emma Lou. Forever putting others before herself. One day, Eliza Lee would solve the mystery of her breakup with Clay. *Apparently not today.*

"I'm over Austin." Eliza made eye contact to prove her truthfulness. "He asked me to go with him to Boston, but I belong here. No way was I gonna let him turn that internship down. It was the best, for both of us."

"What's the problem, then?" Emma Lou threw up her arms, nearly knocking her glass over in the process.

Ever since the two of them were kids, Emma Lou had always been able to read Eliza, draw out the deep parts of her like water from a well. But this? She couldn't explain the problem when she didn't understand it herself. If she was looking, Bennett would make a fine suitor. Kind, sweet, respectful. Except he'd turned his back on her when she'd needed his help most. Despite retracting the refusal and offering his assistance as of late, Eliza couldn't move past his initial response. She did not want to tell her friend that, though. With Emma Lou's forgiving nature, she'd tear that reason to shreds.

However, an aversion to office romance would be entirely acceptable. Bennett was her boss. The man with the power to cut her loose from the railroad should their relationship turn sour. Emma Lou would understand her reluctance since it endangered her career. Plus, his time in Pine Valley was coming to a close. Another perfectly acceptable reason to keep herself firmly parked on the just-friends side of the track. *Yeah, let's go with that.*

"Bennett's my supervisor, and he's only here to oversee the transition. Once the job is done, it's back to the city he goes.

Besides, being alone is good for me. I'm finally learning to stand on my own two feet. Adding a man to my life right now is the definition of what I don't need."

"*Need* and *want* are two very different things, and from that blush you're wearing, I'd say you know what you want by now. Or should I say *who* you want?"

Eliza's jaw dropped as her cheeks grew even hotter. *Want* was fickle. So what if his kiss made the earth shake beneath her? Or that his chocolate eyes were the perfect blend of sweet and heat? Or that his scent made her breath catch?

Smiling, Emma Lou tapped the table. "What we *need* can start as *want* in the beginning, and we all need someone. You included."

Eliza shrugged and speared a piece of lettuce with her fork. *Dang, her hide. If that ain't the truth.*

"You're right, I do need someone." As Eliza spoke, Emma Lou covered her hand with hers, pride beaming in her smile. So much so, Eliza thought twice about what she was getting ready to say. "I need someone to bring me that birthday cake, like yesterday."

Without hesitating, Emma Lou lifted her fork. Was she agreeing with her? Seemed to be, but the mischief in her eyes warned Eliza she had no intentions of giving up.

After a day filled with food, shopping, laughter, and more food in the form of delicious donuts on the way back to the office, Emma Lou dropped Eliza Lee off earlier than planned. The poor thing had forgotten to stop by the community center to sign up for the dance-a-thon. Eliza didn't mind, though. An early night would do her good.

Eliza collapsed into the driver's seat and took a breath before turning the key. The engine roared to life, sending a heavy burst of cold air out the vents. She shivered and adjusted the fan. While the vehicle warmed, Eliza replayed the conversation from earlier, realizing Emma Lou had been spot on, about Austin as well as Bennett.

Until the social, it'd been months since she'd thought about Austin, probably since the week she'd mailed him her engagement ring. He'd said to keep it, but it was too hard. Even tucked away in the bottom of her jewelry box, the ring burned her finger. In the days that'd followed, she'd rewound their relationship a dozen times, finding herself mostly to blame. It hurt to admit that, but it was true.

Grandpa's passing had cut her too deep for words. The lack of communication kept Austin on the outside looking in while the grief inside her twisted like a tornado stuck between the mountains. Even though he begged her to open up, the few times she'd attempted to talk to him had ended with her locked in the bathroom and streaks of his taillights trickling between the blinds. Eventually, the canceled dates, ignored calls, and space apart pushed him past the point of no return long before he decided to move. After passing the CPA exam, he had every intention to set up shop in Pine Valley until a buddy from college landed an internship with an up-and-coming accounting firm in Boston. The company had one more spot available and Austin applied. A few weeks later, he accepted the position and let Eliza down with a heartfelt letter and hug goodbye. The breakup had come so close after burying Gramps, it was hard to know which she grieved for more.

Had she loved him? No question. Did she still love him? Yes, but not in the marrying kind of way. She'd yet to prove her ability to love after his rejection. *Did she want to love again?* Maybe. Which meant she needed to stay away from Bennett. The two of them would never work. His need for corporate permission to help save the Run proved his allegiance to the business and subsequent profit trumped tradition and community. While she hadn't expected him to defy Mr. McCoy, she'd hoped he cared enough about Pine Valley—enough about her—to at least open a discussion about the Run. When he didn't, she'd lost faith in him.

Now, saving the Santa Run was her solo mission. The only way to preserve Grandpa's legacy and her newfound purpose. If she couldn't rescue the event, what good could she do? She had nothing left to offer the town or her family except the Run.

Walking away from Bennett before things got started was best. Better to never fall than to love and risk being left alone again. If the last year had taught her anything, it was that loving and leaving go hand in hand. People die. Others choose to say goodbye. In both instances, pain followed, and she'd had her fair share of that for a while.

Eliza turned the radio up as the first hint of warm air flew from the vents. She tightened her grip on the steering wheel, backed out, and started toward home. The traffic light on the corner of Main turned red and she slowed the car to a stop. Stifling a yawn, she cracked a window to keep from falling asleep. After a deep breath of cold air, a loud whistle sliced through the night, snapping Eliza from her slap-happy-sleepy-state as the light turned green. In seconds, she'd parked the car and started jogging toward the sound.

Eliza scanned the park grounds, finding the swing set empty and the merry-go-round still. The scene appeared safe and sound. Through pursed lips, Eliza blew out a heavy breath. She turned quickly toward the playground but didn't make it three steps before the squeal pierced the silence again. Her feet continued their trajectory, only faster, while she glanced over her shoulder. The fear of being followed gripped her.

"Ouch!" A yelp sounded in front of her. Eliza Lee gasped, froze midstep, and snapped her head forward. Lily Anne Montgomery's pained eyes stared back at her.

Eliza Lee threw a hand against her chest as she took in a deep breath. "Good gracious, Lil. You about scared me senseless. What are you doing here?"

"The same thing you are, I suspect." She smiled and shrugged her shoulders. "I heard a loud whistle and couldn't resist investigating. I thought if I found a good story, Howard might be willing to give me a shot at reporting."

Eliza's jaw dropped. "The newspaper needs your life hack column, Lil. You can't quit it. Do you know how much time you save me?"

Lily Anne's smile grew wider. "I'm glad the hacks h—"

Another screech sounded behind them, sending the girls spinning in search of the source.

Lily Anne pointed to the sky as a light fizzled out.

"Was that a—"

"A bottle rocket?" Lily Anne's guess cut in, melding with Eliza Lee's voice as they chorused the answer in perfect unison. Laughter erupted from along the fence, sending both of them running toward the sound. When they finally made it and stepped behind the bushes, Lori waved. Jenny wrapped her arms tight around her daughter's shoulders.

"Hey, girls. Wanna fly one?" Lori's eyes twinkled as she put another rocket in the empty soda can.

"Nah, I'm beat," said Eliza as Lily Anne shook her head. "Want me to snap a pic for Jonah, though?"

Lori clapped her hands as Eliza Lee took the phone from Jenny. After a few flashes and grins, the pair returned their attention to the fireworks.

"Thanks, sister." Jenny slid the phone back into her pocket and gave a quick hug to Eliza Lee. Bending down, Eliza squeezed Lori tight, tugging on one of her twin braids after she released her. She smiled at her sister-in-law and niece, waving goodbye before shuffling her worn feet in the direction of her car. Walking along, Eliza Lee spotted Lily Anne swinging near the gate. The peace radiating from her friend tugged Eliza her way. Before she knew it, she was sitting beside her and pumping her legs, sending the swing closer to the night sky.

"So, Black Friday, huh?" Lily Anne's face softened as she spoke.

Swallowing hard, Eliza Lee willed the lump to dislodge from her throat. "Yup."

"I, uh, read somewhere that over 170 million Americans go shopping between Thanksgiving and Cyber Monday." Lily Anne halted her swing and twisted to face her. Eliza Lee felt the movement and drug her feet to stop too. She squinted and hoped by some miracle the tears might stay subdued.

"I know what today is, Eliza. I ran into Emma Lou at the community center. You wanna talk about it?" Lily Anne's gloved hand squeezed Eliza's knee, softly punctuating the question.

"I don't know if I can." Eliza Lee covered her mouth. She hadn't spoken about Grandpa's death since the day it happened. There was no need to burden her loved ones with the memory she harbored and, while a stranger might relate, pity was sure to follow. She had no need for pity. Silence was her only option.

Until now.

Lily Anne represented the perfect in-between. Neither stranger nor family, not even a friend of the family, like Emma. Instead of being stuck like glue the way she and Emma had been growing up, Eliza and Lily Anne's friendship hadn't fully blossomed until after their ten-year high school reunion. Talking about Grandpa's death wouldn't hurt her like it would Emma and her family.

Lily Anne cuffed Eliza's wrists and lowered her hands from her mouth. "You'll never know if you can talk about it unless you try."

The warmth in Lily Anne's voice broke the dam inside that had been building for a year. Words gushed out as Eliza shared the story for the first time.

"We'd planned a surprise breakfast for Grandpa. Mom cooked up a storm and all us grandkids finally found a way to make it home. I ran upstairs to get the guest of honor and when I knocked on his bedroom door, he didn't answer." Eliza took a breath. Her shoulders shook, not from the cold of the

November night but from the weight of the words tumbling free.

"I knew something was wrong." Eliza gulped in more air as she let her tears fall. After a good cry, she forced herself to go on. "When I opened his door, Grandpa lay covered up with his hands folded on his stomach like when he napped in his recliner. That man could sleep anywhere." Eliza chuckled slightly.

"I called his name again, but he didn't move a muscle. No twitching, no snoring, no nothing. Before I made it to the bed, I knew he was gone. I knew it, Lily Anne, but I didn't wanna believe it. So I shook his shoulder. When he didn't open his eyes, I put my ear over his mouth to listen for breathing. All I heard was my own, and when I slipped his palm in mine, his hand was like ice. That chill, it stays with me, even in the summer when the heat is so thick you can see it rising on the mountains. Even when I'm fixing chicken over a cast-iron skillet. Even when I-I—" The sobs were too heavy to talk through, so Eliza Lee pressed her lips together. She straightened her shoulders, hoping it'd be enough to still the shivers running through her. It didn't work, not until Lily Anne's arm wrapped around her, pulled her into a half hug, and shushed her gently through her tears.

After minutes that passed like hours, Eliza Lee calmed enough to stand up, freeing herself from Lily Anne's grip not so gracefully as she did. Lily Anne rose, too, and enveloped Eliza Lee in a bear hug, rocking her right to left. It wasn't funny, but Eliza Lee laughed anyway. Lily Anne broke the embrace and ticked a single eyebrow up. Her expression only made Eliza laugh harder. The snickering became contagious. Before long Lily Anne howled right along with her as they staggered to their cars together.

"Thanks, Lil. I needed that."

"No thanks needed. You kept the night from being a total bust. I'll take a swing set story with a friend over breaking news any day."

"Lil, don't lie."

"All right." Lily Anne raised both hands, admitting her attempt at deception. "I'll only take your story over breaking news."

"Much better." Eliza Lee grinned. Her cheeks, sore from ugly crying, hurt all the more. But the joy rising inside eclipsed the pain, just as Grandpa's love overshadowed the grief a hundred times over.

The conversation with Emma Lou resurfaced in her memory. Was Eliza playing it too safe? Could falling in love again be worth the hurt?

Chapter Sixteen

―――

The ribbon looked perfect from the front, but when Bennett tilted his head, it seemed off. The twist of the bow? Maybe. A groan pushed through his parted lips as he pulled ever so gently. First up, then down, and to each side. Better? From the side view, it seemed so, but when he righted his head, he wasn't sure.

Bennett glanced at the clock in the office. Eliza Lee was running late, as usual, but he was glad. He still needed to sign the card and arrange the flowers. Goldie's Rods and Blooms had done a fantastic job with the bouquet, but none of the vases did it justice. A quick trip to Powell's Apothecary had solved the problem.

In the gift section, a tall, slender travel mug stood on the shelf by its lonesome. The green matched Eliza's eyes. To make it even more fitting, lemons covered it from top to bottom. One look rewound the week. Back to the recipe box, the man catcher, their kiss. It seemed an eternity ago, but as he thanked the cashier, the taste of candy canes lingered on his tongue.

How he'd missed her birthday in a town so small was beyond him. No one had said a single word. Maybe she'd dared them to. Then again, between the pie social, Thanksgiving, and his annoyance with his father, he might've missed it even if someone had let it slip.

Today was a new day, not her birthday anymore, but a day to celebrate together since Emma Lou had kidnapped her yesterday. Technically, he wasn't breaking his resolve, either.

Flowers weren't the same thing as a kiss. A grin spread across his face at the thought of her lips against his. Despite his wariness of workplace relationships, Bennett couldn't regret the kiss if he tried. The spontaneity, the undeniable spark, the connection. His breath grew heavy at the memory.

Get a grip, man. The ball's in her court. The reverie faded as a mental lens refocused, homing in on the ground he needed to make up. This was a decent first step, but it was just the start. Was that the plan now? Jump ship on Project Pops and full steam ahead on the love boat? No. He couldn't give up on his father, not when Bennett longed for a family so much.

He foraged a pen from his bag and opened the card. It was short, sweet, and to the point. Nothing sappy, but a simple, safe birthday prayer. All he had to do was sign, but Eliza deserved more. Hoping to convey that sentiment, Bennett reiterated their conversation from the commons, tacked on a promise, and sealed the envelope. He no sooner sat back down than the door slowly opened.

With a click, he opened a new email and narrowed his eyes on the screen as Eliza stepped in. She paused momentarily before hanging her coat up. A sigh escaped, barely, but loud enough he noticed. Worry lines creased her forehead when she faced him while dark circles shone through her made-up face. He tried not to stare, but her appearance startled him. She rarely wore makeup to work and never to hide her lack of sleep. Was she ill?

"Good morning, Eliza Lee." His greeting broke the silence and her concentration. With a squeal of fright, she dropped her coat. Bennett jumped and ran to where it fell.

"It's just me." Scooping up the garment, Bennett chuckled and hung it up. "I'm sorry. I didn't mean to scare you."

She didn't laugh back. In fact, she didn't even smile. More worried than before, Bennett searched her face intently. Had she been crying? The whites of her eyes were bloodshot, and the rims around them tinted red.

Eliza Lee huffed on an exhale. "You about made me jump out of my skin. Why are you here? Doesn't Hanna work this morning?"

"She was supposed to, but her shopping spree yesterday took its toll on her ankles. You're stuck with me instead." Her disappointment to find him in place of Hanna stung. Not exactly the start to the day he was hoping for, but it was early still.

"Love her heart." Eliza shook her head. "And I bet she was wearing those awful heels yesterday traipsing through the stores, wasn't she?"

Bennett went back to his desk and sat down. "I plead the fifth." No way, no how was he getting in the middle of those two.

He cleared his throat and watched as she faced her desk, eyes wide. The corners of her lips turned up into a smile. First at the flowers, then at Bennett. Afraid of making her uncomfortable, he shifted his gaze to the screen, watching her from his peripherals.

Gingerly, she touched the petals. Tulips of all colors, some fully bloomed, others readying to open, stood pretty and proud. Closing her eyes, she breathed in through her nose and smiled again, freeing her dimples.

"They're stunning." She met his gaze with a knowing look. "And my favorite."

Now, it was his turn to blush.

"Hanna?" She raised a brow as she asked, giving him a better look at her eyes. Shadow still lined the rims. Something held the moment at happy instead of joyful. But what?

"Hanna." Bennett ran his fingers through his hair, embarrassed he'd enlisted help with the present.

After bending down to smell the flowers once more, Eliza moved onto the box. Carefully, she slipped the ribbon off, sat down, and moved the present from the desk to her lap. She scanned each side for a tag. With the present resting on her knees, she looked for a loose seam to pull, before giving up and grabbing the scissors to poke a hole. Then, she ripped. When the front peeled far enough to expose the picture, she stopped and jerked her eyes toward him again. The shadow was gone, but they glistened in the light. *That's a first.* He'd never seen a coffeepot bring waterworks out.

Eliza blinked a few times before offering him the sweetest of smiles. "Thank you. So much, but I can't accept this."

Before he could ask her why not, she was on her feet and down the hall. He followed, puzzled. She was standing with her back to him, gripping the sink, when he made it to the door.

Bennett leaned against the facing, adopting a casual pose meant to hide his confusion. "Eliza Lee, it's just a coffeepot. The office needs one, and I know how much you love your caffeine, so I thought why not kill two birds with one stone?"

"Well, for one, it's not my birthday. Emma Lou knew what yesterday was, so she gave me a pretend birthday to distract me."

"Oh." Bennett knew he was probably setting himself up to be shot down, but he had to try. "What was yesterday?"

Eliza shook her head adamantly. "I don't want to talk about it."

"If it was bad enough for your best friend to give you a second birthday, talking might help." Needing to see her face, Bennett put a hand on her shoulder in hopes of motivating her to turn around. Instead of facing him, though, Eliza tightened her hold on the counter.

"I talked plenty to Emma Lou, and last night to Lily Anne. All it did was confuse me. I don't want to make the same mistake again today, especially not with you."

"Why not with me? Maybe I can help." His voice cracked on the last word. Facing her, it was easy to follow her train of thought, but while talking to her back? Cues to help wade through the troubled waters remained hidden.

Eliza shrugged him off as she twisted around, her green eyes blazing. "Even if you could, I wouldn't ask you. The last time I did, things didn't go so well. I don't like making the same mistake twice." The pain in her voice made him flinch.

Kneading the back of his neck with more force than necessary, Bennett blinked at Eliza. Why couldn't she let him in? She was just like his father, holding the past over his head while refusing to acknowledge the present or hope for the future. "I get it, Eliza Lee. I know I hurt you and I'm sorry." Bennett clenched his jaw. He hadn't meant to snap, but her rejection reminded him of his father's, cracking his heart anew.

Eliza turned, slowly, and sighed. "I'm sorry too. Look, Bennett, I know you mean well, but I don't want your help."

"I know you don't, but I'm offering it anyway. That's what the card said if you'd opened it instead of running away." Blowing out a breath, Bennett took Eliza Lee by the hand. "I really do care. About Pine Valley. About the Santa Run. About you. Please, believe me."

"How can I?" Eliza spoke quietly, slipping her hand free from his grasp. When her eyes finally found his again, the shadow from earlier reappeared, darker than before. Bennett finally recognized it for what it was. Disappointment.

"Let me prove it to you. You can do that, can't you?" As the seconds passed, silence stretched until a high-pitched voice rang through the office.

"Eliza Lee, I've got it. I know what we can make for the night market. Eliza Lee?"

"Coming." Eliza stepped past him with quick steps. He followed, hoping to finish their conversation as soon as they were alone again.

But with Lori standing in the front of the office, that might be awhile. Bennett stalked to his seat while Eliza held up her hand for a high five. "What's up, sweet stuff? Where's your mama?"

"Outside talking to Austin." Lori slapped Eliza's palm and kept on talking. "Taking for-ev-er."

Austin? Bennett tensed at the name. He'd only seen the man once, at the social when Hanna pointed him out as Eliza Lee's former fiancé, but he'd left a lasting impression.

Eliza placed her hands on her hips and mock scowled at Lori. "Oh, and you were in too big of a hurry to wait, huh?"

Lori nodded.

"Well, let's have a look-see. Show me what you found, girlie."

"Pot people," she said, holding the paper out to give them a better view. "Bennett, you come look too."

He did as he was told, stepping behind the desk and crouching to get a better look. It was precisely what she'd said, a person made of pots. A medium terracotta planter created the core, an attached cord and smaller pots formed the arms, and baby pots made the feet. It was painted with bright blue eyes and a jersey.

"We can paint them into basketball players, elves, even Santa. I found the picture today at the library. Hanna bought up a whole slew of these pots the other day at Stop-N-Save when they were on clearance. I bet they still got some. Maybe they'd even donate the rest. Do you like the idea?" Lori looked to him, then Eliza, trying hard not to bounce.

"I love it. Mom adores painting, so this is right up her alley." Wrapping both arms around Lori, she squeezed tight before planting a kiss atop her head. "Why don't you guys stop and show Mom too? Tell her to call me so I can make a supply list."

Lori's face lit like a candle while she skipped toward the front. She swung open the door and started to run out. The entrance wasn't empty, though. In all her enthusiasm, she nearly knocked Austin into Jenny as they entered.

"Slow down, Lori, and don't go off the porch," Jenny warned as she cleared the threshold.

Austin stepped toward Eliza and handed her what looked like a business card. "Hey, Eliza Lee. Do you have a few minutes to chat?"

"About?" Her eyebrows hiked beneath her bangs as she took the card from his hand.

"Us."

Bennett crossed his arms against his chest. He'd never been a jealous guy before, but the green-eyed monster had grabbed hold of him. Breathing in and out, he tried to shake its grasp.

With a sigh, Austin's expression turned solemn. "Eliza Lee, I'm so, so—"

"Stop right there, Austin Stone." She shook her head back and forth. "You don't get to apologize."

"But—"

Bennett felt his eye begin to twitch as Eliza Lee cupped Austin's shoulder. "You didn't do anything wrong to say you're sorry for, unless you want to talk about that breakup letter. I expected better from you."

Casting his gaze from Eliza's face to the floor, Austin paused a few seconds before looking back up. When he did, his cheeks were the color of an antique caboose. "I didn't know how else to talk to you. I tried so many times, but then I'd see you and the words just disappeared."

"You don't have to explain. I'm only teasing. We're good." She smiled and patted him on the shoulder. Not a hint of sadness shone from her eyes. Only the care of a longtime, faithful friend.

"I mean, you've seen my driving." Her grin widened. "If I'd followed you to the city, I'd have killed us both by now."

Austin chuckled. "When you put it that way, I guess I made the safest decision for both of us."

"You truly did, Austin." More laughter rang out, so pure, Bennett had no choice but to join in.

"That's my card with all the firm's contact info. When you call, ask to speak to Riley. She's in charge of donations."

"Let me jot that down or I'll forget." Eliza squeezed past Austin and leaned across the desk to snatch a pen. "You said Riley?"

"Yes, Riley French," Austin's eyes brightened. "She keeps all us accountants in line, and I know she'll take good care of you."

As Eliza wrote down the name, Lori burst through the door. Immediately, she pointed above their heads. "You're under the mistletoe. Kiss! Kiss!" She snickered as she covered her mouth with her hand. When she caught her breath, she pointed again.

Eliza froze. Bennett watched as her gaze swept around the room, to Lori first, him last. Minding his manners, he refused to return the eye contact, barely holding back a nonchalant shrug. Movement beside Eliza pulled his attention away, serving as a perfect distraction. He looked at Austin just in time to see him wink to Lori. Bennett took a breath and braced himself, clenching his hands into fists at his side.

"For luck." Austin pressed a peck to Eliza's cheek and stepped back.

"Thanks. For the luck and the card." She pulled Austin into a hug before he opened the door. "I'll call next week."

"Be sure to. Riley will be expecting you." With a wave, Austin bounded outside and away from sight.

"We better go too. Mama needs to be brought up to speed about the pot people. Right, Lori?" Jenny looked down into Lori's face while she nodded. Gently, she herded her to the door.

"Bye, y'all. Don't work too hard. Call me, Eliza Lee, so we can make a plan."

The smile Jenny shot their way told Bennett the conversation would be less about pots and more about Austin. He took another deep breath as she looked his way, tilting her head slightly. From that look, he knew his name would come up too. Ignoring the impending gossip, Bennett waved goodbye.

"I'll call later. Drive like ya got eggs to sell." Eliza shut the door behind them and scooped the half-wrapped gift in her arms. Bennett bolted from the chair, but before he was able to snatch it, she was gone. Leave it to him to blow a birthday present, a pretend one at that.

Eliza returned and sat down in front of him, wrapping both her hands around the vase. She bent her head down for another sniff.

"These really are beautiful. Thank you." After turning her chair around, she booted up the computer and started talking. "I guess the coffeepot is great, too, even if it cost more than my first prom dress. I'll set it up after I check my email."

Though she spoke without turning around, Bennett didn't need to see her face to figure out her feelings this time. He felt it too.

Like. A lot of like.

Chapter Seventeen

Growing up, Eliza used to pretend she could jump into snow globes the way Steve from *Blue's Clues* could do with paintings. The picturesque towns seemed so inviting with the ice skating and the toy shops. She found their charm irresistible, so much so that she dreamed of living in those tiny Christmas towns. Walking up to the night market, Eliza Lee wondered if her dream had finally come true.

The commons looked magical. Strings of Christmas lights circled the concrete columns and red bows dangled from every streetlamp. Storefronts were dolled up to the nines with displays featuring snowmen, reindeer, and elves alike. Even the weather cooperated. Mother Nature had reverted to the usual crisp but not cold air, instead of the unseasonably frigid conditions of the last couple weeks. The night market was special any time of year, but tonight it felt perfect.

The girls had been right too. Not only did the vendors unanimously decide to donate proceeds to saving the Santa Run, but Dottie from the Stop-N-Save gave Eliza the remaining inventory of clay pots. Never one to be outdone, Goldie at the floral shop heard about it and chipped in from her storage room too.

By the looks of things, the night market seemed poised to bring in a fairly decent haul. Voices clamored all around her, and the night was still young. Eliza smiled. Maybe there was hope. The office had been booming the entire week, but in the spare moments, few and far between as they were, she squeezed in painting pots.

Eliza sighed as she pictured Bennett. He'd seated himself directly in front of her Sunday morning at church but left before Mom roped him into dinner again. They'd yet to pick up their previous conversation, but it seemed he'd taken her friendly chitchat and light banter as a green light for proving himself.

He'd lived out the message from her birthday card too. Beneath the prayer and his apology, Bennett had promised to support her as a leading lady, not because she needed saving but because he cared too much to let her fight alone. Despite Eliza's determination to fly solo, he found ways to help beyond her control. If the phone rang while they were painting, he grabbed it. Takeout trays had been carried in all week for lunch, at his insistence and on his dime, giving Eliza more time to paint. Tonight, he had agreed to help set up the booth, per her mother's request.

Eliza shut her trunk and picked up the cardboard box from the pavement, careful to hold the bottom to keep it from busting open. Individually, the pot people weren't heavy, but three of them made for a hefty load. This was the last of her contribution. She hoped it'd be enough. It had to be. After tonight, only the dance-a-thon remained.

As she made her way through the crowd, she nodded and smiled, thanking everyone she passed for coming out. Joe was just flipping the decades-old foldout table upright when she made it to the booth. That thing had seen better days, for sure. She was more than happy to let him do the setup. The last time she tried, it took all her strength to get the rickety metal legs to snap securely in place.

Squeezing between Jenny and Lori, Eliza set the box down, waved, and headed toward Joe to say thanks. Somehow, her foot caught on a seam in the sidewalk, sending her wobbling toward the hard concrete and embarrassment. Feeling the impending fall, Eliza closed her eyes tight, thrust her arms forward, and took in a deep breath. She waited for the blow, but it never came. Instead of pavement, a broad chest crashed into her as two arms closed tight. In all senses of the word, she was caught, as citrus and pine encircled her. She warmed from the inside out.

"Whoa, there. Are you OK?"

Without opening her eyes, she knew who'd saved her, yet again. *Bennett.*

Her instinct to push him away, shake it off, and excuse herself to gather her thoughts flared immediately. But that wasn't a viable option. Aside from causing more of a scene, it'd elicit a talking-to from Jenny, and Eliza did not need that. Instead, she remained still with her palms resting on his chest. Was she imagining his heart racing beneath them? Of course she was, but only because her pulse had skyrocketed.

She opened her eyes. "Yeah, I'm fine. Sorry." She whispered and forced herself to look up. At the sight of his chocolate-drop eyes, her legs went weak again, and his arms tightened.

"Are you sure you're OK?" Bennett's lips lifted in a smile as a loose tendril of hair fell across his brow.

Eliza fought the urge to brush it back. Realizing she was still leaning on him, she nodded and stepped backward as warmth filled her cheeks, second only to the heat beneath her palms planted on his chest.

"Mm-hmm." Eliza took another half step back, going as far as she could with Bennett's arms still around her. "Thanks."

He opened his embrace, and she turned on her heels toward Joe to say her thanks. Walking away, she felt his eyes on her back. His watchful stare made her more conscious of each step and extra careful not to trip again. Though if she did, he'd be in no position to catch her. That should have been comforting, but instead, the thought forced a frown. Was there anyone else she'd rather be saved by? *Yourself, silly girl. You don't need him, remember?*

By the time she'd hugged Joe, she'd managed to calm down. Unfortunately, the peace was short-lived as Jett led Hanna across the commons to where she stood.

"Mom's car won't start and Dad's doing some repairs at the church. Someone has to go get her." Jett explained as Hanna caught her breath.

"OK. Can Joe do it? I just saw him a second ago." Eliza scanned around, expecting to find his smiling face, but came up empty.

"He got a call from one of the engineers, so he'll probably be gone awhile." Hanna answered and grabbed Jett's hand before he could open his mouth. "And I need your brother here with me. The due date's getting close, ya know?"

"I know." Eliza's excitement boiled over at the thought of chubby cheeks and the new-baby smell. "Can y'all man the booth while I run and get her?" Eliza stepped out from behind the table to let Hanna have her seat. Jett unfolded a chair leaning against the wall and slid in beside her.

"You know we can. Be careful." Hanna grabbed her hand and squeezed. Eliza nodded and headed toward the parking lot.

Falling in step beside her, Bennett matched her stride for stride. "Eliza Lee, where are you going? Are you sure you didn't twist your ankle or something?"

She rolled her eyes before looking up. When she did, guilt pinched her chest as worry lines surfaced on Bennett's forehead. Oh, for pity's sake. Something twisted when she fell all right, but it was her heart not her ankle.

"From the way you're scrambling to keep up, I'd say that's a no." Eliza bumped him with her shoulder, needing to keep the mood light and her nerves in check.

"Right." He chuckled before flashing his signature half grin. "Where are you off to in such a hurry?"

"Mom's car won't start. I gotta go get her." She kept walking, trying to ignore his smile, the one that made her forget she needed to keep her distance.

"Do you want some company?" Blinking, Bennett waved those long lashes and she thought about saying yes. An image of her, Bennett, and her mother in a car together chased that thought, changing her mind and making her wince.

"Ouch." He stepped back. "It was just an offer."

Reflexively, she grabbed his hand, goosebumps pebbling as her palm met his. She hadn't meant to offend him.

"I'd love some company, but . . ."

"But . . ." He watched her, their hands still locked like their gazes. Why did he have to look through her like that, causing cracks and fissures to emerge in the strongholds she'd worked so hard to build against him? She squared her shoulders.

"But it won't take long and the backseat will be full." She let go of his hand and darted her eyes to the patch of dying grass beside them. Sensing his stare, she returned her gaze. He looked comical with his best I-doubt-that look chiseled on his face, one eyebrow popped up, head tilted, and arms crossed against his chest.

"It will be full"—Eliza snickered—"with Mom's pot people."

Bennett joined in the laughter, and Eliza quieted her giggles in hopes of hearing him more clearly. He had a great laugh, hearty and full, but he still needed more practice. She'd wanted to help him with that since the first day they'd met, before learning of his mother's death. Before her traditions were in jeopardy. Before the man-catcher pie and their first kiss. Dang it. She still wanted to help him have fun, even though she knew she shouldn't.

"Fair enough," said Bennett. "Just don't take too long, OK?"

Eliza hiked a brow at him. "Why? What are you planning, City Boy?" He was up to something. Whatever it was had led to a momentary lapse in judgment on her part. She hadn't called him that since the social, a fact seemingly not lost on him. As the name registered, his eyes lit up.

"This city boy is keeping his mouth shut, but do try to hurry." Bennett nodded before heading to Jett and Hanna.

Flustered, Eliza followed him with her eyes, tapping her toes as he strolled away. *Patience, Lord, patience.* Did he know what he was doing to her? *Of course, he does, Eliza Lee.*

"I'll see what I can do." She yelled after him, hoping to get another look at those puppy dog eyes, but he threw a hand in the air and kept on walking. She watched him longer than she should've before worrying about getting caught. If Jett saw her, she'd never hear the end of it. The fear sent her jogging to the car.

True to her word, she made it there and back in less than fifteen minutes. Jett met them at the car to help carry the crafts. There were oodles of them. Some sports figures, some elves, and a few iconic princesses and cartoon characters. Once arranged, Eliza handed the cash box duties off to her mother to make her rounds. It was important to her to thank each of the vendors for their contribution.

There were too many vendors to count, from jewelry makers to bakers to aspiring artists to individuals with pieces of estate sales. She decided to go down the right side first, then hit the left. As she made her way down the rows of booths, her thoughts wandered while she scanned the crowd for Bennett. The teasing comment from earlier intrigued her, but she tried to pretend otherwise when he caught her staring at him.

Eliza came to Mr. Stone's booth and paused. In addition to the walkway pavers and garden accents showcased by Austin's father, she expected an awkwardness, too. Instead, she found acceptance. Seeing Austin at Nonnie's had erased the guilt and shame she'd allowed to stand between not only the two of them, but herself and Austin's family, too. Smiling, the man who nearly claimed the title of father-in-law waved her over.

"Eliza Lee, you've done a wonderful job. Come here and give me a hug." In seconds, Mr. Stone had folded Eliza tightly in his arms.

Eliza averted her gaze as heat filled her cheeks, slightly embarrassed to make the night about her. "Thank you, Mr. Stone, but I barely did anything. The town's been so good to pitch in."

Mr. Stone hugged her once more before letting her go. "Right you are, but you were the push to get the ball rolling."

She nodded as her blush deepened, feeling more eyes on her than his. Bennett was watching. She sensed it, but before he came into view, a familiar face landed in the crosshairs of her sites.

"Mason Montgomery, I can't believe you snuck in on me. Lily Anne didn't tell me you were coming tonight." Eliza scooted behind the table, wrapped her arms around his neck, and squeezed too tight from excitement. "I'm so glad you're here. These photos are incredible."

"You don't gotta lie to make friends." Mason chuckled, and she let him go.

"I thought you were on some photoshoot out west. When did you get in?" She looked him over, admitting time, or maybe his new marriage, had treated him kindly. His skin was tanned, his dark brown hair cut shorter than she'd ever seen, and he sported a trimmed line of a beard along his jawline. It suited him.

"Yesterday. I swore Ma and Lil to secrecy in case the weather delayed my flight. I didn't get to bring as many prints as I wanted because of the time crunch, but these are some of the better-known photographs. Not exact replicas, but close to the published shots. Pick out one for the office. It's on me."

"No, no. You've done enough, mister. It's not every day we have a nationally renowned photographer selling portraits for the Santa Run."

Eliza wrapped Mason in another hug, overwhelmed by the moment. Way before his photography career had taken off, they'd met through 4-H and became lifelong friends. His work had been featured in more magazines than Eliza could keep track of. But here he was, selling images at a local night market for less than they were worth, all for a good cause. *Her* cause.

"Eliza Lee, you know I'm happy to help. It's a privilege. Grandpa Walt was one heck of a man." Mason grinned as she released her hold. Fighting back tears, she nodded and gestured to Country Confection's booth, moving herself along before she lost her composure.

Danny Jo supplied the sweets and comfort necessary for an emotional stabilizer. She liked to say a full belly made a light heart and Eliza tended to believe her after indulging in a couple of donuts. Her mood had brightened considerably when she started back toward the front until a loud clang crashed her sugar high. Following the sound and stream of gawkers, she quickly found the disruption in front of the pot people booth.

Eliza gasped at the collapsed table and scattered clay pieces. "What happened?"

Bennett raked a hand through his hair, tugging sharply on the ends. "I don't know. There was an empty spot after someone purchased the last of the ball players, so I took one from the box to fill it. When I put the replacement on the table, the whole thing collapsed."

Groaning, Eliza began cleaning up the mess. Bennett bent down to help, but she instructed him to keep taking care of the customers. After surveying the damage, she quickly realized luck was on their side. Only two or three of the pot people were unsalable.

She picked up the destroyed pots, placed them in an empty box behind the table, and stood, ready to comfort a still-shocked Bennett. Before she could, though, Jett grabbed her attention by motioning for the crowd to quiet down. Once they had, he found a spot toward the center of the commons and cleared his throat.

"Hey, y'all. Thanks for making this the best night market of the year. Give yourselves a round of applause." Jett's warm voice filled the summoned silence and chaos ensued. Vendors and customers alike whooped and hollered as thunderous applause filled the area. Lori whistled as she squirmed in her mother's lap.

"To show our appreciation, we've got a little treat for you tonight. Bennett, you ready?" Eliza's eyes widened as she watched him walk over to Jett.

"Ready." Bennett smiled wide as the crowd looked between the men, the excitement building with each passing second.

"We thought we'd start a new tradition for the Valley with a night market tree lighting. Sound good?" Clapping commenced again as the men pointed to Joe who was ever so gently pulling a tree behind him along the walkway. He and the tall evergreen came to a stop where the rows of tables began. Bennett rushed over with an extension cord.

Once again, Eliza felt like her snow globe dream had come true. Silver and gold garland wrapped delicately around the tree while glittery balls dangled from the branches in the same shades. On the lower half, candy canes kissed the needles, waiting to be plucked by children in the crowd. A few bells and stars peeked out occasionally, too, completing the metallic theme. At the very bottom, a red velvet skirt trimmed with white fur covered what must have been a rolling stand.

"We don't have all night, Jett. Count it down." Bennett yelled.

Jett held up his hand to start. "Five. Four. Three. Two. One." Voices melded together as they counted, cheering as the last number rang out. Bennett plugged in the cord and the lights sparkled on. Strands of bright white shimmered in the dark with the most luminous star atop the pine Eliza had ever seen.

The applause grew louder as more yells fell around her. Eventually it slowed as spectators left the display and commenced their shopping. Feet shuffled around Eliza for hours more until the market closed. She thanked the last of the stragglers as they finished their purchases and sank into her chair. The night had gone better than expected. The pot people had been a huge hit. Only one box left to carry home.

The sound of footsteps caused her to look up. When she did, she found Jett guiding a waddling Hanna.

"Sis, I love ya, but I gotta get my lady off her feet." Jett bent across her shoulders and pulled Eliza close for a pitiful excuse of a hug. Too tired to stand, she took the feeble attempt and ran with it.

"Yes, you do. And you need to get off your feet too." Eliza pinned him with her most intimidating stare. He needed to catch up on rest before the baby came.

"OK, Eliza Lee." Jett made a show of crossing his fingers. "I'll go straight to bed."

Rather than respond to his dramatics, Eliza moved on to more pressing matters. "Are you taking Mom home?"

Jett nodded. "Drive safe. See ya at church."

"See ya." As Eliza watched them stroll away, the tree caught her eye again. "Oh, and Jett?" Standing, she cupped her mouth with her hands for a makeshift megaphone. "Thanks for the tree."

"Don't thank me. I was the grunt work, not the mastermind." Without further explanation, he disappeared down the walk, leaving Eliza alone to figure out the meaning behind his message.

Only she didn't try to decode Jett's words like she usually would. Such an attempt required more energy than she had to spare and it was getting late. Only herself and a few vendors remained in the commons. After securing the cash box, she took it to her car and locked the doors. Then, she returned for the remaining box of pot people.

As she walked through the square, the breeze from earlier picked up. A light smell of rain swirled around her, short and sweet, but enough to pull the bangs across her face. She let the strands assault her cheek and drew in a mouthful of crisp air. Puffing her cheeks out like a blowfish, Eliza held her breath for a few seconds before pursing her lips and releasing it.

Eliza stopped in front of the tree. It was pretty as a painting, with its colorful lights and shimmering tinsel. Snippets of Christmases past flittered by, rekindling the magic of the season as her gaze rolled from star to trunk. In all the chaos of this year, Eliza had forgotten what it was like to see the world through the snow-globe wonder of her childhood. The tree reminded her.

"See why I said to hurry back?" Bennett's voice fell an octave as he drew near, close enough that his breath tickled her ear. A shiver ran through her, excitement shooting straight down to her snowmen socks. Turning to face him, her breath caught as Jett's words echoed through her mind.

"You planned this?" Throwing a hand in the tree's direction, Eliza tried to slow her heart rate before it reached a full-on gallop.

"I did. I thought the town might like it." He raised his shoulder slightly, attempting to make light of the time and effort it had taken to pull off such a feat, especially keeping it a secret.

She slapped his forearm lightly. "You thought right, City Boy. They loved it."

"And what about you?" Bennett took hold of her hand. "Do you like it?"

Staring down at her, he waited for an answer. The hope reflected in his eyes shone brighter than the lights behind them.

Eliza nodded. Words were impossible when his gaze captured her so completely. Her feet inched closer to him of their own accord. By some miracle, she managed to still before their toes touched.

Glancing toward the tree, Bennett grinned. "It was as close to Rockefeller as I could get you."

Eliza's heart went to fluttering at his tender words. Between the rapid beats, she managed to whisper. "You didn't have to do all this."

"I wanted to." With a wink, Bennett unlaced their fingers and returned his hand to his pocket. "I know you're tired, so I'll let you finish packing. Unless you need some help?"

He paused, giving her ample time to answer, but not long enough to silence the voices inside causing her head to shake no.

"Next time, then." His determined tone almost camouflaged his disappointment, but a wavering smile betrayed him before he hurried toward the parking lot.

Part of her wanted to run after him, throw her arms around his neck and kiss him like her life depended on it. Logic nudged the intense emotion to the side until the impulse passed.

The lighting ceremony had been beautiful, but nothing had changed. *Had it?* The tree was sweet, no question, and utterly romantic. Heck, it was the kind of thing Hallmark made movies about. Still, the facts remained the same. With the company transition in its final stages, Bennett's time with her was winding down. He'd return to the city and her life would go back to normal. Well, a new normal, but she'd be able to walk into the office without him looking over her shoulder. That was what she wanted, right?

Taking a deep breath, she decided not to think about the answer. She closed her eyes, hitting replay on one of Daddio's moral-of-the-story sayings. *If you stretch life out, it'll scare ya to death.*

Hearing her father's smoke-laced voice as loud as ever, she opened her eyes and went to clean off her table. There was nothing to be done about Bennett. Her future with him was out of her hands, but saving the Santa Run wasn't, not entirely.

Knowing this, Eliza decided she was better off chasing the country train instead of the city boy.

Chapter Eighteen

"Daggonit. That's all I need." Mama Deb mumbled to herself and any bystanders within earshot of the church steps. Bennett debated following her as she passed. After a sermon on helping hands, offering his services seemed like the right thing to do. Not that he'd had much luck helping the Elliott women, but it couldn't hurt to ask.

An image of Eliza from the night market flashed before him as he walked toward his car. The lights of the tree had cast a glow across her delicate features, making her even more beautiful. When she'd turned to him, the look on her face knocked the wind out of him. The gold flecks dancing in her eyes made it hard to think, so he winked and covered his daze with a smile. Desperate for her to understand, he'd taken her hand, hoping to show her the lighting was for her.

All for her.

Her eyes had confirmed the comprehension, but her actions disputed it. The choice to clean up alone proved he still hadn't earned her trust. Why was it so hard for her to let him in?

Bennett shook his head as a rambling Mama Deb passed him in the parking lot. She'd found Luke James and her mouth was going ninety miles a minute.

When she finally took a breath, Luke huffed. "It's gotta be the alternator, Deb. Looks like you didn't leave the lights on Friday night after all."

As he made his way to the Blazer, Mama Deb followed close behind, nipping at his heels. "I told ya I didn't. Is Jett still here?"

Seeing Mama Deb look his way, Bennett pointed across the lot. Jett was closing the passenger door after helping Hanna in.

Mama Deb cupped her mouth. "Jett, can you help your daddy for a minute?"

Before starting toward her, Jett motioned for Bennett to come over and he obliged. He owed it to him. Organizing the tree lighting had not been easy and Jett had worked himself to the bone. Together, they walked to the Blazer.

Luke James put a hand on Jett's shoulder and jerked his head toward Mama Deb. "The car won't start again. I might have to change the alternator, but I gotta get the dinosaur home first. Give me a boost, son?"

"Sure thing," Jett answered, without hesitation. "Let me just move the car around. Got some cables?"

"Yeah, in the back." Luke whipped up the hatch and pulled out a black pouch, holding it in the air proudly.

Bennett snuck a peek at Hanna. Closing her eyes, she laid her head back against the seat. She looked in need of a nap, or three. Stepping closer to the vehicle, Bennett broke into the conversation. "I can do it if you want to take Hanna home."

Jett toggled his gaze from Luke to Bennett, contemplating the offer. "Are you sure? It won't take a minute."

"Positive." Bennett nodded with a smile, remembering seeing the couple seated during the altar call while everyone around them stood. He'd thought it odd until he saw Hanna's shoes. She was in flip-flops, not her usual heels, putting her swollen feet on display for all to see. His heart hurt for her.

Jett turned to his father, eyes begging for permission. "That all right with you, Daddio?"

"Fine by me." Luke James answered over the creaking sound of the hatch closing.

"And me." Mama Deb chimed in. "As long as Jett'll drop me off so I can finish supper." Not waiting for an answer, she hooked her arm with Jett's and gave him a pretty-please smile.

"Can do. Holler if ya need me." Jett waved goodbye as he started down the lot. He patted his mother's arm and slowed his steps, matching Mama Deb's leisurely gait. The tender sight took Bennett by surprise, reminding him of happier days when his family was complete.

As Jett helped his mother climb in to the back seat of his car, Bennett's eyes began to sting. What he wouldn't give to be able to do the same with his mother.

Luke James cleared his throat. "I'll pop the hood while ya get that purdy car of yours." As he spoke, he patted Bennett on the shoulder. The touch pulled him back to the present and away from the loneliness threatening to take over.

Bennett jogged to his car. In the security of the front seat, he tried to steel his nerves by taking a few deep breaths. It wasn't the lap across the parking lot that left him winded but the image of Jett escorting Mama Deb. The breath in his lungs had seized as he watched them. Mama Deb wrapping one arm around Jett's waist and squeezing out a quick hug as they walked. Jett opening and closing the car door for her, careful to make sure she'd tucked the hem of her dress inside the vehicle. A longing usually sealed tight swelled fit to bust while Bennett nosed his car in front of the Blazer. Stepping out of the driver's side, he sent a silent prayer heavenward.

After securing the open hood, Luke James clapped him on the back. "Thank you kindly."

Bennett blinked hard, amazed by the impact such simple words had on him. There was a shift inside. A knot tied far too tight for much too long loosened. Relief rushed through him, chased with a joy he'd nearly forgotten.

"No thanks needed, sir." Bennett kept his eyes downcast, fixed on the cables needing unrolled.

"You can drop the *sir*, son. My friends call me L. J."

Bennett nodded and kept unwinding, willing his fingers to go faster. This was the last way he'd envisioned his Sunday playing out. Bennett didn't consider himself a sensitive man, but L. J.'s gratitude and Jett's stroll with Mama Deb had steamrolled his emotions.

Before he had time to reason away his unusual response, the church door slammed shut and a clickety-clack of dress shoes prompted him to look up.

"Where's Mom?" Eliza stopped in front of the Blazer beside Bennett, cocking her head slightly. "She said the car wouldn't start and we might ride home with Jett, but one of the children from class roped me into playing dolls with them before I made it out here."

Bennett averted his attention back to the task at hand but snuck in sideways glances as he worked. Soft waves were tied loosely at the nape of her neck, letting tendrils fly free around her face. The black blazer she donned was left open with a lace emerald blouse peeking beneath it, flowing free over a silk-looking skirt that skimmed the cuff of her ankle boots. The look suited her, cute and classic.

"The car won't start, Eliza Lee, but Jett's long gone. Guess you'll just have to wait here until Bennett gets the Blazer going for us."

Eliza glared, first at L. J. then at the stationary vehicle, before letting her hands fall to her side. "Well, it's my week on the cleaning schedule. I'll go ahead and get it done. Yell at me when we're good to go, Daddio."

"Sure will." L. J. waved her on as he connected the cables to the corresponding posts. Once done, he turned his attention back to Bennett. "Bet your folks miss you being around to help them like this, huh?"

Bennett's lips drew tight against the question, a cold reminder of how much he missed having a family. "I'd like to agree with you, but it's only my father and me, and we rarely spend time together."

L. J. stood back to check the connections. Though everything looked ready to try, he didn't move toward the Blazer. Instead, he turned to Bennett and waited, silently insisting he go on.

Bennett focused his sights on the battery as he shared his story. "My mother died when I was in high school, and after that, life went sideways. I changed from my father's pride and joy to a punk kid to a runaway. Thanks to strangers who saw past what I was to who God could make me, I ended up in Maryland with a second chance. While working on a farm there, doors started opening for me. I finished my GED. Then, I started back to school and buried myself in books, trying to become someone I could be proud of. Someone my father might welcome home."

Drawing in a ragged breath, Bennett shook his head. He'd been so foolish to think what little he'd done could put his family back together. Years later, he still hadn't managed to replicate the prodigal son's ending. *Not yet.*

With that hope in mind, Bennett went on. "After I became that person, or thought I had, I went back home to the city, college diploma in hand. Things were good between Pops and me, at first. He was so forgiving and more understanding than I deserved. But we drifted apart."

L. J. raised an eyebrow. A knowing glance passed between them and Bennett sighed. No wonder he was a man of few words. L. J.'s eyes could ask a thousand questions, and right now, he was asking for the truth. "Well, not drifted. He pulled away. No matter how hard I try, he stays just out of reach. I can't wrap my head around it. That's why I agreed to come here, hoping the time apart might make us closer. Silly, right?"

"Nah. Not silly, but wrong as a drunk on Sunday." L. J. rechecked the connection. "You probably think I'm the last person that hears what you're saying. Heck, I can't spit without hitting family land. But I get it. Must be hard, for you and him."

Him? How is it hard for him? It's his fault, not mine.

L. J. pushed up his sleeve and huffed. "Forgot my watch again. Say, what time you got?"

Bennett glanced at the time on his phone, still biting his tongue to keep from blurting his thoughts about his father. "A quarter past one."

With a nod, L. J. looked past the vehicles before cutting his eyes back. Beneath the weight of L. J.'s stare, Bennett surrendered his attention. He didn't want to miss a word of what L. J. had to say.

"Jonah's supposed to FaceTime us at two. I missed his last one." L. J. took a step back from the Blazer and straightened his spine. "When he was a little boy, he was my shadow. I had to watch about turning around for stepping on his toes. Jonah being away is rough. Worrying has never kept me up at night, until now." With that, L. J.'s eyes grew glassy.

"I'm a big enough man to say when I'm scared, and right now I am scared of losing our connection. Guess that's why I worked at the church instead of talking to him last week, even though I miss him something awful. I reckon it's my way of keeping the fear and the pain away. It hurts less to love him from a distance."

Before he knew it, Bennett's eyes matched L. J.'s as tears began to form. His breaths came in slow, shallow puffs. Another realization hit, striking his heart like a bowling ball. No wonder Pops held back. Bennett's history of leaving warranted a gun-shy attitude, especially if he shared L. J.'s mentality.

L. J. laid a hand on Bennett's shoulder and jerked his head toward the front seat. "Go on and start yours up. Let's see if we can make it back to the house in time to see Jonah."

Without another word, L. J. climbed inside the Blazer and stuck the key in the ignition.

Bennett did as instructed, revving the engine a few extra times for the heck of it. The Blazer sputtered to life. L. J. laughed as he followed Bennett's lead, revving the motor before letting it idle. The old man hopped out, undid the cables, and motioned Bennett to roll the window down.

"I'm gonna go grab, Eliza," L. J. said. "Do you care to follow us home? There's a Sunday supper in the deal if you do." Soft and low as usual, his voice warmed Bennett like sunlight through a windowpane.

"I'll follow you, but no dinner. I've got a phone call to make myself." Bennett looked at the dash, hoping to avoid any further discussion. He'd spilled enough of his guts for one day.

"Suit yourself." With a nod, L. J. strolled to the church. In no time flat, he returned with Eliza by his side.

Her cheeks had settled into a lovely cream color the blush from earlier must've hid and her ponytail was gone. Loose waves fell around her shoulders. The look reminded Bennett of beach days when the humidity would make his mother's hair curl on the ends. Did his father remember that? He'd have to ask when he called later.

Eliza waved and smiled out the passenger window as they passed. Bennett did the same, hoping his grin didn't look as weak as it felt. A new revelation began to take shape. Suddenly, Eliza's repeated rejection of his help made sense. By refusing to challenge the Santa Run's cancellation, he'd let her down once already. She wasn't about to put herself in that position again. How had he been so blind? There were so many wrongs he needed to right.

As he turned onto the road and headed for the Elliott's, Bennett let out a loud exhale. It was time to step back and let God clean up his mess. Starting with a timely mistake involving a red sack and a special someone determined to succeed. With or without him.

Chapter Nineteen

"Lori, what'd I tell you about running with those scissors? Sit your butt down before I bust it." Eliza Lee's voice rang loud over the madness around her. The community center was filled to the brim, especially for a Tuesday night. Then again, the packing party elicited quite a crowd every year and this year proved no exception.

Despite the latest fundraising numbers falling well below the mark needed to reinstate the Santa Run, Eliza Lee had forged ahead with the packing party. Now, looking around the room and seeing how the town had come out in spades, she wondered if she'd made a mistake. What would they think if the Run didn't happen and all their efforts lay in vain? She'd be a laughingstock. Worse, she'd be a disappointment.

Lori murmured a half-hearted apology and slowed her steps while Eliza Lee tried to round up the rest of the children. "All right, all right. I need my kids to head toward the front table, please."

The kids continued running circles around the room, hooting and hollering as they played. Eliza took a breath and tapped her toe three times. Determined to at least be seen this time, she grabbed the nearest chair, climbed on, and crisscrossed her arms in the air. "Hey, children! This is my circus and y'all are my monkeys. Get over here."

Laughter flared. Kids and adults alike covered their mouths as the joyous chorus pealed through the air. Unfortunately, no one moved toward her or the table reserved for the littlest of the Santa Run helpers.

A whistle screeched through the room before she tried again. The children froze as she climbed off the chair and turned in the direction the sound had come from. When a familiar male figure strolled toward them, Eliza bit back a groan.

Of course.

Bennett, calm and collected as usual, walked through the room looking better than ever. The top button of his collar had come undone, and one tail of his steel-gray shirt had wriggled its way out of the tuck. His black trousers were covered in wrinkles, and his longish hair was disheveled. The strands softened the strong jawline pricked with stubble. From the looks of it, he'd come straight from the office to the packing party.

"Children." He somehow managed to get their attention with a single word. "Over here."

Eliza smiled, a silent *thank you*, which he accepted with a boyish grin that made her insides crumple. How did he always do that?

Chairs screeched across the floor as children gathered round. In minutes, cheerful faces and eager little hands surrounded the table. Eliza opened the boxes on the table and spouted out directions. The toys needed to be unboxed, sorted, and put in the right bag to be handed out. It was the easiest job to do, so it went to the children.

After doling out instructions, she focused her attention on the coats along the wall. Several women stood ready to organize them by size and gender. Mom, Sue, Trish, and a few other ladies from church swarmed around the rack, buzzing like bees, but with gossip instead of honey. Snickers roared from the group as coats were separated.

The few men dispersed among the room. Without a word of guidance, they went to work, lifting heavy bags, labeling the finished boxes of donations, and knotting a child's temper tantrum before it had ample time to unravel. They knew what they were doing. By all standards, Eliza was still the newest member aboard the Santa Run. Without Grandpa at the helm, though, she'd found herself in the captain's seat. Her heart swelled with pride as she looked around the room.

She sat and started with the grocery certificates. Halfway through the first stack, Bennett joined her.

"This is quite a scene. Is it like this every year?"

Begrudgingly, she set aside the stack of papers and looked up. His dark cocoa eyes warmed when her eyes met them, sending her spiraling into the sweet heat shining at her.

"Yup. I told ya. Our town may be small, but we do Christmas up right." Eliza caught herself as she nodded to an empty chair.

"You weren't lying." He chuckled as he sat down. "Do you want some help?"

Bennett held her eyes for a moment more before dropping his gaze to her hands. She winced at the pain in his voice, hearing the hurt she caused by continuously rejecting his offers. A brick from the wall around her heart crumbled.

"Sure. Go through these and separate by store, please."

Sliding the stack across the table, she accepted defeat. A woman could refuse a kindhearted man only so many times before her resistance wore thin.

Before long, the toys were finished. The kids retreated into the halls, taking up what sounded like a vicious game of hide-and-seek as the wall clock chimed. Ten o'clock already. Soon the volunteers would start sneaking out. As urgency set in, she worked faster on the certificates.

"Can I ask you something?" Eliza surprised herself as much as Bennett when she spoke. They'd worked in silence for most of the night.

"Of course." He smiled and folded his arms on top of the papers he was sorting, giving her his undivided attention.

The intensity in his eyes nearly stole her breath, but she rushed on before she chickened out. "Do you think this is stupid? Going through with the packing party, I mean. There's no guarantee the Santa Run is gonna happen at all this year. Am I spinnin' my wheels?" She tried to keep her voice upbeat, but the sadness was audible even to her.

Bennett covered her hand with his. "No, not at all." With his free hand, he motioned around the room. "Eliza Lee, the whole town came out tonight. It's far from stupid."

Though she nodded, doubt still bubbled up. "Daddio always says to hope for the best but prepare for the worst. I'm doing the complete opposite." She forced a laugh to cover the crack in her voice.

If the Run was going to be saved, it'd come down to the wire. The night market had done well, but the funds were still short. The dance-a-thon was slotted to be a success. What if it wasn't enough? What if she let the town down? Let Grandpa Walt down?

Before Eliza lost herself on the bunny trail of worry stretching in front of her, Bennett spoke up.

"All due respect to L. J., he's wrong in this case."

The steadiness in his voice soothed Eliza's heart, like fresh aloe to a blistering burn. She wanted so badly to believe him, but she felt foolish. The time to face facts had come. As much as Eliza hated it, the Santa Run was in real danger and her best efforts might be found lacking.

As if reading her mind, Bennett went on. "Several years ago, I heard a story about two farmers who prayed to God for a good harvest during a drought. One farmer prayed and stayed inside, biding his time. The other prayed, then plowed and planted, readying his land for the rain. Who do you think did the right thing?"

Eliza looked away until she felt his hand tighten, making her face him. The tenderness in his eyes sparked a boldness inside, forcing her to straighten in her seat like the heroine she'd set out to be. Regardless of the outcome, she knew God had a plan.

"Thank you, Bennett." Slipping her hand free, Eliza pulled the next pile of papers in front of her. "Did your daddy tell you that story?"

Bennett did the same with his set and the two of them got back to work. "I'm afraid not. My father isn't known for his optimism."

"Oh, yeah?" Hiking a brow, Eliza repositioned the certificates. "What is he known for?"

Bennett cleared his throat. "Money management. Staying on task. Negotiation."

"Yikes. Another Mr. McCoy?" Eliza scrunched her nose, pausing a second too late as the impolite reaction registered in her brain. "Sorry, that was rude. I mean, wow. He sounds accomplished."

"He is." Bennett smoothed his collar. "Among other things."

Glancing behind her, he lifted his chin as if he was being beckoned and excused himself from the table. Had someone needed help? One of the kids? Or the women rushing around? *Most likely.*

Eliza dove back into the work. By the time Bennett had returned, she had finished with the certificates. Itching to start on the vouchers, she looked around the table. She found empty water bottles the kids had left behind, candy cane wrappers, and even a sweater. But no vouchers.

"Drat."

At her exclamation, Bennett's head snapped up. His brows furrowed as he studied her. "What's wrong?"

"I must have left the vouchers in the storage room." Eliza smacked the table as frustration boiled over.

"No big deal." Bennett stood up and stretched his arms high above his head as he yawned. "I'll get them for you. It's the door next to the restroom, right?"

She nodded. "Yes, but it's getting late and you look worn out. I can finish up here."

"Eliza, you don't have to be a one-woman show all the time. I'm staying." Bennett ran a hand through his hair, giving him that bedhead style that only men knew how to master.

"Are you sure?" Having an extra pair of hands would be nice, but the line between help and hurt blurred together when it came to Bennett. The more time the two spent together the more painful his departure to the city would be. She needed to distance herself. Especially when that messy hair of his begged her attention.

Not giving her time to take back the question, Bennett took hold of her hand. "I'm entirely sure. Every leading lady needs a sidekick."

The joke silenced her. Arguing with such sweetness would be a crime against southern etiquette. Together, they trotted through the hallway to the storage room. She gave the knob a quick twist and pulled back on the door. It didn't budge.

"Oh, no. No, no, no." Her voice echoed in the silent hallway as she unlaced her fingers from Bennett's and tried with the other hand. Another turn. Another fail. "This can't be locked."

"Maybe it's just stuck." Bennett nudged her to the side and leveraged his shoulder against the door. Then, he gave the knob a sharp turn and pushed his body into the door face. Nothing.

"Who would lock the storage room up? Why?" Eliza moaned and touched her forehead to the door separating her from the rest of the donations.

A warm hand landed on her shoulder, the contrast to the cool metal against her skin striking. The hot-and-cold sensations warred against each other, much like her thoughts as she tried to tamp down her mounting frustration. Blowing out a breath, she turned around and started back down the hall.

"Do you want to call someone? Mr. Hart, maybe?" Bennett trailed after her. "He takes care of the community center, right?"

"Right." Glancing at her watch, Eliza Lee shook her head. "But it's too late. He goes to bed with the chickens and gets up with the cows. So much for getting the job done in one fell swoop."

"Another twenty-four hours won't hurt." Bennett fell in step next to her. "If you can get the key from Mr. Hart tomorrow, I'll swing by and help you wrap things up. How does that sound?

"Like music to my ears." Her answer stopped Eliza midstride. Bennett too.

Apparently, neither had expected such a quick agreeance. *I must be more tired than I thought.* The annoyance over the vouchers had merely left her spent. Fatigue and not Bennett's kindness explained her momentary lapse of self-sufficiency. She needed sleep. After a good night's rest, she'd be herself again.

Without being asked, Bennett pushed chairs beneath the tables in the center while she snatched leftover ribbon and wrapping paper from off the floor. They divided the big stuff. He swept; she mopped. In no time flat, the center sparkled. Not a trace of the packing party could be seen, except for the sorted coats and toys that Trish would pick up the next day.

The two of them walked through the parking lot, chatting about the work week ahead. More than once, Bennett's hand brushed hers igniting tiny fireworks from the point of contact. She ignored both the reaction and her desire to take hold. Despite what she had told herself about rest and sleep, she couldn't help but wonder if she'd truly bounce back after seeing Bennett's devotion in action.

Worse, she didn't know if she wanted to.

True to his word, Bennett met her early the next morning. Together, they knocked the vouchers out before Trish picked up the donations. The progress tickled Eliza Lee pink, and she didn't even like pink. Unfortunately, the feeling waned as the work week stretched on. Her emotional high dissipated entirely with a last-minute registration check the night of the dance-a-thon. On the last of the printed pages meant to identify participants, 26—the number reserved for her and her dance partner—stood out.

Eliza paced the sideline of the gym, trying to figure out how her name landed on the sign-up sheet. She didn't dance. Period. Except now when a question mark punctuated the situation. *What on earth happened?* To make matters worse, she had been paired with Bennett. He epitomized an unsafe partner with his long lashes and let-me-help attitude. His efforts at the packing party had gone a long way in deconstructing the barricade Eliza had built around her heart. For the first time in months, she had opened herself up to more than the work that drove her or the grief that plagued her.

Bennett had slipped through her isolation and the two of them had connected. Her need for distance? All the reasons she didn't need romance? Forgotten, at least temporarily. Any more consideration from Bennett could cause permanent amnesia. Letting herself fall for her boss posed a serious threat, but she couldn't back out of the two-step now. The Santa Run needed her.

I can do this.

Eliza slapped the paper sticky side down on the sleeve of her jumpsuit. She'd chosen to abandon her usual faded jeans and plaid button up for an outfit more suited to the event. The burgundy one-piece had been comfortable enough to work in but still fit in with the dresses and skirts of the dancers beginning to arrive. Thank heavens she'd worn her studded black flats instead of the heeled boots she usually paired with the ensemble.

She heard her name called from multiple spots around the room. Everyone needed something and Eliza had no idea how to get it all done. The DJ required help with setup, the lights on the stage weren't working, and a couple of teenagers looked a little too friendly with each other in the corner.

"Can I help with anything?"

A tap on her shoulder followed the offer. When Eliza turned around an underdressed, handsome-as-the-day-is-long Bennett greeted her with a wide smile. His genuine expression caught her off guard. Despite seeing her at the office for eight-hours prior to the dance-a-thon, Bennett looked truly happy to see her, like there was nowhere else he'd rather be. How could she not accept his offer?

"As a matter of fact, there is. What do you know about PA systems?" She pointed toward the stage and the frazzled man behind the turntable.

"Sound systems are not my specialty, but I'll give it a go." Bennett glanced back at the registration table. "Just let me get my number."

"Yeah, about that." Eliza Lee sucked in a breath and exhaled loudly, hoping the rush of air would make her explanation come out easier. What little she had of one, anyway. She still hadn't figured out how her name had been added to the list. "You know how all the single participants were supposed to be paired randomly?"

Nodding, Bennett's brows furrowed. "Yes?"

"I hate to be the one to break it to you, but you're kinda stuck with me." She chewed her bottom lip as she studied his reaction. It was about as far from hers as possible. He practically beamed as a bright smile widened across his face. Granted, he signed up to dance, so it wasn't the same shock factor for him that it had been for her.

"I didn't think you were dancing?" Bennett's voice grew husky as he studied her.

Beneath his perusal, Eliza shifted from one foot to the other, trying to focus on the question instead of the man asking it. "I wasn't. But when I got here tonight, I'd been given a number. No idea how my name found its way to the registration, but it did. So, dance I must."

"That's wonderful." Bennett's shoulders relaxed as he let out a long breath.

Eliza folded her arms in front of her, wondering if Bennett had anything to do with the dancing mix-up. *He wouldn't. Would he?* She shook her head. *No, that's ridiculous.* Bennett was complicated, but he wasn't cruel, even if he was smiling at her like the Joker.

As if reading her thoughts, Bennett ran a hand down his face, wiping the smile away. "That didn't come out right. It's not wonderful because you have to dance but because I already know my partner. I was nervous I'd have to introduce myself to a total stranger. *Awkward.*"

"Right." Eliza smiled tightly at his failed mimicry of a teen girl with the last word. "Well, Jenny's got all the numbers. You can grab it after you fix the sound system." She started walking toward the roll-away stage, quickening her stride with each step.

Bennett followed close behind. "I said I'd try, Eliza Lee. I can't be blamed for any damages that may occur as a result of my aid. Understood?"

She nodded as they began examining the sound board and wires. After a few minutes of tinkering, the system still refused to work, sending a high-pitched squeal through the air instead of dance music. Eliza redid the hook-ups before having Bennett try again. When the mic still didn't work, she sank onto the floor. Tears pricked her eyes as the last of the couples checked in. They needed to get started soon.

Bennett crouched down in front of her. "I'm sorry, Eliza. I'm not having much luck."

Refusing to look at him, she traced the cords one last time. Red peeked out at her a few inches from the outlet. She snapped her fingers and stood. "Maybe our luck just changed."

Eliza stalked toward the wall, grabbing Bennett's hand and pulling him along with her. When they were close enough to the wire to get a good look, she bent over, searching the length of the cord with eagle-eye precision until she found the frayed spot. Bennett saw it, too, and asked if she'd brought any electrical tape. Nodding, she pointed to an open toolbox near the other side of the stage. After instructing her to unplug the cord, he ran over and grabbed the box.

When Bennett returned, he hastily wrapped the cord with the black tape he'd retrieved. He nodded for her to try again. Eliza prayed and flipped the switch on the microphone before hitting it gently with her forefinger. *Tap, tap, tap.* People turned as the sound echoed. She clapped twice and turned to face the audience.

"Thank you all for coming out tonight to support the Santa Run. It means so much to me, not only because of my role at the railroad but because of all the special people gone on before us. Their dedication and enthusiasm will drive the tradition forward. All of you here tonight prove that. So, thank you." She stepped back and started clapping. Every man, woman, boy, and girl deserved so much more than a round of applause, but it was all she had to offer. After it got quiet again, she took to the mic once more.

"The rules are simple. Dance, boogie, cut a rug, shimmy, shake, or jive. Just keep moving. If you need a bathroom or water break, you can call time as long as your partner remains on the dance floor and keeps going. For every hour you make it through, you will earn the predetermined donation from each of your sponsors. Once you've had enough, raise your hand, and one of our volunteers will notate your end time. Any questions?" No one spoke, so she rushed on. "Well, then. Let's get this dance-a-thon started."

Another big round of applause roared as Eliza stepped off the stage. When the music started, Jenny spun Lori in circles toward the middle of the room. Giggles followed their trail. In the back, Eliza's parents shuffled along the wall, reminding her of a classic movie couple, eyes only for each other. Wearing a poodle skirt and saddle shoes, Emma Lou hand-jived next to a stone-faced Davey Barnes. The two of them made a comical pair. Near the front entrance, Hanna took the first shift at the timetable with Jett by her side. As Eliza's eyes skipped from one couple to another, the scene took her by surprise.

Since Grandpa Walt's death, Eliza had distanced herself from her family and friends. She'd determined getting close meant getting hurt and convinced herself she needed to grieve alone. But seeing her loved ones gathered around made her think maybe she'd been wrong. Instead of pushing everyone away, bent on making it by herself, maybe she needed to accept the love and support they silently offered. *It was worth a try.*

Eliza processed the realization while searching for her partner. When she saw him standing with outstretched arms, she gulped. Her feet and hips had enough difficulty moving together to walk, let alone shimmying. *Breathe, Eliza Lee. Breathe.* She inhaled.

I can do this. For Grandpa Walt. As Eliza crossed the room, she jiggled her hands by her side, an attempt to work the frazzled nerves to the surface and out through her fingertips. *It's just dancing, moving in time with the music for a good cause. One step, two step, three step, four.*

Bennett bowed when she finally made it to him. Laughing at his mock chivalry, she gave her best effort at a curtsy and slipped her hand into his open palm. Like ice on a coal stove, her fears melted at his touch.

"See? It's not so bad." One corner of his mouth tugged upward into a half-grin as they found the beat. He was right. With him holding her, it wasn't a bit bad. It was actually nice, not that she'd admit that.

Eliza gave him the evil eye. "Not yet, but the night is young."

"True," said Bennett. "What do you have against dancing anyway?"

Eliza Lee sighed, but answered as honestly as she could. "Dancing is like driving. You always know what you're gonna do, but it's the other people you have to look out for."

Bennett cocked his head to the side as Eliza Lee felt herself shrink. Brown button eyes wore her resolve until her mouth snapped open to explain. "See those boots?" She gestured toward a middle-aged man with steel toes on, cautiously guiding his five-foot-nothing lady friend around the floor.

Bennett's brows tiptoed to his hairline. "Yeah, and?"

"And . . ." Eliza stressed the words as she tried to clarify. "Those boots hurt when they hit. They'll bruise you badly if you're not careful. Maybe even cause some breaks. It's not safe, not at all."

Bennett stared at her like she'd just explained the theory of relativity using emojis. She didn't blame him. No doubt, her reasoning sounded funny, but it was true. For dancing and for love. *Love? Where on God's green earth did that come from?*

Bennett didn't give her time to figure it out as he spoke up. "I hear what you're saying, but you won't get stepped on if you're letting those boots lead."

His words poured over her like honey, thick and sticky, clinging to all the places in her heart she tried to hide—from her family, from him, from herself. Bennett had silently called "olly olly oxen free." The declaration convinced her heart to abandon cover, opening more with every beat.

"Excuse us. Pardon me. Comin' through." Lori muttered, pulling Jenny along behind her.

As the pair slipped behind Eliza, someone to her side stepped back, smacking her into Bennett. The top of her head grazed his chin. During the madness, her hand slipped from his shoulder to his chest. The other followed suit. Both palms warmed as strong arms tightened around her waist, hugging her close.

When he cleared his throat, she realized it was her turn to talk. But say what? *The truth, Eliza Lee.*

"I've never been good at following." Her whisper sounded small even to her. All the air had been sucked from her lungs as her heart drummed against her ribcage. The woodsy notes of him circled her, starting a buzzing beneath her skin and causing her to lose track of the rhythm. She nearly tripped over his ankle.

Without missing a step, Bennett righted her and got them back in time with the music. "You don't have to follow, Eliza Lee. Just move *with* your partner. Trust they've got your back, that you're safe and heading to a good place for them and for you." Was he still talking about dancing? She didn't know, but the butterflies in her stomach testified against it.

"I guess." As soon as she spoke, she wished she hadn't. She sounded childish. Shutting her eyes tight, she tried to focus only on the music. Gary Alan crooned in her ears, talking about where he needed to be.

Bennett bent his head closer. His breath sent a few flyaway hairs to ruffling and the butterflies from earlier to fluttering. She willed her ears to open wider, intent on hearing Bennett loud and clear.

"Besides," he whispered. "Not everyone wears boots."

Forcing her eyes open, Eliza took in the loafers covering his feet, the same ones she'd mentally mocked the day they met. *He's right, Lord. Oh, he's right. I don't know if I can trust him, but I know I can trust you. Lead us both, Father.*

"True." Eliza closed her eyes once more instead of searching his face like she wanted, too afraid of what she might see. More than that, she feared what her own expression might reveal.

Hope? No doubt. *Adoration?* Certainly. *Love?*

Maybe.

Chapter Twenty

The display window on Bennett's computer had taunted him all morning. *Error 49*. The number meant nothing to him, except that the printer had decided to check out. Google told him how to clear the code in supposedly simple step-by-step directions. He followed the instructions to the letter four times, but the error refused to budge.

Such a Monday. Before the printer's meltdown, Bennett had actually expected the opposite of Monday blues. Especially after the text he'd received on the drive over. Janet wanted him to know she'd moved on. Her correspondence had caught him off guard, but didn't bother him the way seeing her in the office had. Rather, he'd found himself happy for her. He'd taken the response as proof that he was over her for good.

As Bennett thought about the text, a different message came to mind. One from his father on Thanksgiving. Did he know before about Janet's new boyfriend? Was that why he asked about her? Before Bennett could tack another what-if onto the scenario chain, the printer tried to fire up again. Tried and failed.

"Still won't work?" Jett sipped from his cup as he took a seat.

Bennett let silence provide his answer as he narrowed his eyes at Jett's grin, making his employee snicker and spew coffee all over his newly organized desk. The closer Hanna's due date loomed, the more diligent he became. Every night he made sure to finalize the next day's schedule. If he couldn't verify a shipment, he left a detailed list of what needed to be addressed along with the customer contact information.

Tossing a roll of paper towels in Jett's direction, Bennett aimed for that smug smile. "At least the new phone system is finally up and running."

Jett caught the paper towel roll as Eliza walked past Bennett's desk to her own at the front of the office. As if on cue, her phone started ringing. She answered with a smile.

Like much of the time when Eliza spoke to customers, Bennett found himself mesmerized by her southern drawl. The long vowels came out more a song than conversation and Bennett could have listened all day, but Jett had other plans. He tossed the paper towels back at Bennett. "Give it up with the printer, man. Normally, I'd send Hanna to Staples for you to save the day, but I don't want her driving by herself. Why don't you go grab a new one?"

"I think I will." Bennett snatched his key from off the desk. "Do you still have the company card?"

Jett nodded. "I forgot to give it back after the lunch with Thatcher Trucking." He shifted in his seat to get to his back pocket but stopped short. "Crud. I left my wallet at home today, on the stove of all places."

With a wide smile, Hanna rose from her seat and waddled over. "I may not be able to drive, but I can let you in the house. Do you mind if I come too? I'm dying for a joyride in that fancy-schmancy car of yours."

"Of course you can come." Shutting his laptop, Bennett stood up. "Let me go start the car so it'll be warm for you and the little one." With quick steps, he headed toward the door as she murmured a thank-you. "It won't take long to heat up, five minutes tops. I'll wait for you out there. Do we need anything else?"

Jett shook his head as he switched on the headset. Bennett watched Eliza from the corner of his eye as she typed out an email, her fingers tapping furiously.

"How about you, Eliza Lee?" He smiled as she mulled it over, propping her elbow on her desk to cradle her chin. It was her signature thinking pose. The fact she had such a thing was too cute, but the thoughtful expression she wore made it adorable.

"Nope." She popped the *p* in her usual way. "But thanks for thinking of me."

I always do.

Bennett tied his tongue to keep silent, but it didn't stop his heart from skipping. It was becoming harder to concentrate on anything except Eliza Lee Elliott. The way her hair smelled of sweet vanilla, the way she tapped her toe when she was mad, the way her eyes lit up whenever she talked about the Santa Run.

At the mental reminder of the Run, Bennett's smile slipped. The fundraising had fallen short and he dreaded to break the bad news to her. Not now, though. Later, when she turned in the final number after adding in the dance-a-thon profit.

He dismissed himself from the office and headed through the parking lot. The car purred while he contemplated the situation. The crazy idea of pleading with Pops rushed through his mind. If he asked for more funding, his father would be more apt to relent. On the flip side, though, supporting the Run meant talking his father into a yuletide celebration. Pops didn't celebrate Christmas. The last time Bennett had tried a holiday intervention in the form of a catered dinner at the office, his father threw away his plate. The two didn't speak until after the New Year. Bennett knew better than to back the Run. His endorsement would be seen as a personal attack, a betrayal of sorts on his father's mode of grief, and would undoubtedly jeopardize what little progress he'd made with his dad.

Since Bennett and L. J.'s talk, Bennett had been intentional with his communication. He'd sent text messages just to say hi, friendly emails with links to a few of his favorite podcasts, and a playlist of some classic rock he thought Pops might enjoy. Earlier in the week, his father had sent him a snapshot of himself from high school. Bennett had never laid eyes on it before and when he asked his father about it, he'd received more photos and an in-depth story of Friday night bonfires and football. Project Pops was moving in the right direction. If Bennett questioned his dad about the Santa Run, the forward motion might cease altogether.

He couldn't sacrifice his chance at a family to save the Run. But could he break Eliza's heart by abandoning the cause? Bennett shook his head. There had to be another way. Pulling up the financials on his phone, he hunted for something he might have missed. A hidden loophole in the budget or funds to be reallocated. He hadn't gotten far when the passenger side door swung open and Hanna slid in.

"Ooohhhh. So toasty." After she fastened the belt under her baby bump, she freed her hands from the knit gloves and ran a finger across the dash. "And shiny. You know your cars."

"Actually," Bennett paused, wondering if he should go on. It had been so long since he'd shared the story his memory felt brittle. In the city, he'd not spoken of the car's origin to a single soul, afraid someone would slip and mention it to his father. But in Pine Valley? He was safe. Bennett went on. "My mother picked out this car. Open the glove box. There's a pocket album in there."

Leaning forward, Hanna retrieved the book. While she flipped through the pages, Bennett did the same in his mind. He knew the order of the photos by heart. First, the Jag in the showroom. Then, his mother holding up the keys. The two following photos were each of them behind the steering wheel. Finally, his mother leaning against the front bumper and blowing a kiss at the camera. That image had been blown up and placed in the driver's seat the day it was delivered. Christmas Day. When his father had sworn off celebrating.

"What amazing pictures. You look a lot like her." Smiling brightly, Hanna closed the album. "I hope after such a thoughtful present you let her drive this beauty occasionally."

"I would love nothing more, but she died not long after those photos were taken." Bennett cleared his throat. "The Jag was a present to my father."

"Oh, I'm so sorry." Brows furrowing, Hanna returned the album to the dashboard. She patted Bennett's hand that rested on the gear shift.

Blinking the sting away from his eyes, Bennett tried to smile. "Me too. I think you would have gotten along well with her. She loved donuts almost as much as you."

"Smart woman." Hanna made a show of looking around the cab. "She knows her pastries and vehicles about as good as you know your way around an office. The changes have helped a lot. Eliza agrees with me, even if she's too stubborn to tell you so. Thank you, Bennie."

Hearing that name always aged him back ten years, but when Hanna said it, the loneliness ushered in by his mother's memory fell away. He felt seen, like a brother welcomed home.

Home?

Bennett didn't know when Pine Valley had wiggled its way into that word, but the realization surprised him. So much so he pushed it to the back of his mind and focused on the sunlight streaming through the bare tree branches. Hills on either side surrounded the two-lane road. Though their colorful array had passed, the scenery remained as beautiful as ever. The land rested quietly and undisturbed.

Red streaked across his peripherals as Hanna resituated her gloves. "Thanks for letting me tag along."

"Don't thank me yet." Bennett shot a glare her way, narrowing his eyes. "I'm mad at you, young lady."

"Oh?" Her reply mimicked confusion but the expectancy in her voice gave her away. She knew where this was going.

"Why didn't you tell me it was a pretend birthday?" Bennett drifted into the next lane as he readied to turn. "I've not asked before because I didn't want to say anything in front of Eliza, but I think I deserve an explanation."

A slight blush colored Hanna's cheeks as she played with a tassel on her coat. "Because if I had told you it was pretend, you would have asked why she needed one. And me, being a pushover, would have buckled under the weight of your puppy dog stare and told you Black Friday is the darkest day of the year. The day Grandpa Walt walked through the Pearly Gates. It's been tough for all of us, but more so for Eliza Lee. She found him that morning." Hanna angled herself to face Bennett better. "But it wasn't my place to tell you, so I kept my mouth shut."

Slowing the car, he stopped at a red light. He'd never been more grateful to be caught in traffic. The light gave him time to process. Blurry images in his memory sharpened as Eliza's fake birthday and her emotional roller coaster on Black Friday began to make sense.

Hanna's eyes turned demanding. "It still isn't my place. So, let's just keep this between us?"

Watching the light turn green, Bennett gave a half-hearted nod and rolled through the intersection. The action earned a huff from Hanna.

"Look, Bennett." Seemingly unimpressed with his subpar response, she crossed her arms. "Walt's death broke Eliza Lee slap dab in two, cracked a canyon in her heart a mile wide that none of us could cross. Every time we tried to build a bridge, she set it on fire. The poor child refused to lean on a solitary soul. She shut herself off, stitched up the parts she could, closed the parts she couldn't, and hid both away from everyone. Including us. That's why we didn't have this talk."

Now it was Bennett's turn to huff. Hanna spoke in riddles that made his head and his heart hurt, for Eliza Lee and himself. *Why, Lord? Why show me her pain if I can't help?* It didn't make sense.

"Hanna, don't ask me to keep quiet about this. You, of all people, know how I feel about Eliza."

"I do know." Hanna's voice turned sharp, matching her steady gaze from earlier. "That's why I'm putting you in a cone of silence. You bring back the old Eliza Lee, the girl with fire in her belly and a smile on her lips. But if you push, she'll run for the hills."

"What then? Do I pretend I don't know? Wait for her to tell me?" Bennett hiked a brow at his absurdity. *Like that'll happen.*

Hanna pointed at him like he'd given the perfect answer to a million-dollar question. "Exactly. Because when she tells you, she'll be ready to love you the way you love her."

Love?

Did he hear her right? It was too soon to say that. Wasn't it? Bennett had dated Janet for months and the two of them had never spoken that word. Such a thought hadn't even crossed his mind. Of course, Janet wasn't Eliza either.

Bennett tightened his grip around the steering wheel until his knuckles burned. Was Hanna right? Afraid of the truth, he focused on the road instead of searching for the answer or a rebuttal to the observation. Even if Bennett had some sort of response, Hanna didn't care to hear it.

She rushed on. "Turn here. Second house on the left."

Bennett followed her directions and pulled into the drive. With the car in park, he ran his sweaty palms up and down his thighs. He still didn't know how to reply. *Fake it until you make it.* Though he had no words planned out, Bennett started talking. "Uh, Eliza and m—"

"Forget it, Bennie." Hanna slapped his shoulder lightly, ending the conversation. The usual warmth had returned to her face as she smiled at him. She opened the door before he was able to protest. "Come on. You gotta see the nursery while you're here. It's too cute."

While Bennett followed behind, Hanna's words pinged back and forth. She saw love when he looked at Eliza? A better question rushed to the forefront. When Eliza looked at him, did she see the same? Did he want her to see love?

Maybe.

Oblivious to his thoughts, Hanna looked back as she stopped in front of an open door. She motioned him through before walking in herself. "Ta-da."

The light hummed to life at the flip of the switch. Walls of pale yellow surrounded him. An antique crib sat along the back wall, a matching rocker in the corner. Sweet animals with big happy eyes covered the curtains, presumably from Noah's ark, if the rainbow rug in the center of the room was any indication. Hanna clapped her hands. "Ain't it just the berries?"

"I don't think I've ever heard it put that way before, but, yes. It's all the berries. Strawberries, blueberries, raspberries. Truly lovely."

She beamed back at him, her eyes glistening as she rested her hand on top of her belly. "Thank you, Bennett." She pointed back the way they came. "Grab a seat in the living room. I've got the wallet, but I need a potty break. This kid is using my bladder as a trampoline."

"Take your time."

Bennett waved her away as she laughed and disappeared, leaving him alone. The couch did look comfy. He sank down and let the cushions mold around him. Pictures hugged the walls and lined the mantle above the fireplace. Smiling faces, happy people, a loving family. A twinge of sadness ran through him. He'd had that once, but it felt like a lifetime ago. Lord knew he wanted it back. *Why can't Pops want it, too? I just need him to meet me halfway.*

Lacing his fingers, he cradled the back of his head in his hands and leaned against the couch. As he did, a photo in the center of the wall caught his eye. Bennett walked over for a better look. Behind the glass, bundled children—two boys and a girl—huddled around a red-clad St. Nick. The little girl bore an uncanny resemblance to the images of Punky Brewster he'd found online.

"All set." Hanna stood beside him and followed his gaze to the picture. "They were cute, huh?"

"Is that Eliza Lee?"

"Yup, And Jett Lawson and Jonah Gray. The Elliott crew at their finest."

Bennett's mouth went dry as he toggled from one rosy-cheeked face to another, eventually landing on the jolly man himself. He didn't want to know, but he had to ask. "And Santa? Who's Santa, Hanna?" She laid a hand on his arm and he prayed he was wrong. *No, no, no, Lord. Tell me it's not—*

"Grandpa Walt."

There it was, sprawled out in all its splendor. Why the Santa Run was so special, why Eliza's eyes lit up at the mere mention of it, and why she had to save it.

But knowing her motivation didn't change the situation. Pops would need a Marley-like visitation to alter his stance on Christmas, and Bennett didn't dare hope for such a miracle. *Then, again, maybe he should. Maybe this was all in God's plan. Maybe the Santa Run c—*

"There's only been a handful of men to wear that get up." Hanna interrupted his thoughts. "Each counted it a privilege and an honor, Walt especially. The boots were his for more than three decades. Jett's thrilled to follow in his footsteps."

With one final look at the picture, Hanna crossed the living room and opened the front door. "On to Staples?"

Unable to speak, Bennett nodded. The inside of his mouth had transformed from talkative tissue to desert sand. It was turning out to be a Monday to write home about.

Write home? Bennett sucked in a deep breath as he reassessed his faith and the situation. *What did he have to lose?* A few football stories and high school memories swapped between father and son? He'd made progress toward Project Pops, but the results lacked the depth needed to forge true family ties. Like those that prompted his mother to pick out the Jaguar sitting in the driveway and like the kind that fueled Eliza Lee's do-or-die-trying attitude about the Run.

Perhaps asking Pops about the Santa Run wasn't such a bad idea. Instead of sinking the ship, doing so might right his efforts to save his family once and for all, and Eliza Lee in the process. The Pine Valley tradition brought family together. Why not Bennett and his father?

Is it that simple, Lord?

There was only one way to find out. As Bennett slid into the driver's seat, he fished out his phone and found a notification flashing. Somehow, he'd missed a text from Eliza Lee asking for manila folders and paper clips. Bennett tapped out a reply and opened a new text screen. Determined to strike while the iron was hot—and before he talked himself out of it—Bennett wrote out a message to his father. Pressing send, he sucked in a breath and attempted to channel Tiny Tim with his childlike faith. His father's phone would soon light up, and Bennett needed as much Christmas magic as he could get.

As the new printer awoke a few hours later, Bennett smiled at the heavenly sounds the machine made. Knowing he'd solved at least one of Monday's problems put a little pep in his step.

"You look happy as a lark." Eliza Lee propped a hand on her hip and smiled. "Glad to see it. Now that you're in a better mood, can we talk about the paint for the train cars. That color is atrocious."

Bennett pinched his nose and blew out a loud exhale. "Eliza, I can't change the McCoy Railway logo. There's nothing I can do."

"I understand that, but our freight cars have always been tagged with silver." Armed and ready, she pulled a photo album from her desk drawer and handed it to him. She pointed at the picture she wanted him to see. "Can't we change the red to the color we're already using? The logo will stay the same, but we'll be keeping a little nostalgia from the Appalachian Express."

"Why are you so against the change?" Bennett took the book from her, closed it, and set it on the desk. "It's just a railcar."

"To you it is." Narrowing her eyes, she stepped forward. "To Pine Valley, it's tradition."

"Not all traditions are made to last."

Eliza flinched as Bennett realized a moment too late how his words must have sounded. Before he could apologize, the front door swung open and his father stepped in. Bennett froze as Pops wiped his feet on the welcome mat. Eliza Lee, however, slipped into business mode and went to greet him.

With all the poise of a good owner, Mr. McCoy extended his hand. "Good afternoon. Mr. Oliver McCoy. And you are?"

"Eliza Lee Elliott, sir." She accepted Mr. McCoy's hand and shook. "Nice to meet you." Though her eyes were wide and her face had gone pale, she kept smiling.

Pride surged through Bennett. Despite being in the midst of an argument and the arrival of their unannounced guest, Eliza sounded every bit the capable woman he knew her to be. Standing toe to toe with the man who'd turned her world upside down, she exuded confidence with a tried-by-fire strength. Bennett had seen men cower in his father's presence. But not his Eliza.

His Eliza? Where had that come from? She'd smack him for that one.

Bennett's father smiled as she let go of his hand. "A pleasure, Ms. Elliott."

"Eliza, please. We're all family here." Though addressing Mr. McCoy, she found Bennett's gaze. *If she only knew how true that was.* Instead of reassuring Bennett, the sentiment unearthed his worry. Would she renounce her declaration after realizing the connection between Mr. McCoy and himself? When his father stepped toward him, Bennett knew he'd soon find out.

"Don't look so shocked, son. You said you needed to see me, so I snagged the first flight I could from New York to Pine Valley. It took me a bit to get my rental car, but here I am."

To punctuate his words, his father enveloped Bennett in a hug. Bennett stiffened beneath the unusual demonstration. How long had it been since his father's arms were around him? Months? A Year? Longer?

Not wanting to squander the opportunity, he returned the embrace. "It's good to see you, Pops."

As Bennett looked past his father's shoulder, Eliza Lee stepped into his line of vision. He winced beneath the daggers of her glare. Gently, he pulled out of his father's hold, intending to go to her. Before he could, she motioned his father over to where she stood next to Jett. "Mr. McCoy, I know you've spoken with my brother already, but let me introduce the two of you properly."

Jett extended his hand and Mr. McCoy shook with a terse nod before asking about the new phone system. While the two of them chatted, Eliza drew close to Bennett.

Laying a hand on his forearm, she whispered, "Can I talk to you in the break room?"

"Sure." Bennett stood up straighter despite the waver in his voice and waited for her to lead the way. When she did, he followed.

In no hurry to face Eliza's wrath, Bennett shuffled his feet despite knowing his resistance to be futile. He'd been in town long enough to know when a southern woman wanted to talk, a man stood and listened. If not, she'd follow him until he did. Bennett had a sinking feeling he'd much rather keep their conversation private.

"Please don't jump to conclusions." Bennett started talking before he'd even cleared the hall.

"Why didn't you tell me you're Oliver McCoy's son?" Eliza clenched her fists at her side. Her petite frame stood straight as an arrow, except for her head tilted like a dazed puppy.

"It slipped my mind?" Bennett took the humor approach, hoping for an eye roll at worst or a chuckle at best. He received neither. Just a scorching stare from those unforgettable green eyes he'd grown to adore.

"Cute, Bennett. Real cute." Tapping her toe, Eliza took in a breath. "So, what, you've been helping at the fundraisers to clear your conscience? You thought it'd be fun to string me along, to make me believe you care about the Santa Run? About me? Because seeing you and your father together made it pretty clear where your allegiance lies."

"No, you've got it all wrong." Bennett shook his head, holding his hands out in front of him as a sign of surrender. "Pops and I haven't been close in years. I came to Kentucky hoping to change that. The whole absence-makes-the-heart-grow-fonder thing? Like you with Jonah."

At the sound of her brother's name, Eliza's frown softened. "But why hide who you are?"

"At first, I kept my identity hidden because I wanted the crew to accept me—or reject me—because of who I am, not because of my father. I've never been able to climb out from under the McCoy shadow. Until now."

"Right." Eliza tapped her toe faster. "And what about after?"

Listening to the rhythmic beat, Bennett ran through a list of responses, deciding to go straight for the heart of the problem. No use delaying the inevitable. "You mean after the cancellation?"

"Yes." Eliza nodded slowly. "That's exactly what I mean. After your *father* scrapped the Santa Run."

"Everyone would have hated me. Jett, Hanna, Mama Deb." Bennett stepped closer, letting his shoe kiss hers. "You."

From down the hall, a deep voice belonging to Mr. McCoy bellowed. *Really, Pops? Again with the timing?* Bennett ignored the summons. He knew his father's bark to be much worse than his bite. With Eliza, he wasn't sure. Crazy enough to find out, he reached for her hand.

She pulled back, glancing toward the hallway. "You shouldn't keep the CEO waiting. Besides, further explanation isn't necessary. I should have known better than to think you were more than the cutthroat city boy I pegged you for. Now that I know who you are, everything makes sense."

"What are you talking about?" Bennett cringed as a chill seeped through his voice. It seemed Eliza's anger was catching.

"Hanna's dropped pies. The collapsed table at the night market. The locked door at the packing party. My mysterious sign-up at the dance-a-thon." With each instance, Eliza held up another finger, presumably tallying up the offenses. "You didn't come to help me. You came to help your father. Mr. McCoy never wanted the Santa Run to happen and you were making sure it didn't. You were at the fundraisers to sabotage me."

Bennett stumbled back at her accusation. "You don't honestly believe that." His voice rose an octave to match Eliza Lee's as she suddenly decided to study the floor. Her unwillingness to face him kicked like a boot to the mouth.

Blowing out a long breath, Bennett continued. "I was wrong not to tell you who I was, but I would never sabotage your efforts. You know that, don't you?" His whisper screamed between them, deafening Bennett until he was sure he'd never hear her answer. That is, if she answered.

"I thought I did." She finally raised her head and met his eyes. "But now? I don't know what to think."

"Well, at least you're honest." His father called his name again. Bennett cringed. "Listen, I've got some business to discuss with Pops. That'll give you space and time to think. Can we pick this back up later?"

"Bennett, I don't think that's the best idea."

"Please."

It had been a long time since Bennett begged on the streets. When he returned to the city, he swore he'd never do it again, but he was seconds away from falling to his knees when Eliza broke the silence.

"Maybe."

Praise the Lord. It wasn't a yes, but it wasn't a no, and he knew it was more than he deserved.

"Thank you, Eliza Lee." He studied her. Anger still danced in her gaze among hues of emerald and sage, but not quite as fervent. He smiled at the change. "I'll find you when I get back."

With that, Bennett turned and hurried to the door. He didn't want to give her a chance to change her mind.

Chapter Twenty-One

"Slow down with that or you'll get sick, Eliza Lee."
Emma Lou scolded through the phone screen—half-disappointed, half-amused—judging by the traces of her smile.

Eliza had clocked out for break and practically ran to the lounge minutes after Bennett had left. Longing for comfort, she'd swiped Hanna's pint of ice cream out of the freezer and went to town. *Desperate times call for desperate measures.* She'd replace it over the weekend.

As the sugar worked its magic, an impulse to spill her guts rushed through her. She had to talk things out with someone or she'd explode. Jett—with his fix-it attitude and logical mindset—didn't fit the bill. Neither did Hanna, since she'd blab everything to Jett. So, she'd dialed up Emma Lou for a vent session.

Being as unladylike as possible, Eliza Lee shoveled another spoonful of ice cream into her mouth. "Good, maybe then I'll have a legitimate excuse to go home and avoid Bennett. I mean, *Mr. Bennett M-stands-for-McCoy Olsen.*"

The name sounded foreign on her lips. She'd been foolish to fall for a man she barely knew. Worse, to begin relying on such a man. Channeling all her energy, Eliza dug with her spoon like she was searching for hidden treasure. She struck gold in the form of fudge fish and marshmallow. Holding her haul up to the phone, currently propped up by the coffee can, she tipped her spoon in a cheers motion.

Emma Lou's face glowed on the video chat as one of her newest cat adoptions batted at her hair. "Calm down and tell me what happened. From the beginning, thank you very much."

Try as she might to stay on track, Eliza stumbled over her explanation. The story snowballed as she recounted the dropped pies, the locked storage room, the broken table, and the father-son relationship between Bennett and Mr. McCoy. She saved the dance-a-thon for last, wondering if it really mattered how her name ended up on the list. Being in Bennett's arms hadn't been so bad. By the end of the night, she'd found a new love for slow songs.

Maybe for her boss, too, which made his secrecy hurt all the more. Despite the pain, though, she still cared about him. Even if she didn't like him—or his father—one iota at the moment. To be fair, she hadn't liked his father at any point in time.

Satisfied she'd caught Emma Lou up to speed, Eliza inhaled another spoonful of ice cream.

"Wow." Emma Lou's eyes doubled in size. "That's a lot to process in a short amount of time but I am confident in what I'm about to say. Listen close. OK?"

Eliza leaned closer to the screen. "OK. I'm all ears."

"Wake up and smell the roses." Emma Lou smiled, looking like the cat that got the cream. "I know for a fact Bennett Olsen has not been sabotaging you."

"No, you don't." Eliza shook her head. "You can't. Were you even listening? Hanna Bell told me herself he dropped the pies."

Cutting her off, Emma piped up. "Pies he paid for out of the kindness of his heart."

"Yeah, well, it gave him a cover." Eliza plunged the spoon into the soft chocolate and scooped the next bite.

Emma Lou remained undeterred. She nodded dramatically, letting Eliza know the crock of crap she thought that was. "Sure, honey."

"I know, right? If I had suspected him of being behind all the mishaps, I'd never have let him near my night market table."

An orange furball leapt at the phone. With a sigh, Emma Lou shooed the cat away from the screen. "You mean, the same table we used to set up bake sales as peewee cheerleaders. That the table you're talking about?"

"Yes," Eliza answered, trying to ignore her friend's sound reasoning.

Emma Lou guided the purring feline off the couch and resituated the camera. "Correct me if I'm wrong, but that table's seen better days. The last time I used it for the PTA, the legs didn't even want to snap in place. If you want my opinion—"

"Which I don't." Eliza chimed in, but she didn't sound convincing.

"Too bad. I give it freely, like smiles and hugs." Emma Lou flashed a wide grin as an example. "I'd say Joe didn't get the peg in good enough and when Bennett leaned on the table, his weight became the straw that broke the camel's back."

Feeling her train of reason derailing, Eliza switched routes. "OK, can you explain the dance-a-thon, Ms. Smarty Pants?" Eliza crossed her arms over her chest. Even if Emma Lou made compelling arguments for the rest of the incidents, she had no hope of reasoning the dance-a-thon away.

"Yes, I can." Scratching behind a kitten's ear, Emma Lou's smile turned sheepish. "I signed you up to dance with Bennett."

"What?" Eliza blinked at her friend. "Why?"

"His name looked so lonely on the sign-up sheet, and it was obvious you have a thing for him. It was my duty as your best friend to put your name with his." Emma Lou wrapped up the explanation with a shrug and her signature you-know-I-got-you-there expression, a look that ended more than one squabble growing up.

Tapping the screen where Emma's forehead was, Eliza groaned. "You're unbelievable. Ya know that? I'm gonna kill you deader than four o-clock."

Eliza had so much more to say, but when a high-pitched snarl followed by a hiss rang through the speakers, Emma Lou frowned. "Sounds like I've got a tiny cat fight to break up. I gotta go, bestie."

"Watch out for the claws." Still processing Emma Lou's confession, Eliza licked a dab of chocolate that had dropped onto her hand. "Thanks for talking me down but not for playing matchmaker."

She giggled and Emma Lou did too. When the laughter subsided, Eliza was ready to get serious. "I know you think I'm crazy for suspecting something like this, Em. Even I have to admit your reasoning sounds good, in theory, but aside from the dance-a-thon, that's all they are. You can't say for certain Bennett isn't behind our string of bad luck."

Emma Lou rolled her eyes. "I can, Eliza Lee. I've read enough love stories to know that a man can't look at a lady like Bennett looks at you and harbor cruel intentions." With a small smile, she pulled the screen closer to her face. "I'll say it one more time. Wake. Up. And. Smell. The. Roses."

"OK, OK." Eliza groaned as she looked at the clock. "Go get your kittens, crazy cat lady, and I'll take over the phones for Jett. My break was over forever ago."

"All right, but if I don't get a text from you praising my impeccable judge of character no later than the end of the week, be prepared for a visit." The screen shifted as Emma Lou rose from the couch, sending her sideways in the video.

"I'm hanging up before you get the big head. Bye." Eliza Lee waved as she ended the chat. She made her way back to the front of the office, and had no sooner sat down at her desk than two pint-sized arms circled her from behind.

"Guess who?" A small voice squealed excitedly.

"Well," Eliza started, drawing out her answer to seem like she was stumped. "Since it's Christmas break and I'm on babysitting duty, I'll go out on a limb and guess Lori."

"Ding, ding, ding. We have a winner. But I'm not a baby, Eliza Lee." Lori placed both hands on her hips and scowled at her like she'd taken away her birthday.

"You're right. You're not. Do you like the sound of kidsitter better?"

Lori narrowed her eyes but nodded anyway.

"Well, kid, are you too old for games too? Or do you wanna play something with me? Hide-and-seek maybe?" Lori wrinkled her nose at the suggestion and plopped down in Hanna's vacant chair. She rolled it to the front of Eliza's desk, snatched a pen from the cup, and started doodling on the desk calendar.

"No hide-and-seek." Lori stole a highlighter. "Not after the packing party."

The packing party? Eliza did a mental rewind of the night. She thought her niece—and the rest of the kids—had a great time. Softly, Eliza placed a finger under Lori's chin and tilted her face up. "Why not? I thought you loved the party."

"I did," said Lori, coloring a heart neon yellow. "But I sorta ended up in the storage closet and I think I lost my bracelet in there. Matt was dragging me back to the lobby and it must have slipped off. I hain't seen it since."

Eliza plucked a green sharpie from her drawer and uncapped it, looking for a blank space to draw in. "Well, did you retrace your steps?"

"I tried, but the door wouldn't open. Guess I hit the lock button on my way out. Will you take me later to look for it? Daddy sent it to me."

Eliza shut her eyes tight, letting the dust settle on Lori's words. It wasn't Bennett who locked the door but a beautiful little girl making memories with friends. It wasn't Bennett who signed her up to dance, but a meddling bestie wanting to see Eliza happy. It wasn't Bennett who canceled the Santa Run, but the father he happened to work for. *It wasn't him.* Eliza had never been so happy to be wrong in her life.

"Hey, did you hear me?"

Eliza's eyes opened to find Lori with her arms crossed over her chest. "Yes, baby girl, I heard you. I'll take you to look for your bracelet, right after I wipe the floor with you at checkers."

Eliza Lee jumped from her seat and made a mad dash to the shelf. She expected Lori to race her. When she didn't, Eliza hurried back and started setting up the board. Lori remained solemn. In silence, the little girl repositioned her chair on the other side of the desk and folded her hands in her lap, imitating grace and composure well beyond her age. Until she giggled.

"You're on." Lori laughed again before directing her attention to setting up the board. Just like that, she was back to being a kid again, ready to take life as it came, win or lose.

Eliza Lee prayed to do the same, and for the courage to end the day better than it began, with an apology and hope for tomorrow.

Chapter Twenty-Two

"Now that we're in no man's land, care to tell me why I needed to make this trip?"

Bennett's father peered out the window, both eyebrows raised, as he surveyed the rundown houses and dilapidated school building.

"Sure thing, Pops." Bennett shifted in the driver's seat.

The emergency text he fired off may have been two weeks late, but better late than never. It was time to up his game, with his father and with Eliza, in the same spot where she had shared her heart with him.

"But first, tell me what you see." Bennett pointed toward the windshield. The scene played out as it had been before. Mobile homes in desperate need of new roofs, porch steps screaming for repair, swing sets long past their prime. To the right, a playset with rusted monkey bars stood against the December wind. Children swung from one rung to the next, smiling despite the cold.

His father put one hand over his eyes in an attempt to block the sunlight and gazed out. The minutes ticked on, so long Bennett thought he might have to repeat himself. As he was about to, his father turned to face him.

"This is nonsense." The words were matter of fact, but intrigue lined his voice. Not much to work with, but it was enough.

Bennett pressed on. "Humor me, Pops?"

"Fine." His father thinned his lips and shifted his gaze to the window again. "Run down trailers. An old school. A crappy park."

"What about the kids?" Bennett echoed his previous conversation with Eliza. He needed to walk his father through this like she had done him.

Mr. McCoy leaned back in the seat. "What about them? They're swinging, laughing, having fun."

"Anything strike you as odd?" Bennett pointed out the window again.

At first, Mr. McCoy shook his head, but the longer he sat there scrutinizing the scene, his face softened. "They need heavier coats, and gloves."

Bennett snapped his fingers. "Yes they do. The Santa Run gives children, like these, coats, gloves, even toys. It helps their parents, too, by putting turkeys on the table through the grocery vouchers handed out."

"So that's what this is about," said Mr. McCoy, rubbing his chin as he found Bennett's gaze. "Have you gone soft on me, son? I can't afford to lose money with this venture right out of the gate, and you have no right to ask me to."

"You're right. I don't." Laying a hand on his father's shoulder, Bennett cleared his throat. "Just like I don't have the right to ask you to celebrate Christmas, either, but I'm going to. For me, and for mom."

"Leave your mother out of this." His father bolted upright in the seat.

"I can't." Bennett's eyes started to burn. "She's here. In the lights, the tinsel, the trees. This car."

Clasping his hands together, Mr. McCoy stared at his laced fingers. His shoulders drew tight and his back stiffened. "Son, please."

"No, Pops. It's my turn to say please." *Like I should have done years ago.* "Please forgive me. I know I don't deserve your help. I ran away when you needed me most. You were only trying to move on when you started dating again, but when I saw you with that woman? All I could think of was Mom, that she was being forgotten. That's why I adopted her maiden name as soon as I could. I needed to know her memory, her legacy, wouldn't die with her like Christmas did."

With slow movements, his father squeezed his hands tighter. "Bennett, I loved your mother dearly. She wasn't—isn't—forgotten. But seeing this car show up when she was barely in the ground destroyed me."

"You took the tree down that night and sold the car the next morning." Bennett swallowed hard. "You didn't even talk to me about it. In fact, you still don't talk to me, except about work."

Pops dropped his hands at his side and leaned against the console. "Son, I d—"

"Wait, let me finish. It's not all your fault. When I came back to the city, I should have tried harder with you. Instead, I got mad when you distanced yourself. I messed up all the way around. Running away, changing my name, putting all the blame on you. I was wrong."

Pausing, Bennett looked his father over. His furrowed brows and thinned lips gave nothing away. He'd hoped to see forgiveness and encouragement. Perhaps a new understanding. If Pops felt any of that, he hid it well.

Despite his father's stunted reaction, Bennett had gone too far to turn back now. More than the Santa Run depended on the conversation. Project Pops did, too, and Bennett had to give both his best effort, regardless of the outcome.

Kneading the back of his neck, Bennett rushed on. "Maybe it's not too late to start over? I can't undo the pain I caused you, but maybe we can build memories to lessen it in time. It took me over a year to be able to drive this car after I tracked down the buyers, but I kept trying. Now, when I sit behind the wheel I don't cry from loneliness. I smile because of Mom's love. Don't you want that?"

"I do, but . . ." The timbre of his father's voice turned heavy. His breathing grew rapid. In his lap, his hands trembled. It was the most emotion Bennett had seen out of his father in years. After a deep inhale, his father continued. "Sitting here without her is so hard."

"I didn't say it was easy." Bennett shook his head. "Grieving never is. But working through the pain is worth it. Can you at least try, Pops?"

Bennett expected rejection, maybe even a lecture. He received silence instead. Uncomfortable quiet filled the cab until his father turned away, choosing to look out the passenger window once again. Bennett stared at the floorboard.

The stalemate continued long past the point of awkward until sobs broke through the hush of the car. When Bennett faced his father again, he didn't know what to think. His head was buried in his hands, and his shoulders heaved as the sobs grew heavier.

After a ragged breath, his father raised his head and everything Bennett had prayed to see for so long shone back at him. Forgiveness. Grace. Love.

Unable to hold his tears back anymore, Bennett let the first drop roll down his cheek.

His father cried harder. "I'll try. The pain of losing your mother won't be easy to get through. Neither will the fear that grips me every time I see you." Pops laid a hand on Bennett's bicep and squeezed. "When you came home from Maryland, I didn't know how to love you without setting myself up for more hurt. I was afraid you'd leave again. I'm sorry. I've been a pitiful excuse of a father, but that changes today. You're worth the pain."

Pops stretched across the console and pulled Bennett into a bear hug. Both cried on the other's shoulders for the first time since Bennett had returned to the city. The embrace lifted the weight of loneliness he had been carrying and love surrounded the two of them. Bennett's family had been reunited on a country lane atop the highest mountain in Pine Valley. In the car that broke Christmas, no less. The prodigal son ending he'd been chasing had finally been found. Could he find a holiday miracle too?

Taking a chance, Bennett threw out a final question. "What about Christmas, Pops? Is it worth the pain too?"

His father sighed. "I can't lie. Celebrating will be hard, but I'm willing to try."

"Starting with the Santa Run?"

"Bennett, I can't." Eyes that matched his own squinted, making the crow's feet on either side deepen. "The board would have my head."

"But these people have my heart." Bennett looked through the windshield again. "This town has shown me what give-and-take looks like in a family, and I can't let them down the way I let you down."

His father shrugged. "The numbers aren't there."

"What if they are?" Smiling, Bennett held up his phone. He pulled up a saved file and pointed to the highlighted section. "I may have a solution. If we take the money from all the fundraisers and combine it with the amount allotted for the crew's Christmas bonus, we'll have enough to cover the Run. It's not ideal and I have no clue if the crew will go for it, but it's worth a shot."

After examining the document several minutes, his father looked up. "This is a good plan, son. Well done."

"Thanks, Pops."

"When you come back to the city, we might look into doing an event like this." His father clapped him on the back "If you're up to spearheading the project."

Thinking about the city, Bennett cringed. He didn't want to talk about leaving yet, but since his father had opened the door, he might as well.

"About that, maybe it's best I stay a while longer. Jett and Hanna are having a baby and they'll be on leave for a while. Hanna will be gone at least six weeks, probably more. I can be useful here."

"Of course. Stay if you want." His father nodded but his smile morphed into a frown. "But be honest with me. It's not about needing help. It's about Janet. Isn't it? Henry Johnson, that know-it-all intern, warned me she'd run you away from the city. Away from me. His words more than your text rushed me into coming here. I was afraid I'd lost you for good."

"You haven't lost me, Pops." Understanding dawned on Bennett as the meaning behind his father's text at Thanksgiving revealed itself. His father wasn't feeling sorry for him. He was worried. Project Pops had worked. In a weird, roundabout way.

Bennett chuckled at the irony. "I admit Janet played a part in me leaving the city, but when I came here, I had every intention of returning to the city. Staying in Kentucky has nothing to do with her and everything to do with Eliza Lee."

"Ah." His father's brows shot up as he nodded. "I see."

"I know romantic relationships in the office are frowned upon, but I can't help it." Bennett's face filled with heat. "Pops, she's the one an—"

With a laugh of his own, his father held up a hand. "You don't have to explain. I met your mother working as a temp. I couldn't help it either. What do you say I tell you all about it over dinner on Saturday?" Mr. McCoy opened his blazer and pulled his phone from the inside pocket.

"Saturday, Pops?"

"That is when the Santa Run is scheduled, isn't it?"

Bennett tilted his head. "Yes?"

"Well, I can't promise I'll ride along for all the stops, but I'd like to see this famous run in action. If the inn can extend my stay, I'll be there. Afterwards, we'll catch up. I think we have a lot to talk about."

Sitting on the mountain, Bennett reached a pinnacle of his own as understanding passed between him and his father. For the first time since his mother died, he saw a future for them. Not as coworkers but as family.

When they made it back to the office, the men had a game plan to reinstate the Santa Run. Bennett spoke with Jett and, though he seemed hopeful, he didn't know if the crew would be willing to sacrifice their bonus. The one person who would know? Eliza Lee. Unfortunately she scooted past them on the steps, nearly knocking him over.

"I'm sorry." Eliza touched his arm briefly and stormed on. "I have to go."

The urgency in her voice made him follow her. "I know you're upset and you have every right to be. But I can—"

"It's not that, Bennett. I'm sorry for jumping to conclusions earlier and I promise we'll talk, but I have to go. Dad's hurt." Fear flickered in her eyes as she glanced back at him.

A gust of wind picked up, making a few leaves on the steps scatter, and Bennett shuddered. His father, who had decided to trail along, adjusted the collar on his coat and passed him by. With long strides through the parking lot, Pops called out to question the severity of L. J.'s injury.

Eliza stopped halfway to her car. "Not sure. Mama said he cut himself changing that stupid alternator. She took one look at him and passed out colder than kraut. She does that every time she sees blood, so it's not safe for her to drive him to the hospital. None of the neighbors are home either. I hate to leave so suddenly, but I have to take him to the hospital. Please, excuse me."

The words spun in Bennett's head as he continued after her, sending his lunch hurdling to the top of his stomach. "Wait. Let me take you."

"No." Eliza waved toward Mr. McCoy. "Go be with your dad. He's come all this way to see you. I'll be fine."

Bennett wasn't certain, but her voice seemed lighter than before, softer, and much less angry. The change in tone gave him the courage to press on. "And what about L. J.? Will *he* be fine?" Though wrong on so many levels, the insinuation served as his ace in the hole. "My car's faster."

"And smaller." Eliza pointed to the Jag. "Dad can't get in the back of that."

Bennett passed his hand over the top of her head and smirked. "No, but a shorty like you can. The front has plenty of leg room for L. J."

"I hate it when you're right." Eliza shook her head as she made her way to the car. Pulling the driver's side door open with a good yank, Bennett tried to hide his excitement. It had been a while since he'd put the pedal to the metal. Getting L. J. to the hospital was the perfect excuse.

L. J. insisted on being dropped off at the front entrance. He claimed he didn't want to "clodhop" through the hospital parking lot with a dish towel around his hand. Though Bennett didn't know if such drop-offs were allowed, he did as instructed.

"Wait here, Punky." L. J. pointed at Eliza. "I wouldn't let your Mama come hold my hand and I'm not letting you either. I'll call if I need you."

After a long hard look, Eliza Lee ceded to her father's orders, and he went into the building. Watching the two of them together solidified Bennett's suspicion that she came by her stubbornness honestly. Once L. J. was safely inside, Bennett drove around to the nearest parking spot and stashed the Jag between the lines. He patted the empty seat. She glared at him but climbed over the middle console and into the passenger side.

Without a word to him, she started scrolling through apps on her phone. Bennett bit back a groan. Whether she liked it or not, they were going to talk. Leaning into that mindset, he started. "I'm sorry I didn't tell you who I was. You have every right to be upset, but at least hear me out."

A heavy silence filled the car. Desperate, he took her hand in his. *Let her see, Father. Give me the words to explain.* When he opened his eyes, Eliza squeezed his hand and leaned closer.

"Eliza Lee, my dad and I haven't been good in a place for a while. The long and the short of it is that I messed up and he gave me a second chance by allowing me to work with the railroad. But our family isn't like yours."

Taking a breath, Bennett paused. Why was talking about his father always so difficult? He thought about his advice to Pops and reminded himself the pain was worth it. "If I had tried to step in with the Santa Run, he would have seen it as a betrayal. Businesswise, he hates to be questioned. More than that, Pops swore off Christmas after my mother died. The last time I tried to convert his Scrooge ways, we didn't speak until after the New Year."

"I wish you'd told me this from the beginning." Eliza repositioned her hand, lacing their fingers together. "I would have understood."

Bennett felt his brows shoot to his hairline, which made Eliza roll her eyes. "Not right away. But I would have once I calmed down. Case in point, I've had time to think and I know you didn't sabotage the fundraisers. I shouldn't have accused you the way I did. You're a good man." Eliza tightened her hold on his hand. "A man I wish I knew as well as I thought I did."

When she cast her gaze to the floorboard, a dam broke inside Bennett as he realized their time together had been tainted by his secrets. No wonder she'd jumped to conclusions. He'd never opened up to her, exposed himself as the lonely man desperate to earn his father's love. Now, the time had come to show her all of him.

Softly, Bennett released her hand and laid his palm on her cheek, turning her face toward him. "You had every reason to believe what you did. I wanted to help but went about it entirely wrong, starting by not showing you the real me." Leaning against the door for a better extension, he moved his hand to her palm, gripped it, and shook like when they first met. "How about a new introduction?"

"You're crazier than I am. But why not?" She shook back, cocking her head slightly. "Hello, I'm Eliza Lee."

"Nice to meet you, Eliza Lee. I'm Bennett McCoy Olsen, your new supervisor, heir to McCoy Railway, and runaway son of Oliver McCoy. He's the CEO of this fine company and by working in your lovely town of Pine Valley, I'm finagling a way back into his good graces. I'm desperate to make us a family again. Please let me know if I can be of assistance to you. If it doesn't jeopardize the fragile father-son relationship I'm attempting to piece back together, I'd be more than happy to help."

Bennett's eyes never moved from hers as he spoke. Somewhere in the middle of his speech, Eliza began to cry. Encouraged, he went on.

"The truth is, after my mother died, I gave up on family. I went so far as to drop Dad's last name after seeing him on a date. I became a runaway living on the streets. Being eighteen made it easy to do both, but my actions destroyed Pops and me. We haven't been the same since."

Out the window, the hospital stood tall like a lighthouse welcoming Bennett home. The ocean he'd been sailing along to find his father finally ending in safe shoreline. "As ashamed as I am to say it, I would have never brought my father for stitches a month ago. We don't have the kind of relationship where he would have asked me to. After watching you and L. J. together, I want to do better. And now, Pops is here and I'm getting a second chance. Because of this town and your family. Because of you, Eliza Lee."

Another tear rolled down Eliza's cheek. "I'm happy for you. So, so happy. It's good to know the Run didn't end in vain."

"Don't give up yet."

"Bennett, it's over." Slipping her hand free, Eliza shook her head. "We gave it our best, but we haven't raised enough money and we're out of time."

Leaning over the console, Bennett cupped her shoulder. "Pops is here because I texted him. We went to the spot you showed me and we've got a plan to keep the Santa Run going."

"Oh, Bennett. Thank y—"

Interrupting, Bennett held both hands up in the air to quiet her. "Hold on, now. Pops still doesn't want to lose money."

"You're not making any sense." Eliza's watery eyes searched his as her mouth bent into a frown. "Explain, City Boy. I'm in no mood to dance in circles with you tonight." They both laughed, but he could tell she meant business.

"If you add in the amount set aside for the year-end bonus, there's enough." He smiled softly as he delivered the news, waiting for relief to replace her disappointment. It didn't. If anything, disappointment grew to despair.

Eliza sniffled. "Thank you for trying, but I can't ask that of the crew. Those bonuses make Christmas for most of our employees."

A good gust of wind could have knocked Bennett over. He'd finally found a way to save the Run and she didn't even want to try? Bennett shook her shoulder, trying to knock loose the fire and passion he knew ran in her veins. "The whole town has rallied around you, Eliza Lee. I know the railroad will, too, but you have to give them a chance. You owe it to them to at least ask."

Clenching her fists in her lap, Eliza glared at him. Bennett straightened, determined to get past her head to the place in her heart that still believed in Christmas magic. If Hanna hadn't sworn him to secrecy, Bennett would have reminded Eliza of Walt. But he'd been placed in a "cone of silence" by the soon-to-be mother, so he couldn't. *Lord, what can I do? Help me change her mind.*

Bennett called to mind the promise he'd written in her birthday card. The show was hers to run, but maybe he could stand in the gap for her and prove his devotion at the same time. He tried to persuade her one last time. "If you don't want to ask, let me. You'd be doing me a favor."

"How so?" Eliza's toe tapped against the floorboard, making him look away to keep from smiling. *There's the fire.*

When he'd steeled his expression, Bennett answered. "Pops wants to stay in town through the weekend. We don't usually do traditions, but I'd like to start. I can't think of anything better than the Santa Run."

Bennett knew the moment she relented. Her foot stopped midtap.

"Fine." Eliza blew her bangs away from her face and side-eyed him. "But I don't like it."

Bennett nodded. "Noted."

Liking the solution was optional. Agreeing, however, was vital. Bennett knew she'd get over her frustration. The next step in his plan all but assured it.

Chapter Twenty-Three

Eliza sipped her coffee, smiling after each drink. The Santa Run had finally arrived. Not the way she'd imagined, but it was here at last.

Mr. McCoy's solution had blindsided her. Asking coworkers to forfeit their bonus for the greater good was admirable, except saving the Santa Run was a personal goal. The event benefited the town, but that wasn't the main reason she'd pushed so hard to keep it. She'd fought as much to preserve her own sense of purpose as she had to help Pine Valley.

She'd nearly refused Bennett's offer to ask the staff about the bonus, but Pastor Clemens's sermon on Sunday touched a nerve. Looking a gift horse in the mouth was rude unless the gift giver was God. Then rejection turned prideful, rebellious even. Eliza Lee knew she'd been disobeying God through her stubborn independence. Ever since she'd asked the Lord for help on Black Friday, Bennett had been by her side. If God sent him, she needed to let him in.

As Eliza contemplated a second cup of java, Lori's voice carried through the room. "King me, Ollie."

"But you already have one," Mr. McCoy answered, his reply barely audible from where Eliza sat. "Cut me some slack."

Eliza wasn't sure if he was letting Lori win or if he was the worst checkers player in history. It'd been weird to listen to them at first, but now she didn't bat an eye at their bickering. Since school had let out for Christmas break, Jenny dropped Lori off before work, and Mama Deb collected her around lunchtime. Eliza had been afraid to see Mr. McCoy's reaction to the arrangement, but Lori had won him over within minutes, the same way she had Bennett.

As if conjured by her thoughts, Bennett appeared in the doorway. He stomped his feet on the mat. Glistening snowflakes fell from his hair and dusted his shoulders. "Have you heard from Jett?"

She dug the phone from her pants pocket. "No. I was hoping you had. This isn't like him. I'm gonna call him again." Midway through dialing, Jett's grinning face appeared on the screen.

"Thank goodness. Please tell me you're on your way." Despite her nerves, she managed to keep from screaming, but her hands started to shake. Fear of dropping the phone before Jett spit out an answer caused her fingers to tighten.

"Yeah, I'm on my way, but not to you."

Eliza's jaw dropped and her heart followed. "Jett Lawson, if this is another one of your twisted pranks, I'll hang you up by your toenails and boil you in oil, you hear me?"

"I'm not joking, sis. Hanna's water broke. We're pullin' into the hospital now."

Without a second thought for decorum, Eliza jumped up and down, making the office her very own bouncy house.

"Oh my gosh. How is she doing? What do you need me to do?"

"Hang up and find a new Santa. I'll keep you updated, I promise. I'm sorry, Eliza Lee." His voice sounded so solemn, Eliza hated to laugh, but she couldn't help it.

Between the cackles, she found her voice. "Don't you dare apologize. Tell Hanna I love her, and I'll be there as soon as I can."

"A'ight. Love ya, sis."

"Love you." Eliza jumped once more for good measure. After ending the call with Jett, she turned to Lori. "I've got a job for you, baby girl. Run and fetch your mama from the porch for me, will ya?"

Lori nodded and rushed out the door.

Once Eliza knew she was out of hearing range, she filled the crew in on their new mission. "Guys, we have to find a new Santa."

Mr. McCoy's forehead wrinkled as his brows inched together. "Why?"

"Jett's at the hospital. Baby Boo decided to come today of all days."

"What are the odds?" Bennett ran a hand through his damp locks, sending melted snow dripping down his face. Long eyelashes glittered with moisture as he blinked.

"I know, right?" With her hands on her hips, she took a deep breath. *Get it together, girl. You've made it this far.* Blowing like she would at a birthday candle, Eliza exhaled loudly. "Bennett? Are you up for the challenge?"

After everything he'd done for her, Bennett had earned the coveted role. Not just anyone could fill those boots, but she had no doubt he could. Until he took a step back. Was he going to say no? Surely not.

"I'd love to, bu—"

Eliza Lee interrupted before he could answer. "But nothing. It's fine." With a wave, she walked away. "Maybe Joe can do it. I'll go find him."

As she fled from the office, tears filled her eyes. *Again, City Boy?*

She swiped at the first tear that broke free just as Bennett's voice called out to her. "Eliza Lee, wait."

Instead of stopping, she walked faster, wishing for longer legs with each step. Soles slapped the pavement behind her. He was closing in on her. Fast. As she reached for her driver's side door, a hand grabbed hers.

Instinctively, Eliza curled her fingers, refusing to lace them with his. "Do you have any idea what an honor it is to wear that suit, City Boy? Grandpa Walt was the best Santa this town has ever seen, but I know you'll be a close second." Her voice cracked with the words, but she tried again. "I need you to do this, Bennett. For Grandpa and for me."

The truth rolled out like the hot tears on her cheeks and there was no taking it back, not that Eliza wanted to. As much as needing Bennett scared her, losing him scared her more. Emma Lou had been right all along. She did need someone. Bennett.

Without warning, he stepped back and stood ramrod straight. "I know, but sweetheart, look at me. I'm too tall."

Eliza covered her mouth as the truth of his words registered. *He's right. Goodness gracious, he's right.* The height difference between him and Jett hadn't occurred to her. A good four inches, at least. The pants would be high waters on him.

Heat filled Eliza's cheeks as she lowered her hands, laughter busting free. Bennett joined in, the sound music to her ears. She closed her eyes. Focusing on the tone, she noticed it was different than before. Light and free, renewed. The way she'd always hoped it could be.

Bennett stretched his arms wide, an open invitation. She took a step and he closed them tight around her. Lacing her hands around his neck, she tipped her chin toward him. Her pulse skittered. When he smiled, but didn't move a muscle, her breath caught. What was he waiting for?

"Ahem." Eliza squeaked out the word, surprising herself with the urgency she heard. Bennett's warm chocolate gaze locked with hers and she leaned in closer. Those puppy dog eyes would be the death of her yet. Or maybe the life of her? She wasn't sure which, but her heart stuttered at the thought.

A chuckle rose from his chest, but he remained still as stone.

"Ah-he-hem."

Another laugh but no movement.

"City Boy." The name rang out higher than a cat's back as her face flushed. Bennett smirked. He was toying with her, dang it. She tried to break free, but his hold tightened as he tugged her closer. She placed a palm on his chest and he smiled.

"Can I help you with something?" Bennett's voice, low and husky, shot shivers through her while simultaneously heating her blood to boiling. How did he do that? She'd never met a man who could burn her biscuits and calm her soul at the same time, but he did. And she loved every minute of it.

"Maybe." Eliza rubbed her lips together to hide her grin. "If you can make yourself shrink." Stilted laughter fell between them as he bent his knees and hiked a brow.

Eliza pushed up on her toes and closed the distance between them, pausing a split second before their lips touched. "Thank you."

Her eyelids fluttered shut as her mouth found his, moving sweet and slow. The world around her faded as he stood to his full height again without letting her go. His hands blazed a trail up her spine as her fingers worked their way into his hair. With that, the kiss turned from sugar sweet to blazing heat, melting away the misunderstandings between them. As her toes tingled, she moved her hands to his shoulders for better balance, but instead, she felt herself lean back as Bennett dipped her and kept on kissing.

A slam from the porch startled them apart. Eliza stood back up. Instead of letting go, though, she turned in his arms toward the sound. There, on the top step, stood Mr. McCoy, decked from head to toe in red velvet. A picture-perfect Santa if ever there was one.

The snow fell heavier as the train rolled into the first stop. Mr. McCoy gripped the railing on the caboose with white-gloved hands. He'd practiced his "ho, ho, ho" the entire way. Bennett teased him relentlessly, offering suggestions to create a heartier tone. Eliza shook her head at their banter. The McCoy men were finding their footing as friends quickly.

People of all ages lined the tracks. Volunteers in neon yellow vests directed the crowd, keeping them a safe distance from the train. The conductor blew the whistle wide open, then in short, quick bursts. Cheers filled the void between the notes. To think she'd almost missed this. If not for Bennett, there was no telling how things might have played out.

As the wheels screeched to a halt, a strong arm wrapped around her waist. Warm breath tickled her ear as Bennett's cheek grazed her temple.

"This is more than I ever dreamed. There are so many people." He kissed her cheek and closed his other arm around her. The scent of him mingled with the wind as snow swirled around them. His awe had already made the first stop a success and they hadn't even stepped off the train yet.

"City Boy, we're just gettin' started." Grabbing the toy bag at her feet, Eliza grinned over her shoulder. "C'mon."

His arms loosened, setting her free. Santa chuckled and greeted the crowd. Christmas carols played somewhere in the distance as she descended the steps, careful not to drop the sack of stuffed animals entrusted to her for delivery. Scanning the crowd, she saw a blue-eyed little boy calling out and motioning for her to come closer.

As they walked, Bennett rested his hand on the small of her back. He nudged slightly this way or that to keep them from bumping into the bystanders. The child rocked from one foot to the other as they made their way across the yard. Eliza stopped and opened the bag, surveying the gifts for the right fit. Bears, penguins, and reindeer galore rested at the top, but none that seemed like a match for the boy waiting in front of them. She dug deep until her hand closed around a floppy ear.

It couldn't be. Could it? With a yank, the dog flew over the bag's brim. A tan-and-white beagle peered at her.

"Perfect," Eliza whispered to herself.

"What is?"

The question interrupted the moment playing in her heart. She spun around and Bennett's face replaced the image of Grandpa Walt. The sadness of the memory shattered as her focus transitioned from past to present.

"This. You. Us." Eliza clutched his hand and squeezed. Eagerly, she pulled him along, tightening her grasp around the pup while the sack hung loosely from her forearm.

The little boy grinned when they reached him. Eliza crouched to put them face-to-face. "Hey there, little man. What's your name?"

"Jake. Jake Brown." A snowflake lighted on the tip of his nose, making it twitch. He brushed the flake away with his bare hand.

"Well, Jake Brown. It's nice to meet you." Eliza grabbed his tiny hand and shook gently. Bennett stuck his hand out as soon as she let loose and the child gripped it, repeating the motion. "Something tells me you've been good this year, huh?"

Jake nodded as Eliza handed him the doggy. A tiny gasp escaped him as he hugged it against his chest. Bennett bent down, tapped the boy on the head, and pushed down a fuzzy black beanie to cover his ears.

Jake's smile widened as Bennett handed him a pair of gloves to match. "Thank you, sir."

"You're welcome, Jake. But you can call me Bennett. We're buds now, right?" Bennett closed his hand and held his fist out. Jake bumped it and nodded again.

"Thank you, thank you so much." A small voice rose above the crowd's commotion as two arms pulled Eliza into a bear hug. The embrace took her by surprise at first, but she squeezed back tightly after she realized it was the boy's mother.

When they separated, a stocky man stepped from behind Jake, grabbed her hand, and shook vigorously. "We appreciate you, ma'am."

Eliza smiled as he tipped his hat to her. Tired eyes shone with gratitude beneath the bill, making her heart squeeze beneath her chest. "Most welcome. How are you this morning?"

"Better now." As his mother answered, Jake threw the plush puppy into the air, making a *weeeeeeee* sound while he did. Without missing a beat, she laid a hand on his shoulder and tucked him to her side. "Much better. This is our first time coming out, but it won't be our last."

"Ditto." Bennett chimed in and laughter ensued among the group. When it died down, Jake's dad spoke up.

"We moved back home to take care of my Uncle Derek. He took a fall a few months ago and isn't quite back to his old self yet. It's been difficult to get my hours in at work while running him between doctor's appointments and therapy. I hate to admit it, but our Christmas dinner was gonna be bologna sandwiches until Joe told us about the Santa Run. That grocery voucher is a godsend."

"I'm so glad it'll help." Bennett touched the man's shoulder lightly as he spoke.

The small gesture brought tears to Eliza's eyes. She leaned in for another hug with Jake's mom. "It was sure nice talking to you today. You guys have a Merry Christmas."

With a wave, they said goodbye. Bennett draped his arm around her as they weaved their way to the outer rim of the crowd. The first stop went smoother than she'd hoped. But there were so many left to go. She refocused her attention to the task at hand and smiled. It was time to fulfill Grandpa Walt's legacy and start living her own.

"Mr. McCoy, you're a lifesaver. Those kids thought you were the real Santa." Eliza chattered as they climbed off the train. It had been a long day. The best day, but long. They'd made it to all the terminals on time and met family after family at each stop. The coats, toys, and turkey certificates were long gone, except the one Eliza tucked back for Mrs. Bannerman.

Knowing that Christmas equated to Mr. McCoy's Black Friday, Eliza stopped where she was and turned to face him. Eyes the same color as Bennett's stared back at her and she smiled. "I can't thank you enough."

Mr. McCoy gently took her by the shoulders. "I should thank you, dear. Me in a red suit? That's quiet the Christmas miracle you pulled off."

Eliza blushed as he drew her in for a hug. After releasing her, he grinned back through a yawn. "It did take a lot of me, though. I think I'll head back to the inn. I'm ready for a nap."

Patting his father on the back, Bennett chimed in, offering his services. "Do you want me to take you?"

"No, son." Oliver's smile dimmed slightly but didn't falter. "If I plan on driving myself back to the city, I need to take baby steps. A trip to the inn seems like a good place to start."

Placing a hand on his father's shoulder, Bennett nodded. "OK, Pops. Don't push yourself too hard, though. Take all the time you need."

"Oh, I plan on it. You might even make it back before I do." Oliver stuck his hand into his coat pocket and jingled his keys.

Bennett cut his eyes to Eliza before meeting his father's gaze head on. "Doubt it. We still have a hospital visit to make."

Oliver chuckled. "As long as you don't forget to pick up our steaks from Nonnie's, I'll be fine. Oh, and I'd love a cinnamon roll for dessert. I don't know what Danny Jo does to make them so addicting, but I'm hooked."

As they watched Oliver walk around to the back lot, Bennett wrapped an arm around Eliza's waist, pulling her to his side. The smell of him was intoxicating, pine and citrus. She'd never be able to have a real tree again without thinking of him. Or a peppermint mocha. Or a lemon cream pie.

When they made it to her car, Eliza looked at the empty spot beside hers and panicked. Where was the Jag?

"Your car." Eliza gestured to the space. "It's gone."

"I know." Seemingly unfazed, Bennett spared a glance at the space before turning back to Eliza, not even a hint of worry reflected in the bottomless brown depths.

Eliza cocked her head. "What do you mean, you know? You drove this morning, didn't you?" The words came out staccato as her breathing quickened. She was about two seconds away from a total freak out.

Meanwhile, Bennett remained unaffected. Instead of answering immediately, he dipped a hand inside his coat, retrieved an envelope, and put it in her palm. "Yes, I drove. But that's my ride."

Bennett pointed to a clunker of a truck that looked vaguely familiar. Where had she seen it before? She blinked hard and tried to jar her memory. Goldie's Rods and Blooms? Nope. Maybe Powell's Apothecary? Not there either. Who were they talking to when she saw that truck? Pastor Clemens, that's who, after church. The pickup had a For Sale sign.

Before she could continue her interrogation, Bennett gestured to the envelope. "Open that. Please."

Curiosity urged her on as she followed his instructions. The envelope crinkled as she slipped a finger inside and ripped straight across. She removed the slip and unfolded it, discovering a check written for the same amount the crew had forfeited with their bonus.

"What is this?" Pulling the check closer to her face, she double-checked the numbers, making sure her eyes weren't playing tricks on her.

Bennett took both her hands in his. "The crew needs their bonus." His feet shuffled until the tip of his toe landed against her foot. "You said so yourself."

"But I didn't mean for you to sell your car." Shaking her head, she tried to make sense of it all. "Why did you do this?"

"For one, it was time to reunite the Jag with the rightful owner. Pops bought it."

"Come again?"

"It's a long story that I fully intend on sharing. But not today." Bennett smiled and squeezed her hands in his. "For two, I needed to prove myself to you. I love you, Eliza Lee. Please, tell me you see that now?"

"I—" Eliza's insides twisted as her voice failed. She drew a deep breath, hoping to steady herself. Then she tried again. "I'm stubborn, not blind, City Boy. Can you see I love you too?"

Bennett didn't answer. Instead he lifted her in the air, holding on tight. They spun round and round until dizziness set in, making it impossible for Eliza Lee to walk without help. She didn't care, though.

With Bennett leading the way, she knew she was safe.

Chapter Twenty-Four

As Bennett stood in Mama Deb's kitchen, hints of motor oil, smoke, and stale air tickled his nose. The odd combination of odors overpowered the lingering hints of cornbread and beans. Ignoring the stench as best he could, Bennett dusted the bill off with the back of his hand before passing the offending hat to Jett. That thing had seen better days. The basement had, too, judging from the cobwebs Bennett had braved to find Walt's stuff. Funny, L. J. had neglected to mention the tight quarters in his directions on where to find the trucker cap. All Bennett's trouble would be worth it, though. *Hopefully.*

The best Christmas Bennett and his father had seen in over a decade had finally ended. When he'd told Pops his plan to sell the Jag, his father had reacted the opposite of how he'd imagined. Instead of talking him out of it, he'd agreed to buy it. The turn of events shocked him, but not as much as Pops playing the part of Santa. His father took "try" to a whole new level, jumping straight into the deep end of Christmas. He'd even stayed in Pine Valley through the holidays. At Mama Deb's insistence, they'd both joined the Elliotts for dinner. Then, his father had claimed his stomach too full to drive home right away. He'd started for New York bright and early the next day, but stayed a night in West Virginia and a few in Pennsylvania to stretch the road trip. Still, he'd made it back to the city well before New Year's Eve.

But not without promising to visit soon. Bennett knew it was a promise his father meant to keep. Despite the miles between them, since Bennett was staying in Pine Valley, he felt closer to his father than he had in years. Project Pops had worked better than he'd dared to dream.

"Bennie, hurry up," Lori yelled from the living room.

A whimper sounded. By the time Bennett wiggled into the love seat beside Eliza Lee, the baby's cry had turned into a wail. Jenny bounced the little one and rubbed circles on his blue sleeper.

"Shhhh, now. I gotcha, Nicky." She whispered the words, but the room had grown silent, making her reassurances loud enough to carry.

Hanna scooted to the edge of her seat. "Want me to take him?" As she spoke, she reached her arms out to Jenny and the family's newest edition.

Jenny shook her head. "No way. Aunt Jen's got him. Don't I, sweet boy?"

Nicholas Andrew, rightly named after St. Nick, stirred against her shoulder and drifted back to dreamland. Seeing her boy peacefully settled, Hanna sank back into her chair.

"Sorry, Hanna. I didn't mean to wake him up." Lori hung her head until Jett threw a piece of popcorn at her. "Hey, now."

Bennett's eyes widened as Lori spoke, her voice barely audible. It was the quietest he'd heard her outside of church. He put two thumbs up for her effort.

Eliza Lee snuggled under his arm and laid her head against his chest, making his heart pound. He dropped a kiss on top of her head. Sweet vanilla radiated upward from her hair and Bennett thanked God for the chance to hold her. And for Pine Valley. The acquisition had given him so much more than a second office. He'd been given a new beginning and a bonus family to love.

L. J. nodded at him as he took his place next to Mama Deb. "Happy New Year, boy. Do you think you'll miss the city much?"

Squeezing Eliza's shoulder, Bennett shook his head. "Nope, not at all. The traffic, the noise, the lights. It takes a toll and I had my fill. Pops was thrilled to hand Pine Valley over to me. Less travel for him, he says. Mark my words, though, he won't be gone for long."

Mama Deb chimed in. "You tell him to come down anytime. I'll have dinner waiting for him."

As she spoke, Bennett's phone vibrated on the table with an incoming call. "Looks like you can tell him yourself." He grabbed the device, slid a finger across the screen, and lifted it to his ear. "Hey, Pops. . . . Happy New Year to you too. . . . Yeah, everyone's here. . . . I'll switch to video so you can tell them yourself." Bennett motioned for Lori as his father's face appeared on the screen. "Hold this for me, Lori. Pops wants to say hi."

Jett handed him the ball cap and Bennett turned back to face Eliza Lee. "After I say my spiel."

Cocking her head to the side, she propped her elbow on a knee and rested her chin in her hand. She was thinking. *Good.* As long as her thoughts were about him.

"Do you know what this is?" Bennett gestured to the cap, careful not to drop it as he held it high for a better look. Eliza slowly shook her head.

"It's the trucker hat you told me about the day we met. The one with all the nicknames."

"Oh, OK." Her gaze wandered from Bennett to her parents, seemingly searching for counsel. L. J. sat silent while Mama Deb winked at her. "But I already have a nickname. Punky."

"True, but I think you need a new one." He jiggled the hat in front of her. She giggled but she didn't take the bait. *Stubborn, as usual.* Nodding at the cap, Bennett pushed it closer to her, making the folded slips of paper inside jar together. Each one bearing a name. The same name. "Humor me?"

Eliza plunged her hand into the hat. "Sure, why not." Eyes closed, she circled her hand through the slips, taking her sweet time. As she did, Bennett tried to steady his breathing. If she didn't hurry, he was going to pick for her.

Before he could, though, Lori passed the phone to her mother and beat him to the punch. "We hain't got all night, Eliza Lee."

As Lori's tiny fingers unfolded the slip, Bennett's stomach knotted. So much for his plan. With no way to intervene without giving his intentions away, Bennett let the interruption play out.

Squinting at the paper, Lori read aloud. "Your new name is Mrs. Olsen?"

Bennett barely made it to one knee by the time Lori finished, the ring box closed in his hand. Eliza Lee sat frozen, speechless. The announcer on the television behind them reminded the crowd less than a minute remained before the New Year began.

Wanting to start January right, Bennett rushed on. "I know this seems fast, but I don't mean right now at this second. I mean someday, Eliza Lee. When you're ready, nothing would make me happier than to give you my last name." He paused and stretched his free hand around the room, making sure to catch his father's eye. Bennett had offered to change his name back to McCoy before his father left for the city, but Pops wouldn't hear of it. The memories it brought back were too special, he said.

On the screen, his father smiled and Bennett went on. "These people here with us tonight are all I need in this world. And you, sweetheart, are what I need the most."

When Eliza still didn't speak, worry threatened to consume him, until Bennett watched her eyes go glassy. With trembling hands, he opened the box. He spared a glance to make sure the ring hadn't slipped. Then, he set his gaze on her. The unshed tears reflecting in her eyes gave him the courage to go on. "Eliza Lee Elliott, will you marry me?"

Her gaze pinned him in place as the hint of a blush crept across her cheeks. She nodded and a tear slipped pash her lash line. "Yes, City Boy, I'll marry you. You're everything I never knew I needed."

Before Bennett could stand, Eliza was kneeling in front of him. She circled her arms around him and hugged while the room shook with applause that woke the baby. Through the newborn's cries, the countdown continued and the ball dropped.

Bennett figured as much, anyway. With Eliza's lips on his, it was hard to notice anything except his love for her and a new hope for their future.

Historical Notes

While the story of Eliza Lee and Bennett is fictional, the book was inspired by a real-life event that takes place in my hometown: The Santa Train. The train hands out goods at the start of the holiday season during a route that begins in Pikeville, Kentucky, and ends in Kingsport, Tennessee, every year on the Saturday before Thanksgiving. Unlike the two little towns of Pine Valley and Hickory Hills that The Santa Run aides, there are fourteen stops along The Santa Train's parade route where clothing, toys, and food are handed out. Sponsors include CSX, Food City, Appalachian Power, the Kingsport Chamber of Commerce, and Soles4Souls. The tradition has been serving families in Kentucky, Tennessee, and Virginia for over seventy-five years, even finding safe ways to provide through the pandemic by implementing a drive-through system instead of traveling via the railroad. You can find out more about The Santa Train at https://www.facebook.com/santatrain.

In addition to the inspiration drawn from The Santa Train, this book is a tribute to the most memorable parts of those I've loved and lost. The characters in the book are inspired by those precious souls who made me who I am, the friends and family who carried me when I was too weak to walk, and those whose love lives within me. I believe good fiction begins with a kernel of truth. When writing this story, I took my own truths and worked outward. Eliza Lee's parents inherited many characteristics of my late parents. Mama Deb shares my mommy's name (Debbie) and Luke James carries my dad's initials of L. J., as well as his way with words. My mother, like Mama Deb, refused to wear her hair pulled back because she hated her ears and, though I was given the nickname by my daddy instead of my grandfather, Punky was all my dad ever called me until the day he died. Likewise, the town pride and close-knit community of Pine Valley was fashioned after my own little home tucked away in the hills of eastern Kentucky.

IRON STREAM MEDIA

If you enjoyed this book, will you consider sharing the message with others?

Let us know your thoughts. You can let the author know by visiting or sharing a photo of the cover on our social media pages or leaving a review at a retailer's site. All of it helps us get the message out!

Email: info@ironstreammedia.com

 @ironstreammedia

Brookstone Publishing Group, Iron Stream, Iron Stream Fiction, Iron Stream Harambee, Iron Stream Kids, and Life Bible Study are imprints of Iron Stream Media, which derives its name from Proverbs 27:17, "As iron sharpens iron, so one person sharpens another." This sharpening describes the process of discipleship, one to another. With this in mind, Iron Stream Media provides a variety of solutions for churches, ministry leaders, and nonprofits ranging from in-depth Bible study curriculum and Christian book publishing to custom publishing and consultative services.

For more information on ISM and its imprints, please visit
IronStreamMedia.com